Peter Fahy served as a pilot in the Royal Air Force for seventeen years. In that period he wrote poetry, which was eventually published in six books in the year 2000. In civilian life he worked as a management consultant in the antipodes and the USA. *Roots in the Sand* is his first published novel.

To: June,
With appreciation
for help and advice.

Peter

ROOTS IN THE SAND

ROOTS IN THE SAND

Peter Fahy

ATHENA PRESS
LONDON

ROOTS IN THE SAND
Copyright © Peter Fahy 2006

All Rights Reserved

No part of this book may be reproduced in any form
by photocopying or by any electronic or mechanical means,
including information storage or retrieval systems,
without permission in writing from both the copyright
owner and the publisher of this book.

ISBN 0 84401 649 8

First Published 2006 by
ATHENA PRESS
Queen's House, 2 Holly Road
Twickenham TW1 4EG
United Kingdom

Printed for Athena Press

Contents

The Dilemma	9
The Choice	20
Andromeda	31
Make Deserts Bloom	43
Cairo to Tunis	53
Three More Days?	63
A Trip Up North	73
The Value of Boring Records	83
Victoria Is Three Days Early	92
The Countdown Begins	103
The Original Phaenton	113
The Ice Advances	123
PI Hits Headlines	133
Colgate Advises	142
Beaten By The Opposition	151
When Time Stood Still	160
The Countdown	170
Phaeton the Scorpion	181
The Aftermath	192
"Does The Rain Have A Father?"	202
The Red Crescent	212
Compost In Sand	221

The Dilemma

In his comfortable, high-tech suite of offices in Pall Mall, in the west end of London, Miles Poundmore watched his panoramic telecomputer screen as if he were mesmerised; it brought the reality and threat of Phaeton the meteor to within a few feet of his desk. These pictures, primarily for the media attending a conference at Church House, Westminster, were also being relayed to the world. Dr Laurie Colgate, an eminent physicist, objectively and dispassionately explained that the massive object made of rock, minerals and metal was actually orbiting the sun. However, at intervals of about seven thousand years its orbit crossed that of planet earth. And this time, said Colgate, it was hurtling directly towards us at some thirty thousand miles per hour. In answer to another question he said that international co-operation was excellent and that governments around the world were making plans for dealing with potential disaster.

Miles Poundmore's success in building up his business empire owed much to his pioneering application of computer networks to commerce. Now, instead of tracking world stock markets, or his managerial staff in Europe, the Middle East, the Americas or Australasia, he concentrated on the mindless meteor that was bent on destroying both him and his lucrative empire. The urge to maximise profits yielded to the instinct for personal survival in the face of this catastrophe that threatened planet earth. Dr Colgate's answer to the last question had convinced Miles Poundmore that the time for action had come. He pressed the intercom button, "Eileen," he said to his personal assistant, "get Victoria on the telephone."

"Victoria", he said instead of the usual Vicky, so she knew he was either cross or anxious. "I'll send the helicopter to pick you up in two hours, we're leaving for an indefinite stay on *Andromeda* – I'm sending her to the Med."

The Dilemma

"You can't do that, darling. *Andromeda* is on charter to that nice man, Lord whatsisname – we had lunch with him in the Upper House last month. Remember?"

"You mean Harding-Smith? He's had it. I've told Captain Wenock to let him know that due to unforeseen circumstances, *Andromeda* is not available. Can't be helped. There are more important things than his holiday cruise."

"I'll have to join the ship at Gibraltar. I couldn't be ready in two hours, or two days, or even possibly two weeks."

"Look Vicky, let's not play games. This is a matter of life and death. Scrub your engagements—"

"Miles," she broke in, "I am not missing the services at All Saints, nor the special weekly services at the Abbey. *Andromeda*'s at Lisbon now isn't she? Geoffrey Wenock can sail to Gib. Tell him I'll board there."

"What if I come and collect you? Would that make any difference?"

"You know what my commitments are, Miles. I will not let people down, not for Phaeton, nor even for you when you're being unreasonable." Victoria put the phone down.

"Eileen!" he shouted, neglecting the intercom in his annoyance with Victoria.

"Yes, sir?" She always accentuated the "sir" when she was aggrieved. Her voice came clearly, quietly, irritatingly over the intercom.

"Cancel my engagements for the next ten days. From first thing tomorrow I can be contacted on *Andromeda*. I may send for you to join her at Gibraltar. I'll talk to you tomorrow about that. Get Giles to bring the car round right away. And phone the Docklands Airport; I want *Ariadne* prepared for a flight to Lisbon tonight. Contact Captain Williams and tell him to get clearance for take-off at 10.30 pm local time."

"Mr Poundmore," said Eileen, "the Minister for Trade and Industry is meeting you here at 11.30."

"Eileen," he interrupted, "I said *cancel* my engagements. Begin with him." He growled into the intercom. "First Victoria now her, looking for trouble instead of doing what they're told."

The Dilemma

Eileen told her assistant to get the Minister's personal secretary on the phone, saying she would talk to her herself. Following this she gave the assistant the list of cancellations for the next ten days. "Tell them Mr Poundmore deeply regrets that one of his senior colleagues overseas has been taken ill. He is flying out to appoint a successor. He will be in touch as soon as possible."

She knew that Miles, in his present mood, would neither listen to, nor consider, anyone else. Later he would be contrite and would make some extraordinary and expensive effort to compensate for his bad temper. He knew that Eileen would obey his orders implicitly she would correctly interpret those that were badly expressed: she was invaluable to him. That's why her pay was equivalent to that of his junior directors. She had been with him from the start, more than thirty years ago, when he had made his first lucky acquisition, for peanuts, of a down-at-heel property company, whose assets had far exceeded the imagination of its previous aged and burnt-out owner.

That same company, renamed Poundmore International, was now the centrepiece of a vast conglomerate which in one or more of its guises, had blue-chip status on all the world's stock markets. Although Miles Poundmore exercised a ruthless control over his empire, he eschewed personal publicity. His regional managing directors were the front men; instant dismissal loomed for any staff member who mentioned his name to the press or on any public occasion. This policy served him well and his comings and goings attracted no attention from the media. The more flamboyant of his accoutrements, such as the jet plane, yacht and helicopter, were registered in London in the name of Victoria Miles.

This low profile proved profitable when asset-rich companies were available for snapping up as the competition would be unaware, until too late, that there was an unknown, very well informed predator stalking the game. Whilst the big, publicity seeking moguls discussed bids in public, a discreet agent, acting on behalf of Poundmore International, negotiated secretly only going public at the last moment and, almost invariably, walking off with the prize.

The Dilemma

The dark-blue Rolls drew into the parking slot in front of a house in a quiet street off St. James's. It was about five minutes walk from the Poundmore offices to the Poundmore town house, but Miles expected to travel with Victoria to the Docklands Airport. As he walked into the hall he shouted, "Vicky, where are you?"

"In my bedroom," she called. "I'm going out in ten minutes. If you want to talk, come up."

Miles strode up the stairs and burst into her bedroom. "Look, Vicky, we face an odds-on probability of a strike from this meteor. Do you know what that means?"

"I think so dear," she said, advancing and putting her arms round him. "But don't let something over which you have no control get you into such a tizzy. It's most unlike you. What's happened to your self-discipline?"

"I have just seen the latest expert report on Phaeton. I've seen its line of approach and I reckon it will hit us, somewhere between latitude fifty and sixty degrees north, in ten days time. Instead of sitting here like lemmings, with the option of being blown to bits or roasted by a meteorite, I have a plan which offers us a good chance of survival."

"Darling," replied Vicky soothingly as she freed Miles from her embrace, "lemmings don't sit around, they rush off in a panic and leap to their deaths in the sea. Why leave our family and friends at a time like this?"

"Tell Amabel that she and the boys must join us. Gordon can come too if he wishes." Miles had a troubled relationship with his son-in-law who, having turned down an offer of a working directorship in Poundmore International, seemed to be happy scraping a living as an overworked doctor in a country practice. Furthermore, he had insisted that his and Amabel's two sons should attend their village school, spurning Miles's offer to pay preparatory and public school fees.

"If you have business abroad my love, go and attend to it and rejoin us at home as soon as you can. You know very well that Amabel will not take the boys away from school during term time, and I will not cancel my engagements at such short notice," Victoria said firmly.

Miles recognised the tone. Nothing would budge her now. "On your own head be it," he said. "I'm flying to Lisbon tonight and I shall spend the next three weeks aboard *Andromeda*, sailing in the eastern Med." He looked at her with a mixture of exasperation and devotion. Thirty years of marriage and they were still in love. Somehow they had negotiated those tempestuous passages which assault even good marriages, though their vows had at times come under considerable strain.

"I'm going to the special service in the Abbey at four o'clock. I shall be home about six. What time are you leaving?" she asked.

"Take-off is at ten thirty tonight, so I'll leave about nine-thirty. Giles will be available for the next three weeks if you need driving anywhere. Unless, of course, Phaeton arrives early and makes driving impossible. In which case his orders are to get across the channel before impact and head for Rome. Now, I have a few phone calls to make. But we can have dinner together," he said in a more cheerful manner.

"Yes, see you later," she said.

Miles went to his study, picked up the phone which gave him a direct line to Eileen, and asked, "What did the Minister say?"

"He spoke to me personally, said he quite understood. In fact, he's a bit hard-pressed himself. All your engagements are cancelled for the next ten days, but I have a list of people who want to talk to you as soon as you are available."

"I leave it to you, Eileen. *Ariadne* should be airborne by 11.30 p.m. If you think any of those calls warrant it, please put them through to me after say, 10.30 p.m."

Eileen noted the "please". "Captain Williams has filed a flight plan for take-off at 10.30 p.m.; he has engaged one stewardess. ETA Lisbon is 7.30. He would like to know if *Ariadne* is to return to London."

"Tell him I'm going on to Rome and Cairo. I'll discuss timing with him tonight, after I've spoken to Capelli and Rahman. Get Rahman first."

By 5.45 pm Miles had arranged the immediate part of his Mediterranean itinerary. When dealing with his own empire he seldom gave much notice to people – they all, including top directors, fell in with his plans. His computer screens gave him

The Dilemma

an up-to-the-day – if not an up-to-the-minute — account of all his interests. His talks with his senior people concentrated on aspects of the Group's integrated world strategy. After such discussions Miles pulled the strings, and his senior staff performed.

He decided to look at the recording of Dr Colgate's press conference to see if had missed any significant points. He reckoned that the physicists and politicians were hand-in-glove during the present crisis; stakes were high, and every word must be weighed carefully. He inserted the disc and switched on.

"Ladies and gentlemen," Dr Colgate greeted the reporters of home and international media, "welcome to this briefing on the progress of Phaeton the meteor. In a moment I shall give you a verbal statement. This will be followed," he pointed to a large screen, "by satellite shots of the meteor, and pictures which present an accurate plot of its trajectory in relation to earth. After that I shall be pleased to take questions."

A woman in the front row jumped to her feet and shouted, "There's only one question. Let's have a straight answer. Is Phaeton going to hit this planet?"

"Mrs French," Colgate smiled at her, "you have anticipated the statement I promised to make, which is that the Observatory, after consultation with authorities in countries around the world, is not yet able to say whether Phaeton will hit, or miss planet earth. We can tell you that on its present course it will pass close by, or collide, in ten days, that is a week on Sunday."

Dr Colgate then called on his assistant, Sheila, to present pictures and diagrams which told nobody who watched television, listened to the news, or read the papers, anything they didn't already know. But it was official – life on earth faced the prospect of extinction, and officialdom had no more control over meteors, and the planet's ultimate fate, than the man in the street.

Afterwards a stream of questions hit Dr Laurie Colgate. He raised his hands for silence and said, "Ladies and gentlemen, I can give you twenty minutes for questions. May I remind you that this meeting, your questions and my answers, is being transmitted worldwide by satellite television. I will take the first question from the second row."

The Times correspondent in the second row was first to his feet, "Scientists tell us that some 250 million years ago ninety-six percent of earth's species disappeared. They also tell us that a mere sixty-five million years ago the dinosaur became extinct due to prolonged cold and darkness. If the extreme cold in Scotland and northern England develops into a full-blown ice age, do you think Phaeton might be a blessing in disguise?"

The question raised ripples of nervous laughter which served to ease the tension in the room. Dr Colgate answered, "The fate of the original Phaeton might answer that question for you." Nervous laughter again. He waited for silence. "As you know, the weather men predict more blizzards and severe weather next week. This has little bearing on our tracking of Phaeton. Satellites beam information and pictures of the meteor to television and computer screens every minute of the day and night. International co-operation is excellent – governments have agreed on the best possible plans for dealing with any emergency that arises."

A question came from an American lady in the third row, "Why can't one of our space ships get alongside Phaeton and give it a nudge, or blast a rocket with a nuclear warhead at it?"

"A rocket such as you suggest might, at best, cause disintegration of Phaeton. This would certainly create highly radioactive fragments and dust, some of which would land on earth, exposing people to fall-out over a wide area. Clouds of disintegration dust would reach high altitudes, and deflect more of the sun's warmth away from earth causing lower global temperatures. At worst Phaeton itself might explode."

"Suppose Phaeton misses earth, but passes very close, what would that mean for us?"

"At my emergency office in Church House, Westminster, we have discussed this possibility with colleagues and governments around the world. A near miss, assuming that Phaeton overcomes earth's gravity, would mean that the meteor has a shallow trajectory as it passes us on its solar orbit. It could, therefore, travel in earth's upper atmosphere for several minutes generating tremendous temperatures, well over 3,000 degrees centigrade. The earth's surface, and anything on it, for some miles at either side of its path, would be scorched and burnt. Phaeton might

The Dilemma

explode. Apart from immediate and appalling damage caused by the explosion, molten debris would be scattered over a wide area. Disintegration dust would reach the upper atmosphere and block the sun's rays for months. It would further reduce the abnormally low temperatures which are at present affecting Scotland and Scandinavia."

It was clear to Miles that Dr Colgate was not hiding anything. The next questioner asked what the British Government's plans were.

"The Prime Minister wants the best scientific advice so that she can decide government policy. She feels that if decisive action is the best course, that action must be initiated now. However, a mass exodus to southern Europe because of advancing ice would be unwise, we could be sending millions to the very area which Phaeton might lay waste. If we advise sit tight, and the ice advanced, it may become impossible for anyone to go anywhere."

The next question, in a sarcastic vein, was about the need for cross-checking with other experts. Dr Colgate answered courteously, "We check computer printouts again and again. Before this briefing for example, my assistant, Sheila Maclaren, double-checked with ATM Australia – that is the Australian Asteroid Tracking Programme, and MPC, the Minor Planets Centre in the USA. These are key watchers of the hemispheres, and I assure you that since Phaeton was first spotted, his approach towards earth, his course and his speed have been, and will be, closely monitored."

Sheila Maclaren produced a plot of Phaeton's track and a series of drawings, mounted on transparent sheets, so that the trajectory of the meteor was graphically traced from its first sighting to its present position in space relative to earth.

To end the conference, Dr Colgate summarised the present position: "The facts are these. Firstly, Phaeton is heading towards earth at a relative closing speed of 25,000 miles an hour. Secondly, it is too early to say positively that the meteor will hit us, or, if it does, where it will strike. At best, it will pass uncomfortably close. Thirdly, in terms of astrophysics its present mass is infinitesimal, but as a missile it is enormous – thirty miles across at its widest. Fourthly, it is expected to impact, or pass us, in ten days. And finally, occasionally Phaeton passes through invisible clouds of thin gases, so that a strange glow is added to its pale reflection of the sun's rays. If, or when, it strikes our planet, friction and white-hot heat generated by its passage through earth's atmosphere will have reduced Phaeton to about one third of its present size."

That was how Dr Laurie Colgate presented his case. The known facts, and a reasonable prediction, the accuracy of which would interest comparatively few people after the event. Most of the hard-bitten men and women of the media realised that the danger mankind faced was beyond human comprehension. The destructive power of a nuclear bomb was puny in comparison to the potentially catastrophic phenomenon in the shape of the meteor named Phaeton, that was now confronting humanity in the year 2010. There were those who felt that blame must be attached to politicians, or scientists, or the military. Others simply wished to hear a convincing survival plan. Some merely wanted to be assured that the problem would go away.

Miles switched off the video and telephoned Eileen again. "I've booked seats at Covent Garden for you and Victoria next Thursday, have dinner at Vicky's club. Giles has the tickets. I'm signing off now. I'll talk to you tomorrow."

Eileen sighed. No time for her to say thanks. No chance to choose which night best suited her. He knew that she wanted to see the performance of *Il Seraglio*. This was his apology and his thank you. She and Victoria enjoyed their trips to theatre and opera. The frequency of these outings punctuated the accepted hazards of working for a tycoon like Miles. He would not get involved in business detail; he was the strategist. He employed tacticians, administrators, accountants and others to deal with detail. He kept a controlling hand and eye on his global interests. He spotted immediately anything unusual in a balance sheet. Yet he invariably, and personally, booked seats for Victoria and Eileen when he felt that his account with either of them was at a low ebb and needed a credit item.

Victoria returned to find Miles in the bath, listening to the six o'clock news. She sat in the chair by the bath ruffling his hair. "The Abbey was absolutely packed. The Dean's prayers were very moving," she said.

The Dilemma

"Let's hope his prayers move the snow and ice from Scotland. Was the heating on? Or were they, like everyone else, conserving fuel?"

"Don't be so petulant, Miles. The Dean apologised for the lack of heat and, in any case, the whole service was so heart-warming that people left feeling encouraged and hopeful."

"What did he say about Phaeton?"

"That the universe is in God's hands. That he'd managed it for thousands of millions of years and, whatever may happen to the world, God will look after his people."

"I thought God loved the world? I'm going off him a bit. Why sling a bloody great meteorite at something you love? Why does he threaten all the people he's supposed to love with annihilation? Dammit, the choice seems to be between freezing to death in a sudden, unexpected ice age, or roasting to death in the blasting explosion and flames of a rogue meteorite. I'd rather do something about it myself – and not just sit here waiting like a mindless robot. Aren't we supposed to use our initiative?"

"Of course we are, but not just for our own interests. And I need notice if you want me to rearrange my diary," Victoria reiterated.

"I've already offered all our family a trip to the Med. I aim to follow that up with invitations to Eileen and a few others. Giles will drive the Rolls to Rome. You'll be left here all on your own."

"My love, your efforts are concentrated solely on Poundmore International and your own needs. Be honest, you don't give a fig for anyone else's arrangements, do you?"

"Hell, darling, let's not argue on what might be our last night together." Miles got out of the bath and embraced her. He held her tightly to his wet body, she responded, locking her arms round his waist, then she caressed and kissed him. She released herself from his arms, took his hand and led him to her bedroom. They rejoiced in a relationship, which, apart from occasional incandescent clashes of will and temperament, had never palled in more than thirty years of married life; their love for each other was a certainty in an uncertain universe.

Outside their warm, rapturous world, the promised blizzards hit Scotland. Here, as the arctic temperatures persisted, the ice expanded, heading as if to link up with the northern sheet which, as it thickened, edged slowly, ponderously, inexorably southwards from the Arctic Circle and Greenland.

Miles and Vicky Poundmore were used to parting. He had spent at least one hundred and eighty days and nights abroad every year since PI's foundation, first building up the business and now to keep ahead of worldwide competition. But This parting was different.

"You know, Vicky," said Miles, as they talked over dinner, "even if Phaeton misses us, we shall have to move south if the ice really begins to build up and cover the south of England. If we leave it too late, all UK transport systems will have ground to a halt. We shall be trapped, like everybody else."

The Choice

"I shall come to the airport to see you off," said Victoria. "You know I don't like your spur-of-the-moment panic trips. And this one really *is* a wild goose chase. Capelli wants you to hold his hand because there's been a disastrous slump in demand for fridges and freezers."

"I have to be at the airport by 10 o'clock. I have some figures to cross-check on *Ariadne*'s computer." He glanced at his watch "We'll leave in half an hour. Darling, Will you tell—?"

"Yes! I've told Giles to have the car ready for 9.30 pm."

"You should use the twenty-four-hour clock, saves mistakes," said Miles with an exaggerated sigh. "Has Eileen sent the CDs?"

"Yes, she has. Together with a printout of figures for Rome and Cairo. Anything else, my lord?"

"Well, since you ask—?"

"No, Miles. There isn't time. You know you can deal with Capelli and Rahman inside a week. Tell Angelo to switch production to radiant heaters. You could tell him that on the phone." Victoria deftly turned Miles's mind away from the one activity that rivalled his business interests.

★

Captain Mike Williams telephoned the senior air traffic controller to check that clearance for Papa India One's flight through the London control zone had been confirmed. At 34,500 feet he would be above much of the traffic heading between the Americas and European cities. He intended to skirt Spanish air space but would have to advise the Madrid controller of his route.

The executive Lear jet named *Ariadne* had a flight crew of three and seated twelve passengers in armchair comfort. The main cabin was luxurious and spacious enough to equal the best that international airlines could provide. The galley was small but comprehensive – as was the bar. Behind the captain and his first officer there was an electronic office where two people could sit at a console in which three computers were installed. When the key, high density, Poundmore International compact discs were fed into the system, Miles had available all the information he needed in order to exercise that tight control of his empire which ensured its continuing and phenomenal success. These computers were independent of, and isolated from, the aircraft's electronic control equipment.

Usually Eileen accompanied Miles on flights abroad. This time, if he wanted information whilst airborne, he himself would operate the PI computer system.

At number 10 Downing Street, the PM and her husband were enjoying a working dinner with senior colleagues. No other spouses were present. Winnie Smith had invited final bids for dealing with the crisis. First, she listed the steps, either overt or covert, which had already been taken:

"We cannot repel either of the invasions that confront us. Our strategy must follow that of the Russians, first against Napoleon and then against Hitler. Retreat enabled them to live and fight another day. We are advised that the ice will advance, but we don't yet know how far, or for how long. We have negotiated air bases, as yet secret, mainly with the French but also with other European allies. Five such bases are already manned by skeleton forces and are operational. Naval and merchant shipping is earmarked for evacuation purposes. The channel tunnel will be switched to one-way operation. For obvious reasons these moves cannot yet be announced to the public. We intend to keep a presence in the UK, and to that end an armoured division is at present operating within the Arctic Circle, with specially adapted equipment. This will provide an experienced nucleus for training troops and civilians on survival in arctic conditions. We will deal with supply, water, food, heat, light and tactical problems in full cabinet. Tonight we take strategic plans a step further and agree a timetable."

"Prime Minister," said David Medden, the Foreign Secretary, weary after a strenuous round of negotiations in Madrid.

"Let's keep it informal," said the PM.

The Choice

"Right," he continued, "you have stated our strategy very simply – it is retreat before the ice. We will avoid further tragedies like the one in Scotland if we enforce evacuation in good time. We have seen the incredible speed at which snow and ice render airports, roads and rail impassable. Our people have never before seen this on such a scale. We must stress, in language that will not cause panic, that people who don't get away when they are advised to, won't get away at all."

"There is a very human aspect to this problem," said Myrtle, the Environment Minister, "because, in a property-owning democracy, people become attached to their possessions. There is a natural reluctance to leave one's house, one's furniture, one's car but *especially* one's pets knowing full well that, if they're left behind, they will starve to death, if they don't freeze to death first. Some people would prefer to die with their friends rather than desert them."

"Sheer maudlin sentiment," said Mick Taylor, the Employment Minister, in his blunt northern accent, "ah've already lost ma house up north so ma family's moved to London. Had ter leave animals – no other way, it were kids or animals, simple as that. Ah say, when one's time comes one takes nowt." He now parodied Myrtle, "Our policy should be to get one's youngsters away, all under twenty-five conscripted for service abroad. And think on." A professed atheist he went on, "A man's life consists not in the abundance of his possessions. Course, a woman's..." he caught the PM's eye and his voice tailed off.

"In that case," responded Myrtle, "I take it that Michael agrees with me. In a democracy people should have a choice – stay or leave."

Heather Moor, the Home Secretary, intervened to prevent a feud between Employment and Environment ministers, "We have taken emergency powers so that we can act, as would a nation at war, in the best interests of the nation. Winnie is right. If necessary we must retreat before the ice. The death rate amongst the aged has risen dramatically in the north due to the intense cold spells which have alternated with short periods of warmer weather. Germs have multiplied in the warm days creating epidemics, which unfortunately, have killed off infants as well as older members of society. I suggest that we firstly agree an age limit up to which compulsory evacuation applies, secondly, get the Chief of Defence Staff to modify his logistical paper on evacuation accordingly, and finally, my department can then work out, with the Chief, a survival plan for the Eskimos – those who remain in the UK. If, initially, we evacuate all up to twenty-five years of age, we must plan to move some 15,000,000 people."

The PM spoke decisively, "Thank you, Heather. We are agreed that evacuation must take place. Are we agreed that all citizens who are aged twenty-five or under, at a date to be fixed by the Home Secretary, are to be evacuated in accordance with the Chief's plans? We know families will be split, but parents will appreciate that this plan is best for their children. Our arrangements must be flexible enough to deal with special cases such as nursing mothers over the age of twenty-five. Heather, you will liaise closely with health, transport and, of course, the Chief of Defence staff. I want a daily report." She turned to the Secretary of State for Scotland, "Mac, how is identification and burial proceeding in the disaster area?"

The meeting continued into the early hours. By the time it ended the ministers had a comprehensive plan of action to put before the full meeting of the cabinet later that morning.

★

The Rolls drew up alongside *Ariadne*, Victoria stepped out and boarded the plane with Miles. An attractive blonde stewardess greeted them: not one who had flown with them before. "Captain Williams will be back from air traffic control in a moment, sir," she said.

"Are we on main power?" asked Miles. "I want to start up the PI computers right away."

"Yes sir," she replied, leading the way forward. Miles sat at the console, instantly oblivious of anything and anyone as he switched on the electronic devices that would give him access to the vital business statistics which were updated several times daily at every national head office of Poundmore International.

"Can I get you a drink, Mrs Poundmore?"

The Choice

"Yes, please, I'd like a gin and French. Would you like to join me?"

"I'd love to, but it would cost me my job. So I have to say no, thank you," replied the girl.

"How very strict," said Victoria, "is it a PI rule?"

"No, it's the agency. But it was the same when I worked for a major airline, although provided one was discreet, it was possible on jumbos to have one small drink. On a small, intimate aircraft like this it would be most unwise."

Captain Williams came aboard, "Good evening, Mrs Poundmore, sorry you're not travelling with us this time."

Victoria smiled, she liked Mike Williams. He was an experienced and competent aviator, and as well as that, he was a friend. "Good evening, Mike," she said, "I just had too much going on, and notice was a bit short." She sipped her drink. Which was exactly as she liked a dry Martini.

She was about to compliment the girl when Mike said, "I hope Mrs Ashby will become our regular member of cabin staff. The agency has promised to let her go if we can agree terms. Now I must go forward. Goodnight, Mrs Poundmore."

"Goodnight, Mike," said Victoria.

Ten minutes before take-off, she went forward to say goodbye to Miles. He left the console and walked her to the Rolls. He kissed her, "Look after yourself, and try to persuade Amabel to take a holiday on *Andromeda* now," he stressed. He waved once, then strode to *Ariadne* and boarded without looking back. Giles drove to the control tower, where he parked so that Vicky could watch the take-off. She was deep in thought. Never before had Miles left the aircraft once he was settled on board. This simple action convinced her, more than all his warning words, that he truly believed that the world faced a cataclysm of global proportions.

★

Miles checked on the vast storage space that would become available to Poundmore International in Italy if all refrigerators, freezers, cool boxes and the like were shipped to South America and Australia. The ships that took them out could return with grain, corned beef, frozen meat, fruit and any kind of canned food that could be stored. His South American office had, on his orders, adapted warehouses, or acquired new ones for food storage, including many deep-freeze plants; these now contained enormous amounts of food. If the politicians, weathermen and scientists were wrong about Phaeton, but right about the advance of ice, a major problem, perhaps *the* major problem, would be shortage of food and shelter.

Some time after it was first realised that Phaeton was heading for earth, Miles had held a long discussion with his son-in-law. "If Phaeton hits us, Gordon," he had said, "there will be a shortage of people. If it doesn't, there will be a shortage of food. Everyone sits around like paralysed rabbits stalked by a stoat. PI doesn't. We've just beaten a Middle East consortium in buying up South American food stocks."

"Did you have to bid up on price?" asked Gordon.

"No. My South American agent told me that governments in the area had agreed to place a news embargo on Phaeton for seven days. This was at the request of the Mexican President who was worried about a European journalist's scare-mongering forecast headed, 'A sixty-five million-to-one chance that Yucatan will collect another meteorite.' We did most of our buying in that week. The buyer for the Middle East consortium was a militant fundamentalist Muslim. At least, that's what my agent said."

"Why bring religion in to it?"

"Money, the universal religion, was already in it. It was a coincidence that there had been some difficulty about oil pricing in which Mexico lost out to the Gulf. It cost them hard currency. They were sore about it. Whatever the reason, we were able to buy from most South American food factors," Miles replied.

"So, if Phaeton hits us, it won't matter anyway. If it doesn't, PI makes a fortune?" queried Gordon.

"I look at it this way," said Miles, with a touch of acidity, "if foreigners had cornered all those food stocks, countries that suffered most from the advance of ice would be most in need of food. They could be held to ransom. As it is, PI will sell it on at a modest profit. Just as doctors sell pills at... er... a modest profit."

Miles and his senior directors in PI had estimated the enormous acreages of arable and pasture land that would go out of production under the ice. "If it's anything like the last ice age, large areas of Canada and north America, as well as most of the UK and land in northern Europe, will no longer grow food," pointed out PI's logistics expert. "If carefully rationed, the stocks we've bought might buy a month or two. What then?"

"I've instructed Rahman to purchase and store as much heavy and light agricultural gear as he can cope with. If Phaeton misses us, tractors, combine harvesters, modern milking appliances, bulldozers – all that kind of stuff," said Miles, "will be needed to make waste land productive and deserts bloom. We have to move now if a worldwide famine is to be avoided. That's our strategy – feed the five thousand – it has been done before. It must be done again on a slightly bigger scale as it's the 50,000,000 this time. I'm betting that Phaeton misses earth. If I'm wrong, there's no future for humanity. But the PI line is business as usual. We've made our decision."

*

David Medden returned to his London home somewhat revivified by the positive note on which the meeting with his cabinet colleagues had ended.

"God knows, darling," he said to Lorna, his wife, "we try to pretend that we have a choice. But we don't! We sit and wait for Phaeton. If it misses, we sit and wait for the ice. In fact we have no choice but to live each day as it comes. Our advanced technology tells us that we might die somewhat earlier than most of us had anticipated. Without modern techniques we would have thought Phaeton was just another new star, exciting to watch at night, but harmless. Matthew Prior was far-seeing when he wrote, 'From ignorance our comfort flows, The only wretched are the wise'."

"Oh, David, we *do* have a choice. We've often discussed this kind of thing in principle. You know very well that if Phaeton were to hit London we, and millions of others, would die. That wouldn't be the end of the *world* but it might be the end of the human race as *we* have known it," said Lorna vehemently. "The real choice is to abandon the old way of self-centred living and to live by faith."

"I know you're right. My problem is that I'm still too close to the bartering that went on to get land and facilities for perhaps fifteen million displaced refugee Britons. My God, when you're at the wrong end of a market economy, you soon find out what a heartless power is in the driving seat. A market economy, where market forces rule, is run by the haves for the haves. And yet, in the not too distant past, I thought our overseas aid was quite generous."

"You sound like an old-fashioned communist, David," said Lorna. "Don't worry about the money side of the bargaining. If Phaeton hits, there will be nothing to worry about anyway. If it misses, the countries that aren't troubled by the ice will have other problems."

"True," he replied. "Over-population and shortage of food. Let's go to bed, there's a full cabinet tomorrow. You can read from Job 42. It might help us to keep things in perspective."

★

The Rolls pulled up in front of the house. Victoria said, "Don't get out, Giles, you can put the car away for the night. Tomorrow I'll let you know by about 10 o'clock what my plans are for the next seven days. Goodnight."

It was 11.30 pm now, a bit late to ring her daughter, but Victoria wanted to talk. She picked up the phone and dialled the number. "Gordon, has Amabel gone to bed? Could I have a word with her? Ammy, your Dad's just flown off to Portugal and I wanted a talk. Have you and Gordon made any plans?"

"Yes, Mother. We have."

"That sounds very definite. Lucky you."

"I understand Dad's concern, and we appreciate his offer of accommodation on *Andromeda*. Gordon and I have talked it over and we've decided to stay put. There's only one thing that might make us revise our decision," said Amabel.

"And what's that?" asked Victoria sharply.

"Gordon has heard a rumour that everyone under twenty-five is to be compulsorily evacuated to southern Europe. We want to live, or die, as a family. The boys are too young to go off with strangers to somewhere unknown, for goodness knows how long. If that rumour turns out to be true, we shall reconsider."

"Yes! The boys must be with you and Gordon. But if this rumour is true, and it becomes law under the emergency regulations, people over twenty-five will need permits to travel abroad, and permits will be granted for business reasons only. Don't leave your decision too late, dear."

"We won't," replied Amabel, "but for the time being we shall stay put."

"I shall get Giles to drive me down to spend a couple of days with you whilst your father is away."

"A good idea. We look forward to seeing you."

★

Laurie Colgate and Sheila Maclaren had just finished another session of late night, unpaid overtime in what they called their panic office in a large room on the first floor of Church House, Westminster. Essential observatory equipment had been duplicated in this office which was convenient for the Prime Minister and others who had legitimate grounds for personal briefing from the experts.

"What did you think of the press do?" asked Sheila.

"I had anticipated questions on trajectory, approach speeds and angles," Laurie replied, "and on relative closing speeds and the crucial difference that the approach angle of a meteorite has on the depth and scope of damage it inflicts. And because I was ready for them, those questions weren't asked."

"There are so many variables," said Sheila, "planet earth orbits the sun at an average speed of something like 66,700 miles per hour. It spins and wobbles about its polar axis. It is subject to a variety of gravitational and magnetic forces, so it seems incredible that a relatively tiny meteor, travelling millions of miles through space, can hit such an uncertain target. And yet, since we know that about a million tons of new material from space falls on earth every year, I suppose collecting a big piece occasionally is not so surprising."

"Remember, Sheila, Phaeton is really orbiting the *sun* we just happen to be in its path. Because almost every major tracker in the world says Phaeton is on a collision course, we have had to inform governments. Frankly I would have been happy for the scientific fraternity to have kept this story to itself. Until it actually hits, we don't know conclusively that it *will* hit! If it does hit, we know that it could be the end of the human race. It's an odd coincidence that it should appear when we are in any case threatened by the possibility of at least a mini ice-age."

"I think the uncertainty is the worst thing about it. But once governments were informed, it had to be made public. I think we should press on with long-term plans to cope with the ice. After all, if Phaeton hits it will, for most of us, mean that our troubles are over. Or do you think we could escape with less than catastrophic damage?" she asked.

"At present this is strictly between you and me. My latest private plotting exercise indicates that Phaeton is likely to have a very flat trajectory in the final stages of its flight through the earth's atmosphere. There is a tiny possibility that, due to this flat approach angle, when Phaeton enters earth's atmosphere not only will it encounter much higher friction, therefore more heat, and therefore more disintegration, it is just possible that its angle will become even flatter, and it will kind of bounce off the relatively thicker layers of the planet's gases."

"A ray of hope," said Sheila very quietly.

"If that tendency does develop, it will become even greater if the meteorite encounters the troposphere at an altitude of seven or eight miles above earth's surface. It could mean that we shall be bombarded by small fragments, scorched in a wide area along its line of flight, but we would escape being wiped out by a direct hit. We are talking about a very tiny change in angle during the last seconds of the meteorite's approach. It is too early, I think, to publicise this possibility, we must first consult with colleagues round the world."

"Can we say yet whether it will come down in the southern or northern hemisphere?" Sheila queried.

"We could, but we mustn't. If it were the southern there's more hope that it would be over the sea. Even then damage would be on a colossal, world-wide scale. The resulting tsunamis would create havoc in the islands and coastal cities of the Pacific and Indian oceans and the south Atlantic. It could cause massive movement in tectonic plate regions, with earthquakes and increased volcanic activity on a global scale."

"So we sit and wait?" said Sheila.

"There is really no other option with regard to Phaeton. The ice is a different matter. We need to get our skates on – an unintentional pun – to deal with problems arising from that."

"Thank you, Laurie. I'd better get home to my family."

"Good night, Sheila. My regards to Jim and give the baby a cuddle from me."

Andromeda

Geoffrey Wenock, a retired RN Commander, finished his inspection of *Andromeda* and declared it, "All shipshape and Bristol fashion." He expressed his satisfaction to his First Officer, Jack White, known on board as Jimmy or "Number one". "As soon as PI comes aboard, weigh anchor and set sail for Gib. What's our sea time?"

"Thirty hours, sir," replied Jimmy, who was as keen on maintaining naval tradition in *Andromeda* as his captain. They referred to Miles Poundmore as PI because, as far as they and the crew of *Andromeda* were concerned, he *was* Poundmore International.

"Is Lord Harding-Smith travelling with PI, sir?" asked Jimmy, who had ordered the steward to make special cabin arrangements in preparation for the peer and his guests. The state cabin, which was double the size of the other cabins, contained a special case of port and bottles of champagne in coolers, as ordered by his lordship.

"No," said Captain Wenock shortly. In the turmoil of contacting Lord Harding-Smith to advise him not to board the plane for Lisbon, he had forgotten to countermand the special orders. "Tell the steward to transfer all the drinks from PI's cabin to mine. And while you're about it, Number one, tell 'Sparks' to make sure PI's computer room is operational – all switched on and ready to go."

"Aye, aye, sir." Jimmy saluted smartly, about turned, and chuckling to himself, went about his duties.

Captain Wenock opened the starboard bridge door and gazed at the ascending banks of twinkling lights that delineated the steeply rising terraces of Lisbon. A myriad pinpoints of light stepped upwards and eastwards in contoured, snaking lines, their reflections dancing in the curving waters of the Tagus as it threaded its way under the blue-black sky, across Portugal and

Spain, to its source in the Serrania de Cuenca. His thoughts turned to his hero Wellesley, and the peninsular war. British troops had marched along the valley of the Tagus, crossed the Spanish border and, at great cost had defeated the French at Talavera. Why, he wondered, did Europe throw up men like Napoleon and Hitler? Pity there hadn't been something like Phaeton to give them a fright.

He had almost chosen to live in Lisbon, but instead had installed his wife and daughter in a flat overlooking Naples bay. It was far from the advancing ice, and further from the flood of refugees who were fleeing before it. Phaeton, he had said to his wife, was a phenomenon beyond man's control, so, if you get the opportunity, watch it through the telescope as it rides the night sky way out in space. Geoffrey Wenock frequently recited to himself words which he had learned as a member of Alcoholics Anonymous, "God grant me the serenity to accept the things I cannot change, courage to change the things I can, and wisdom to know the difference."

The offshore breeze had dropped and the early morning air was still and warm. Much of his service in the Royal Navy had been spent in the Mediterranean theatre – perhaps too much from the promotion angle – but he had no regrets. He knew the key officers in most of the ports, and had many friends in the countries around his beloved Med. That, and his service record had, in spite of his age, clinched his appointment as master of *Andromeda*.

His thoughts were interrupted by the buzz of the bridge intercom. He stepped inside picked up the handset, "Captain," he said tersely.

"Signal from *Ariadne*, sir," said Sparks.

"Read and send copy to the bridge," said the Captain.

"Message reads ETA Lisbon 03.30 hours local stop. Advise car stop. PI will board at 04.00 hours stop. *Ariadne* stop. Message ends."

Geoffrey Wenock glanced at the ship's chronometer. He could retire to rest for an hour. On his way below he told the Officer of the Watch, "Mr Poundmore will board at 04.00 hours, call me in my cabin at five minutes before." It had been a strenuous day.

Captain Mike Williams spoke to his First Officer, "You have control, altitude twenty-five thousand feet, course 205 degrees, La Coruna to port, one hour to Lisbon. We are fifteen minutes ahead of ETA. Advise *Andromeda* and tell the Electronics Officer to inform Madrid and Lisbon." He walked aft, passing the computer console and the EO's electronic panel, to the seat in which Miles Poundmore reclined, reading a book entitled *Myth and Legend*. Miles rested his book on the broad arm of his seat. "You know, Mike," he said, "they shouldn't have called that damned meteor 'Phaeton'. Icarus would have been more apt, don't you think?"

"My knowledge of heavenly bodies is limited to their use for navigational purposes, sir," replied Mike. "We have just passed La Coruna. ETA Lisbon is now 03.30 hours. I have advised *Andromeda* that you will board at 04.00 hours."

"Well, Phaeton inadvertently threatened the world with fire and brimstone, so Jupiter blasted him out of the sky, though not before he'd done a lot of damage. Perhaps the name's appropriate after all. Sit down, Mike, let's sort travel plans out. *Andromeda* steams 360 miles a day in average conditions, so I shall be in Gib early tomorrow. Allowing for business there – I have to tie up contracts for fruit deliveries from Spain for the next two years – I reckon we can set sail for Rome by 16.00 hours. Two days sailing at fast cruise will get me there at about 04.00 hundred hours on Friday. My business with Angelo Capelli will occupy me 'til midday on Saturday. Originally I had intended continuing to Cairo in *Andromeda*. Change of plan, must get back to London. So I want *Ariadne* standing by at Rome International – no, let's make it Naples – at midday this coming Saturday, destination Cairo."

"That gives me time to get *Ariadne*'s Certificate of air worthiness renewed, as she's running low on hours," said Mike, taking the opportunity to remind his boss that aircraft required servicing and inspections from time to time.

Miles frowned, "Any problems likely with that?" he queried sharply.

"No, sir. I had the engineers give her a prelim last week. She'll sail through with flying colours and she'll come to Naples on Friday with plenty of hours for the Med trip and more besides. I'd better get back to the driving seat. Anything else before I go?"

"Yes! Get a signal off to Capelli changing the venue for our meeting to Naples. Tell him to charter a light jet – no a helicopter for his flight from Fiumicino. That saves me the hassle of getting into Rome. Tell Capelli, same day, Friday, and time, 16.00 hours. If we can't berth alongside, *Andromeda*'s motor boat will be at the quayside to bring him aboard. I need two days in Cairo, three if Rahman hasn't got things moving in the machinery business. Say *Ariadne* leaves Naples at 14.00 hours Saturday, arrives Cairo 16.00 hours. Let's aim to take-off for London at 06.00 hours Wednesday. Confirm there's a car to meet *Ariadne* at Lisbon, Mike. I want to board ship no later than 04.00 hours." As he picked up his book he asked, "Are you taking any steps to safeguard your family against ice and Phaeton?"

"As soon as I have time I shall take them to our farmhouse in the Dordogne," replied Mike.

"Why not drop them off at Bordeaux on your way to Naples? It would add less than half-an-hour to your flight time?" Miles made one of those generous gestures that endeared him to his employees, and encouraged them to accept the ruthless efficiency that characterised his approach to business.

"Thanks for the idea, sir, I'll do that," said Mike. He returned to the cockpit in time to hear the first instructions from Lisbon air traffic approach control.

"Have we had a signal confirming that a car will meet us at the specified time?" Mike asked the Electronics Officer on the intercom.

"Not yet, skipper," came the reply.

"Send the silly buggers another signal. I want confirmation that the car will meet *Ariadne* at 03.30."

Confirmation came as *Ariadne* began her final approach to Lisbon's international airport. Mike had unwittingly saved his opposite number on *Andromeda* from an unhappy start to his Mediterranean cruise.

*

"Step on it," Miles Poundmore said to the driver of the big black

Mercedes, "I don't want to miss the boat." He appreciated the speed at which he was whisked to the dockside where he was welcomed by Captain Wenock.

Miles travelled with neither briefcase nor baggage. Wardrobes and toilet necessities were available in *Ariadne* and *Andromeda*, and in PI flats in the important capital cities of the world. For him, briefcases had long been rendered obsolete by computer systems. A few sheets of paper containing a computer printout of the essential monthly statistics were all he needed. These showed totals of sales, purchases, net profits for each major wholesaling line, stock totals, and the estimated monthly and annual profits. New, or experimental lines were listed separately. He had the enormous advantage of having grown up with PI. A kind of mystique had developed around his ability to command, and sometimes confound, experts who came to meetings armed with briefcases full of paper only to find that this man not only knew all the answers – but the difficult questions too.

"Good morning, sir. We're ready to weigh anchor as soon as you board."

"Morning, Geoffrey. I'll spend a couple of minutes with you on the bridge. The best view you get of Lisbon is from a ship leaving the harbour, just before it turns west to negotiate the narrows. It's magic, especially in this predawn blackness."

By the early hours *Andromeda* was heading south in the busy shipping lane that would take her to Gibraltar.

"I'm going to my cabin. Give me a call at seven. Let's breakfast together," said Miles as he turned to leave the bridge.

"Call me if necessary, Jimmy," said the Captain as he opened the door to his sea cabin, a tiny area at the rear of the bridge with a bunk, a wash basin, a shower cubicle and hooks upon which his waterproofs hung. When they were on the open sea, he rarely used his cabin below deck, it was wise to be close to the centre of operations; he slept better that way.

"Aye, aye, sir," replied Jimmy. Apart from the helmsman and the lookouts on the wings of the bridge, he was alone. A competent and experienced navigator, he had gained his Master's certificate. "I shall soon," he had told his wife of two years, "be looking for a command post, but not if bloody Phaeton spoils everything. Who knows what to believe?" Scientists and astronomers were noncommittal; their caginess made people suspect the worst. The tabloid press, and some television news and *Science Now* programmes, married the extinction of the dinosaurs to a Phaeton-type meteorite, separated from us by a negligible sixty-five million years. Being a pragmatist, he had decided to ignore Phaeton until it impinged on his affairs.

The ice was different. He had seen that for himself when his previous ship, a coaster, had tried to sail up the Forth. The ice had compelled them to return to London with their cargo of grain. Ice had already impinged on his affairs. He thought of his young wife and their baby son, and wondered if he should accept the skipper's offer and move them to the flat in Naples. He decided to mention the idea in his next letter. She would like the flat. It had two large bedrooms, and a small one that would take the baby's cot. The living room had a veranda overlooking the bay. The Wenock's had a larger apartment on the floor above, so she would have a friend close at hand when he was at sea.

Angelo Capelli was worried. The computer had just printed the latest figures for that part of the PI empire which he directed. In past years his group of businesses had appeared consistently in the upper ranges of the consolidated return. Now the graphs depicted, with painful clarity, the leaders and the laggards. He was a good salesman, but he couldn't sell fridges and freezers to Eskimos – or potential Eskimos. Added to that, sales of summer clothing, by stylish Italian designers, which had proved so attractive to the ladies of North America, Canada and Europe had slumped miserably. Shoe sales too had fallen. Cars and computers were still doing well. But generally his balance sheet made unpleasant reading. His wholesalers refused to place orders because the retailers were choc-a-bloc with goods they couldn't move. The manufacturers blamed him because their factory lines were grinding to a halt. They were laying off workers. And soon Angelo would try to explain his problems, face to face, to Miles Poundmore.

"Carla," he called his secretary in, "be a good girl and send an email to *Andromeda*: 'To MP. Will report at *Andromeda*'s berth,

Naples, 16.00 hours Friday. Signed AC.' Get it off right away sweetheart. Then charter a helicopter for ten o'clock on Friday. I want to be in Naples in good time. You know, Carla, we have shipped all, repeat all, stocks of fridges and freezers to Australia and South America. That stock was worth millions on our books. Now it's gone. Our warehouses here in Roma, Milan, Turin, Napoli and Brindisi are empty. And what will our balance sheet show? I shall demand immediate credit from PI Australia and Argentina."

The bridge telephone buzzed. Jimmy stared ahead unmoved. The seaman on watch picked up the handset, "Bridge," he said, just as the Captain did.

"Message from AC Roma, sir."

"Read and send copy to the bridge," said the seaman.

Jimmy looked at the message. It could wait. At five minutes to seven he moved to knock at the door of the Captain's sea cabin, but Geoffrey beat him to it. Dressed in his best uniform, he emerged from the cabin, walked over to the chart table, checked their position and said, "Good morning. Did we spot Phaeton last night?"

"No sighting reported, sir," replied Jimmy, suppressing a yawn. He would shortly hand over the bridge to the second officer.

"Tell the steward to give Mr Poundmore a knock at seven, Jimmy," said the Captain as he left the bridge for the dining room on the aft upper deck.

They sat at the same side of the polished table, facing the Spanish coast where it swept round from Almeria to the Cape de Gata. In the distance the shapes and colours of the Sierra Morena glowed, sharply etched and vivid, in the near horizontal rays of the early morning sun.

"What's the family situation with your regular crew members?" Miles asked Captain Wenock.

"Of the ten regular crew, six are married. The two engineers are married to Italian girls. Jimmy has a wife and baby living in Grimsby. Two ordinary seamen have Portuguese wives and homes in Lisbon. The steward's wife is Spanish – lives in La Linea. The other four have girls in every port."

"The only one with immediate ice worry is your Jimmy then? Would he prefer his wife to stay put?"

"He wants to bring his wife and baby to Naples. I think, when he's saved enough money for air fares, he'll put in for leave to go and get them," said Geoffrey.

"Tell him you can arrange for *Ariadne* to fly them to Naples on Friday," said Miles. "You'd better let Mike know, signal his London Docklands Airport office."

"I'll have a word with Jimmy immediately after breakfast," responded Geoffrey, "and if the trip's on I'll signal Mike."

"I want you to keep an eye open for certain types of industry in your travels around the Med. I'm not interested in job lots, I want to buy factories or groups – heavy-duty clothing and goods including boots, oil lamps and stoves, and electricity generators. We're into these lines already but we need more capacity. We also need agricultural machinery. For that we need to buy up distributors in the Med. If you hear of anything signal Angelo Capelli, copy to me. I'm also expanding our property holdings on the northern shores of the Med. I want more blocks of flats like the one at Naples, and well-managed hotels. If you hear of anything suitable, let Ahmed Rahman have details."

Almost effortlessly Miles Poundmore shattered the calm, unhurried routine of life aboard *Andromeda*, except, that is, for the professional and disciplinary aspects of running a ship, which remained firmly in the hands of her captain. He heard Captain Wenock say to his First Officer, "Jimmy, go below to my cabin and phone her up at once. If she can get packed and ready at short notice, tell her that Captain Williams will fly to Humberside Airport to pick up her and the baby. Tell her to remember her passport. Let me know right away if she wants to come, then we can settle the details."

Before morning coffee was served, Jimmy had spoken to his wife.

"Are you in England?" she asked, "you sound so close."

"No, we're off the coast of Spain heading for Naples. Look Rosie, there's a super flat we can have. It overlooks the bay at Naples. Captain Wenock lives in the one above. The boss says his private jet can pick you up on Friday morning. Would you like to live out here?"

"Yes, I would," said Rosie decisively. "My parents won't be too pleased though. Could they come to see us in Naples?"

"Of course. There's a spare bedroom in the flat. I know it's short notice. I should have mentioned it when I wrote last week. There are quite a few English people so I don't think you'd be lonely – even when I'm at sea."

Shortly after landing at the Docklands Airport, Captain Williams received a signal which authorised him to pick up Jimmy's wife at Humberside Airport on Friday morning.

"Bloody hell," he said, "by the time we've caught up on some sleep and put *Ariadne* through the C of A... Oh! Well, all in a good cause."

He turned to his First Officer, "Here's something to keep you busy. We have to be back in Naples in time for take-off at 14.00 hours on Saturday. Allowing time for refuelling at Naples, work out a flight plan to take us from London DLA, to Humberside to pick up two passengers," he glanced again at the rough itinerary he had drawn up. "Then to Bordeaux where we drop off two passengers and refuel, and so to Naples. Allow the usual safety margins for fuel and time. I hope we don't have to make the Humberside pickup at an ungodly hour on Saturday morning. When you've worked it out, I'll have a look at it. Then you can phone this number and tell the lady to be in the Humberside departure lounge in good time."

By lunchtime Miles Poundmore had completed a tour of his yacht. He had spoken to every one of his seagoing employees, addressing each by name, thereby ensuring their continued devotion to Poundmore International and, incidentally, furthering the mystique which surrounded the PI boss.

Angelo Capelli's chartered helicopter whirled him into Naples at 11.00 hours on Friday. He had booked a one-way trip. As they left Rome he said to the pilot, "I meet my boss. After that I cannot afford to hire helicopters, so I walk back to Roma."

"Are you in trouble?" asked the pilot sympathetically.

"You wouldn't believe it. How can it be? Ice in the north of England, northern Europe and North America, a meteorite millions of miles away, and Angelo Capelli is in trouble in Italy!"

"Do you sell ice cream?"

"I might do better if I did. No, I had warehouses full of magnificent refrigerators and freezers. I had the rag trade depots full of lovely dresses for the ladies. I had millions of smart shoes than everybody wanted. I had millinery that was all the rage. All these things everybody wanted, but not now, and never again. The fickle ladies of Europe and North America – they don't want silk dresses and silk knickers anymore. They want wool and flannel. They don't want Ascot hats. They want balaclava helmets. I am millions of lira up the pipe!"

"They can't blame you for that. Ice and meteors are acts of God. The Holy Father says we should pray."

"My boss doesn't look at things that way. He says, 'That's how it is, what you doing about it?' If the sky fell in he phone me, 'Angelo, what you doing about it?'"

"On the television this morning," said the pilot, "there was a report from an American astronomer who reckons that if Phaeton hits in a shallow angle the sky will fall in. We shall go the way the dinosaurs went. Perhaps you should hire me to wait and take you back – what's a few millions of Lira matter?"

"Nice meeting you," said Angelo as he left the helicopter.

He jumped into a taxi and told the driver to take him to the industrial development area which had spread north to Caserta. He directed him to a large site where tractors and various items of farm machinery, all freshly painted and looking brand new, were parked. "Wait for me," he told the driver, "I have two calls here, then we go on to Benevento and after that south to Salerno."

Angelo was not directly bothered by the ice threat. He was even less bothered by Phaeton, which he regarded as a bit of a joke. But the thought of Miles Poundmore's icy blue eyes, which, in a few short hours, would be boring into his from a distance of twelve inches, *that* disturbed him. After worrying about his predicament for days, which stretched into weeks, the imminence of Poundmore's visit had belatedly galvanised him into action. For years it had all been too easy: you find a factory that turns out good freezers and refrigerators. You find another that makes inferior ones. You buy both. In a fairly short time you double output of the best ones at the good factory. The other goes to the wall. Production up, costs down. Exports up. Refurbish the old factory – double output of good fridges and freezers – double profits.

Now, once more, he had to start from the beginning with lines that he knew little or nothing about. His first visit was to the manager of a light agricultural machinery manufacturing company. His next was to a firm that made oil and gas heating and lighting appliances where he spoke directly with the proprietor. The third visit was to an electrical appliance engineer where many kinds of generators were built. He phoned to cancel his appointment at Salerno – pressure of work.

Andromeda was anchored about two miles offshore, her motorboat whisked him through the maze of craft that cluttered the inshore waters. It was 15.55 hours when the duty seaman led him into the dining room where the steward said, "Good afternoon, Mr Capelli, Mr Poundmore will be coming for tea shortly. I hope you are keeping well, sir?"

"Thank you, yes," said Angelo, cross with himself for not remembering the steward's name.

At nearly four o'clock, Miles Poundmore left the computer console with an up-to-the-minute picture of PI's state in the Mediterranean area. His lightweight blue blazer, white linen shirt, blue Poundmore International tie and cream, lightweight flannel trousers gave him a youthful, energetic ambience as he swept into the aft dining room, hand outstretched in greeting.

"Angelo, nice to see you, I trust you and Isabella are in the best of health?" said Miles, his intent, blue eyes searching Angelo's brown face and eyes.

Angelo cursed himself for forgetting to wear the PI tie and allowed a wide grin to reveal his good white teeth, "Thank you Miles, we are both well. I can see that you are fit as ever – is Victoria with you?"

The steward served tea by which time talk centred firmly on business. "How do you propose to make your division profitable again, Angelo?" Miles queried. He listened to the embryonic plans for buying the required manufacturing businesses. "Are draft contracts on the table for the purchase of these firms?" he asked.

Angelo explained the difficulty of identifying the right kind of companies, and then of persuading them that becoming part of the PI empire was in their best interests.

"Don't try to persuade them of that!" Miles said coldly. "That's none of their business. Do your homework first. Show them an independent valuation of their firm, stress rising production costs, wholesalers pressing for increased margins, retailers doing the same. Falling profits in face of stiff competition, shrinking markets, increasing bankruptcies. Tell them that we have already expanded our capacity in their lines. Tell them if they sell to us, their troubles are over. If they don't, life can only become more difficult for them."

Angelo was pleased when he was ordered to follow up the firms he had contacted, and to keep an eye open for more. He was less happy when Miles said, "That's dealt with the minor points. Now for the exciting expansion plans for your division."

Make Deserts Bloom

Captain Williams eased the throttle levers forward, squeezing a few more knots out of *Ariadne* at the expense of higher fuel consumption. They landed at Bordeaux Merignac at 9.15 a.m. As they taxied in to the parking apron he said to his First Officer, "When you've finished refuelling, make sure we are cleared for take-off at 10.00 hours. Ask the stewardess to see that Rosie gets out to stretch her legs. I'm off to see my wife and daughter through customs. Start engines at 09.55 hours – don't go without me."

Mike steered Molly and their daughter through the customs clearance routine for aircrew, which was efficient and quick. A few questions and the four large suitcases were taken out to a taxi. "I envy you the peace and beauty of Brantome, Molly," he said, "and as soon as possible I will join you. I shall probably take a week off when we get back from Cairo."

"It's time you had a break. If Miles Poundmore hadn't been so generous about this flight, I'd have let fly a few sharp words at him. Look after yourself, darling. Give Miles my thanks for the flight, and tell him I expect you in Brantome next Saturday for a whole week." Mike kissed his wife and daughter farewell, watched their taxi drive off, then walked quickly through the departure lounge to the tarmac. As he approached *Ariadne* the refuelling bowser drew away. He boarded as his First Officer started the engines. There was no queuing for take-off. It was after ten o'clock as their wheels left the Bordeaux runway and they climbed on course for Naples. When they had reached their cruising height of 35,000 feet, he went aft to talk to Rosie.

Rosie, too, felt that the last few days had been hectic. "I didn't have much time to arrange things. I told Mum and Dad that it was just a holiday, but Dad insisted on going up to London to have the baby's name put in my passport. What with that, medical forms, seeing my doctor, and packing, I'm ready for a holiday."

Make Deserts Bloom

"You'll like your flat in Naples," said Mike reassuringly. "It's in a very pleasant position. There are quite a few English people in that vicinity, including of course, Captain and Mrs Wenock. I expect Jack will have a few days off to help you get acclimatised. It's not a long flight, but if there's anything you need now – a drink, baby food warming, just let the stewardess know."

"Oh, thank you. We've been looked after very well. But I would like to ask one thing, Captain Williams. I'm worried about my parents. They've had terrible blizzards in north Yorkshire in the last few days, do you think the snow and ice will move south?"

"The forecast is pessimistic," Mike answered, adding evasively, "but at least one expert reckons the snow and ice will last only a few months. Let's hope he's right." He returned to the flight deck.

★

Ahmed Rahman arranged a speedy passage through customs for Miles who arrived at Cairo Airport at 16.00 hours on Saturday. He walked to the waiting limousine with a plan of action in his head, and in his pocket a single sheet of paper on which was printed up-to-the-minute information about Ahmed Rahman's division of PI. Miles considered Rahman to be shrewd, capable, but inclined to shrug his shoulders and say "Kismet!", perhaps too easily, when faced by tough challenges.

"Good to see you, Ahmed. How's the family?" said Miles, nodding to the chauffeur who held open the rear passenger door.

"All well, thank you, Miles." Ahmed moved swiftly round to the other side of the car. As they sped away, he continued, "We shall go to my new office which I have built on to my home. The city is too noisy, too crowded, too hot and too dusty for a modern electronic office."

A twenty-minute drive brought them to a green and pleasant area northeast of the city. The chauffeur drove the car into the driveway of an imposing two-storey house behind which stood a substantial single-level building: "I built this at my own expense," explained Ahmed, "but when our increased profits begin to show, the firm will pay for the office."

Make Deserts Bloom

As Miles thanked the Arab driver, he said, "Ahmed, I would like to borrow your gardener." A handsome, broad pergola, rich with varieties of scented climbers, including purple Bougainvillea glabra, pale yellow and white roses and pale blue Clematis, provided a charming walkway which, after some twenty yards, forked into separate coloured pathways, each perfumed by flowers. One path led to the house, the other to the office block. Small patios, two with pools and fountains, added enchantment to the garden which, Miles noted, also displayed a variety of Japanese Acers and other exotic shrubs.

Proudly, Ahmed showed Miles around the spacious, air-conditioned offices. The computer equipment was standard as in all PI offices. "We have the latest figures for you," said Ahmed, knowing very well that Miles would already have the information in his pocket. They sat in leather-upholstered chairs in a panelled room which Ahmed called his boardroom. A brown-skinned, dark-haired secretary, wearing a tunic type blouse and full length, brightly coloured skirt, brought in a tray of iced tea and two copies of the computer print-out.

"I'm happy with these figures, Ahmed. You should continue pushing all these lines. How are your expansion plans going in the east of your area?"

"A sensitive area." Ahmed was astute enough to recognize the tribute to success matched with a reminder that there was more to do.

"I'm keeping an eye on north European competitors who might be forced out of business by the ice. Also, I now have friends in Iraq and Iran who are not frightened to talk business. There are signs that the pendulum, and the power, is slowly swinging away from the fundamentalists. Patience. As the Chinese say – softly, softly, catchee monkey."

Ahmed's secretary knocked at the door and walked into the boardroom, "Excuse me, sir," she said, addressing Ahmed, "there is a personal call from England for Mr Poundmore."

"Switch it through," said Ahmed, as he picked up the boardroom handset, gave it to Miles, and started to follow his secretary out of the room.

"Don't go, Ahmed," said Miles, "it's probably Victoria. She

said she would call me if anything cropped up that might impinge on our Mediterranean operations."

"Yes?" said Miles. "You think that will have an immediate effect? OK, Vicky. I'll discuss it with Ahmed." Miles put the phone down.

"Snow and ice has moved south of York. It is creeping towards Lincoln in the East and Chester in the west. Victoria thinks we should urge your part of the world to increase food production now, Ahmed."

"There are enormous problems in this region. Soil erosion, drought, overuse of chemicals on good land." Ahmed spread his hands expressively. "There will be no magic growth in food production here."

Miles appeared not to hear. "It may be that this region will be asked to take refugees. So, whatever obstacles there are to increased food production, they must be overcome. One thing is certain – if we are in for another ice age there is nothing man can do to stop it."

"But," protested Ahmed, "the acreage of land that can be cultivated in Egypt is shrinking. And here in the delta region, once our most fertile area, much of the soil is poisoned by overuse of artificial fertilizers. Refugees? You must be joking. Some of our own people don't get enough to eat. My agronomist and agricultural friends see food production going down, not up."

Miles rose to his feet, shook himself and said, "Nevertheless, we must get on with plans to grow food for thousands, hundreds of thousands, perhaps millions of people who will starve unless more food is produced wherever land is free of snow and ice."

Ahmed, realising that Miles's concern was genuine, said, "We Muslims have a saying: Nobility of spirit, which is 'The Manner of God', cannot be learned or taught. It springs forth like a divine blossom when one becomes conscious of its message. Our first concern must not be for profits, but for people."

Miles, slightly embarrassed by what, to him, was flowery language, said, "Have you done anything about supplies of heavy agricultural and earth-moving equipment?"

"I have draft contracts for the purchase of £10,000,000 worth of heavy and light tractors, ploughs, and six bulldozers – all with

Make Deserts Bloom

spares. I am looking for more. We got good prices from Canadian firms who are keen to sell while they can." Ahmed produced lists of equipment all showing prices and discounts, against the names of the supplying firms in Canada and Italy. Some of these firms, in areas not threatened by ice, were to become part of the PI empire. All would provide consignments of the kind required by Poundmore International.

Miles glanced at the papers, "Send copies to London," he said. "Already done," said Ahmed, whose secretary was at that moment transmitting details to London on PI's computer network. "We shall have storage available by the time the first shipment arrives. I have talked to Capelli. It makes sense for him to store the Italian machinery, I'll have the Canadian. But what's the plan when we've got all this agricultural machinery?"

Miles fixed his eyes on Ahmed, and waited: waited until Ahmed felt obliged to look, questioningly, straight into those penetrating blue orbs. "You are a Muslim, Ahmed. I am a Christian. Some call us the people of the Book. I call us men of our word. You know, as well as I do, that if the meteor they call Phaeton hits us, it could mean the end of mankind. That's in the hands of God. Meanwhile hundreds of thousands, if not millions of people, may soon be forced to flee their homes before advancing ice. That's why we pushed production of prefabs, caravans and tents. But that's not enough. Every hectare of ground covered by thick ice will be a hectare lost to agriculture. We already have famine caused by stupid wars. We have food shortages due to drought, and we have vast areas of once productive land that man has turned into desert. What's going to happen when more of Canada, parts of north America, the UK and, maybe, much of northern Europe is covered with ice anything from one foot to 500 feet thick?" he paused, still searching Ahmed's eyes.

Miles had brought the reality of the situation home to Ahmed, who, until this moment, had thought that distance separated him, physically and morally, from the problem. Now he caught a vision of the scale and magnitude of the disaster that faced the whole of mankind, including those who, like himself, were not directly in the path of the ice.

Miles continued, "All true believers should face this challenge squarely. In your Koran, Sura 90, it says, 'We feed you for the sake of God: we seek from you neither recompense nor thanks.' In my Bible, James says, 'What good is it if a man claims to have faith but has no deeds? ...Suppose a brother or sister is without clothes and daily food?' *There* is the problem – or is it an opportunity to serve God and our fellowmen? If the ice continues to advance, we shall soon have a hundred million refugees and a catastrophic food shortage. If it retreats, we shall have started a new initiative to make the wastelands fertile, to make food available for the starving people of our world."

"You are right. We *must* do something about it." Ahmed stressed the last sentence as he visualised a sea of refugees running before an enormous wall of ice. A human flood that would overwhelm the world unless countries beyond the ice prepared themselves for the inevitable.

"I'm working on this in London. Here's what I want you to do. Remind all your friends in the Arab world that their efforts to achieve sensible irrigation, and to extend the acreage of fertile land in their countries, are showing the way to the rest of the world. Remind them that what is now desert in Iraq, was once the granary of the ancient world. You know how to put it, Ahmed. My job is to try and convince English-speaking countries that they should follow your lead. What we can't do, is to sit and twiddle our thumbs in the face of global disaster. We have the means at least to alleviate it."

"I have a friend who is an agronomist at Cairo University, he meets colleagues from most Arab states, I will talk to him. Old and hardened political, as well as religious attitudes, will have to change. If we reclaim land, we must ensure legal rights to grow crops on it for at least ten years," said Ahmed.

"Our legal department is looking into that. PI Cairo must negotiate to buy land, or hold it on a long lease, in Mediterranean countries. Tell your agronomist friend that the time has come for a global, long-term policy on food production. Politicians have had their chance and they've failed. The Food and Agricultural Organisation of the United Nations has spent hundreds of millions a year since it was formed in 1945. It suffers from international bureaucracy that restricts progress. We've tried working from the top down, now it's time to work from the bottom up, just as we must if we are to improve the global environment. The time has come to recognise that man's greatest enemy is man. 'Rend your hearts and not your garments.' That's not a trite saying with a purely local, religious meaning. It tells us what our attitude should be to our world and every plant and animal in it."

In attempting to create a vision that Ahmed Rahman could see, Miles caught more of it himself. It also became clear to him that Ahmed needed no pushing, just encouragement. He was shortly surprised to find himself being pushed, it was a new experience.

"I think you should call on friends of mine on your way home," said Ahmed.

"Who, where and why?" asked Miles.

"The men I shall mention have an interest and an influence on agriculture in their own country," replied Ahmed earnestly. "Jasem Al-Mana heads a flourishing agriculture programme in Tunisia. I think he will be sympathetic to your ideas. Mohamed Ramzi is anxious to extend the advances in agriculture in Algeria. He is ready to listen. A call on him would not be a waste of effort. Times are difficult for him as a moderate in an often immoderate society. Hassen Osman, of Morocco, never refuses to listen to plans to improve agriculture, it is vital to his country's export trade. If you agree, I will speak to each of these men."

"I like the idea, Ahmed. First, have we dealt with all PI matters here? Have you any questions? Are you clear about our expansion plans?"

"You will see! We shall replace London as the hive of activity for the PI bees. You will come and make your home here soon," replied Ahmed.

*

In London the House of Commons had, after a stormy debate, settled on Cumbria as the first English county whose population would be offered evacuation to new, prefabricated towns in

Oxfordshire and Somerset. The human and logistical problems involved in moving half-a-million people from old established, stone-built homes, into what were by comparison, flimsy prefabs, were daunting. After people had exercised the option to stay or to move, numbers would be assessed, and administrative and helping professions would be allocated accordingly.

The plan was to move city, town and village administrators first, the helping professions next, followed by the general populace. The dangers of opting to stay put were clearly spelt out. Cumbria had been chosen because snow and ice had already closed most of the roads, many villages were cut off, and, in some areas, there were now no life-sustaining facilities.

*

Laurie Colgate had arrived early at his office in Church House, Westminster. He had to get work done before incoming telephone calls and visitors put an end to the complicated computer plot which he made up daily from official sightings and timings of Phaeton. In seven days the final countdown would begin. When Sheila Maclaren came in to the computer room she went, without so much as a "good morning" directly to her own console and began work on the same statistics. They would not speak until each had plotted the intricate angles, speeds and distances, which would give them the latest position of the meteorite. If they were agreed on that, they would then work out what its position should be at the same hour for the next seven days, assuming that Phaeton was neither diverted nor changed speed.

*

Victoria Poundmore enjoyed the drive to Dorset. Usually she drove herself to her daughter's house on the outskirts of Wimborne. But with Giles at the wheel of the silent, comfortable Rolls, she saw so much more of the countryside. When she heard the discreet buzz and the red light flashed, she thought it might be Miles, picked up the phone and said, "Victoria Poundmore."

"I'm glad you let me know about the ice advance. At present

it's unreal to most people here. Sand, sunshine and droughts are their problems. The governments of ice-threatened countries should get their information departments working. Maybe we can push them, but I don't want PI's name caught up in it. I'll talk to you and Eileen when I get back. I'm changing my travel plans, will let you know my new itinerary soon. Bye, darling."

At the next lay-by, Giles stopped the car, produced a thermos of coffee, another of hot milk, and a flask of brandy from the cocktail cabinet. He poured out Victoria's coffee, added a lump of sugar, measured a tot of brandy into a glass, put cup, saucer and glass on a tray and gave it to Victoria, "I trust all is well with Mr Poundmore, madam," he said.

"Thank you, Giles, he's well. Just a bit too much sun and sand."

*

The Prime Minister's husband said, "There's no point in worrying about Phaeton, Winnie. Colgate knows what he's doing. As soon as he is certain of a hit or a miss he will tell you. Frankly, the ice business scares me stiff, that is our problem, and the responsibility for dealing with it falls squarely on your government."

"Don't you agree with the steps we're taking, Leo? We're running the evacuation of Cumbria as a pilot exercise. It will give us practical experience of the human and logistical problems, and we will, hopefully, have time to see how the prefabricated city works before the big crunch comes."

"I don't see what more you could do. Except that you might have stood out for compulsory evacuation. You could face delaying tactics. You know, let's wait and see if the forecast blizzards materialise, if they do, we go, and if they don't we stay," explained Leo.

"The compulsion element raised mixed emotions, not only in the House, but in the communities immediately involved. Some even likened it to the mass deportation of Jews in the holocaust. The fact that people have to leave most of their treasured possessions behind raised grave suspicions. The word soon got

Make Deserts Bloom

round that antique dealers and the like would grow fat at their expense. The House was almost unanimous in saying that people must come first. After that, every reasonable step would be taken to safeguard property."

★

On that Saturday evening Miles Poundmore dined quietly with Ahmed Rahman and his wife, Selma, at their home near Cairo. Immediately after dinner, Miles used Ahmed's office computer to check the PI global reports. Ahmed telephoned his friends in Tunis, Algiers and Rabat. Following this, Miles drew up a new timetable and itinerary which would enable *Ariadne* to return to London on Wednesday, but to take-off at 14.00 hours from Rabat instead of 06.00 hours from Cairo. He telephoned Mike Williams at his hotel and gave him the new timetable so that he could prepare and file flight plans.

Cairo to Tunis

After dinner, Ahmed and Miles returned to the office block. "My faith in Allah," said Ahmed, "encourages me to enjoy the good things of life in moderation, so long as I am willing to share them with others." He produced a sandalwood box on which was engraved, in gold letters, "Corps Diplomatique". He offered the cigars to Miles.

"I seldom smoke, Ahmed, but this is a special occasion. I will smoke a cigar on condition that we adjourn to one of those delightful patios to enjoy the sights, sounds and scents of your charming garden as we smoke."

Ahmed produced two brandy glasses from the top drawer of his desk, and a bottle from the bottom drawer. Using the bottle top as a measure he carefully poured a tot into each glass and replaced the bottle in the bottom drawer. He led Miles through the pergola in a balmy night air that wafted the scent of flowers about the pathway; tinted lights, positioned at a height of about three feet, were shaded to deflect their subdued glow downwards away from the eye, their colours blending with the subtle perfumes of the climbing plants. As they passed the first patio Ahmed said, "That is the sunset patio, but we are too late for that. Soon, from the dawn patio, we shall see the moon rise."

They smoked, and sipped their Remy, in a silence which was broken only by the occasional hum of traffic in the distance. Eventually, Miles put the stub of his cigar in the heavy metal ashtray which had a looped handle shaped like a whale's tail, "I need to know something about your friends in Tunis, Algiers and Rabat," he said.

"Made in Israel," said Ahmed, pointing to the ashtray. After a pause, he responded, "Compared with the UK, these countries have much land and relatively few people. For example, the UK has sixty million people and 94,000 square miles of territory, Tunisia has nine million people and 64,000 square miles. Jasem

Al-Mana will tell you about his hopes and plans for his country's agriculture."

"I don't want official government involvement. That can come later, after we've got things moving at the bottom of the heap. Bureaucracy can follow up with what it's best at – paperwork. We have to recognize that when a country increases food production, its population tends to increase. That's why we must look at food and shelter, basic human needs, together with regional population. If we don't do that, when the advancing glaciers force the mass migration of millions, the world could face starvation and epidemics on a scale that would make the Black Death look parochial," said Miles.

"And the roles of Lazarus and the beggar would be reversed," observed Ahmed.

"But you see the danger? The free world mobilised itself to stop the scourge of Nazism engulfing civilisation. Now the world must mobilise in the face of implacable ice, and starvation on a global scale. If Phaeton misses earth, and we mishandle the ice threat, we might live to wish that the meteor *had* wiped us out quickly and cleanly," said Miles.

"I understand your point of view. It would be much worse if, as our physicists say is possible, Phaeton hit the earth at a very shallow angle. It could burn and destroy enormous areas of land, including cities and everything else in its path. It could trigger earthquakes, tidal waves and volcanic eruptions. Its speed on impact will be in excess of 25,000 mph. If it disintegrates there might be survivors, but the human race as we have known it would be decimated. If it were to explode on impact we would probably be finished," said Ahmed.

"It is better to talk about things we can change, and the people who might help us to do it. Jasem Al-Mana, Tunisia?" asked Miles.

"He is past middle age, fifty years maybe; an agronomist who spent some years on the faculty of West Virginia University, America. Like me, after university here in Cairo, he was a postgraduate student at Edinburgh, which was where we became friends. Like me he is a believer with a Muslim background. He is also a theologian and an astronomer. His wife is Scottish and

Christian. His faith is in his heart, for him it is a way of life. It underpins his work with the soil and the stars. Study of the stars and the universe has given him a vision of a universal God whose power is present in the smallest sub-atomic particle – it also ranges beyond all galaxies, as does his love. You will find Jasem a kind, delightful man. He knows Ramzi and Osman well. I think it is true to say that if you win him, you win all three," said Ahmed.

"Ramzi and Osman?"

"Good men. Both have key positions in agrarian circles in their own countries. Industrialisation has caused problems for agriculture in Algeria. Wages in the oil industry are relatively high. Ramzi has tackled his job with vigour and imagination. Osman is the Agriculture Minister's chief agronomist in Morocco. I will give you a short, written brief on each visit at breakfast. We will have time to talk, your take-off for Tunis is 10.30 a.m., your meeting with Al-Mana is at 1.30 p.m. He will meet you at the airport."

★

As soon as Miles Poundmore showed his passport to the customs officer, the rather bored expression on the man's face gave way to a happy smile. "Please follow me, sir," he said in English. Miles was taken through the VIP lounge to a private room where Jasem Al-Mana rose to greet him.

"Welcome to Tunisia, Mr Poundmore, it is a pleasure to meet you."

"It is good of you to spare the time to see me, sir," said Miles.

"My friend, Ahmed Rahman, has outlined the purpose of your visit. I hope you will agee to a discussion of the general parameters within which any such plan as you have in mind would have to work?"

Miles agreed to Jasem Al-Mana's proposition, which seemed reasonable. In doing so, he found, eventually, a friend whose grasp of the limited choices which mankind faced put his own efforts in perspective.

"Phaeton and the ice," said Jasem, "have focused the attention of the wealthy, 'first world' nations, on problems that have forever been part of life in 'third world' countries, and, indeed of the very poor in 'first world' countries too. The simple need for water, food and shelter. The parameters cover many disciplines, some of which might seem unrelated. For example, ecology and agriculture – including fertilizers and pesticides, hydrology, air pollution, forestry, bacteriology, demography, physics, astronomy, religion, and, above all, economics – the power behind the throne of modern civilisation. The mystical figures of gross national product are the key statistics, because Mammon is the god of the nations."

"There must be a sense of urgency in tackling these issues," responded Miles. "I want to keep it simple, get things moving at the grass roots, so that ordinary people catch a vision of what can be done. Then they will push their governments and make them do more. We have seen how bureaucracy can hamstring the most powerful organisations – even the United Nations."

"I appreciate your concern. Methods of improving a country's GNP too often involve a squandering of resources that cannot be replaced for generations – if they can be replaced at all. A one-off, short-term gain is made at the expense of our children and grandchildren who will suffer the long-term loss." Jasem paused to give his words weight. "You wish to reclaim land for crops by careful and energetic husbandry. However, drought conditions now prevail in what were once productive, though not rich, lands. For example, south of us lays the Sahara desert, and south of that is the belt of land known as the Sahel where, until recent times, wandering tribes had a way of life suited to an inhospitable terrain. An increase in population in this vast area has coincided with a decrease in rainfall, in fact with prolonged drought. In these regions occasional food shortages have turned into endemic famine. That is, so to speak, a tragedy enacted in my own backyard, but it is a play that is also performed on the world stage. The last words of this play are, 'Am I my brother's keeper?'"

Miles had listened intently to Jasem Al-Mana. He was surprised by the Arab's grasp of the problem with which so few people were acquainted. "Do you think my efforts are misguided?" he asked bluntly.

"My dear sir, if I had thought that, I would not have put you to the trouble of coming to Tunis. What I would hope is that if we consider carefully all the variables which, throughout human history, have led to some people starving to death whilst others are embarrassed by the weight of food on their groaning tables, we might find a way of assuaging the problem, a way that will outlast the present crisis."

"I'm all for that," said Miles.

"Most of the parameters I have mentioned depend upon human attitudes to this beautiful world in which we live. If the nations continue to worship Mammon, then we shall destroy earth's bounty as we have known it, and probably ourselves as well."

"I see this in practical terms," Miles responded, "a matter of feeding people, not reforming them. Maybe some people do worship money. More fool them. To my way of thinking it would be criminal negligence if, having been warned of an imminent catastrophe, we did nothing to avert it, or at least to mitigate its consequences."

Jasem persisted with his line of argument, "I think it was Dr Johnson who said, 'Depend upon it, sir, when a man knows he is to be hanged in a fortnight, it concentrates his mind wonderfully.' I believe people's minds are at present concentrated, some because of the ice, some because of Phaeton, some because they fear that wave after wave of refugees might soon be swarming into their lands."

"So you agree that now is the time to act?" queried Miles.

"I would like to see practical steps taken. Also, I agree that we should catch this 'tide in the affairs of men' at the flood. But, if we want to change hearts, minds and attitudes, we must change our vision of what the good life is. Deep inside the souls of millions of people is the wish, seldom articulated, that the basis of life should be love, hope and generosity. Too often it is fear, despair and greed. How can we love the earth, conserve water supplies, have a policy of sustainable agricultural crop rotation, use fertilizers with discretion, and cease our pitiless exploitation of the earth, if our basic aim is economic power over our neighbour?" asked Jasem.

The Tunisian's quiet, passionate manner impressed Miles. However, he was still bothered by what he thought were red herrings. "In your parameters you included astronomy and religion. I know the sun and moon influence our weather, but I don't see that we can do anything about that. And I do not want to get bogged down by religion. I'd rather leave that out. You have trouble with fanatics from time to time in your country and we have our troubles too."

"Religion, like the law, is a schoolmaster. It can teach, but it cannot make people good. Unless we grow through and out of it, just as we grow through and out of our schooldays, religion palls, that is, breeds fanaticism or ends in smug self-righteousness. Love is of God. When love and faith go together, they become a way of life. That is one reason why Islam tries to further the concept of the Islamic state, but the vision is so often spoiled by religious bigotry. Another reason is that Islam sees in the advance of secularism a denial of both God and neighbour."

Miles broke in, "I see the validity of much of what you say, but what I'm proposing is a simple, grass roots plan to grow more food." But Jasem persisted in what Miles regarded as irrelevant polemics:

"Arms sales by one government to another swell the selling nation's GNP. But these are acts of folly and greed, not wisdom. And they are repeated in miniature by the sale of handguns to individuals. If Abel has something Cain wants, Cain has every right to go for it. We appear to be saying that it's still OK for Cain to slay Abel. And that, in a world full of manmade weapons of destruction, is a dangerous and diabolical impression to give to anyone – even people of sound mind, don't you think?"

"I'm a simple pragmatist. I wouldn't want food and shelter to be accompanied by religious tracts, or any missionary effort. You can't blackmail people into belief," Miles answered. Immediately he regretted making what might be taken for an offensive remark.

There was a knock at the door. Jasem looked at his watch, "I have ordered tea," he said. A young man brought in a large tray which, besides tea, had a dish of dates and a plate of pastries. Jasem thanked the waiter and sent him away. He smiled at Miles and asked, "Milk with your tea?"

"A little milk, no sugar, please," answered Miles, whose business brain was trying to decide whether, in a polite but circuitous way, Jasem had been indicating that if feeding refugees became a reality, co-operation from him would involve some kind of consideration. He thought of Ahmed Rahman's comment, "I think it is true to say that if you win him, you win all three." He contemplated a blunt question to Jasem, something like, "What would it take to convince you that you should use your influence to promote this idea?"

He was surprised when Al-Mana said, "We are agreed on the parameters. Do you know these words of Teilhard de Chardin? 'Anyone who devotes himself to human duty according to the Christian formula, though outwardly he may seem to be immersed in the concerns of the earth, is in fact, down to the depths of his being, a man of great detachment'."

"No, I don't know those words. They're not the kind of words I read, but I think there's some truth in them. I am a business man. I expect a return on my investments. As you probably know, my international interests cover banking, petroleum, motor cars, property, engineering, computers, clothing, electrical engineering and appliances – other lines now being developed include agriculture and associated disciplines. These must be cost effective too, because if they're not, something is wrong with the way they are being tackled. But I would be happy to see profits literally ploughed back to expand the venture in agriculture."

"I know that you appreciate the magnitude of the task that may fall upon countries south of latitude fifty if, in fact, the ice persists and advances," said Jasem. "Governments, and the recognised aid societies will all become involved. Meanwhile, if we can spread your initiative at grass roots level to catch the imagination of more Arab and African countries, that can only be good."

"Do you foresee any political or ideological problems if unofficial efforts are made to reclaim marginal lands?" asked Miles.

"Provided land is in the ownership of indigenous people, I see no problem. I suggest you consider a series of low-key pilot schemes, which would not attract attention, would seek no publicity, and which would begin work in areas where, at present, funds have not been available to finance such experiments," answered Jasem.

"Could you, a senior agricultural adviser in Tunisia, be a member of an ad hoc, international body without compromising your position?"

"If your proposition had been entirely commercial, even though I like the idea, I would have declined to participate. What you are suggesting, however, is an injection of private effort and capital into a great humanitarian scheme. Ahmed Rahman tells me that you have already allocated £10,000,000 for a range of agricultural machinery. Do you expect to recover that kind of outlay?" asked Jasem.

"If I said 'no', I'd be a fool. You know as well as I do that equipment that comes free gets very poor servicing. What I would suggest is that you allocate certain hectares of scrub or dry land for reclamation. You find young, energetic men who long to farm, and believe that they can make wastelands bloom. Would your government make a grant if, say, we have a charitable trust which finances equipment and supplies for an experimental period?"

"In the past, our Minister of agriculture has tried such schemes, but they have not generally been cost-effective. That is no reason for not trying again. A major problem is irrigation. Drilling for water usually turns out to be another example of a short-term gain which rapidly lowers the water table. If most of that water then evaporates through ill-considered irrigation, it is lost forever to that area. We have also learned that extravagant use of fertilizers and pesticides may result in a short term gain, but in the long run it turns marginal land that might have been reclaimed, into desert. There are no shortcuts in good husbandry." Jasem looked at his watch again. "Mr Poundmore, will you do me the honour of dining with me?"

Whilst Jasem arranged a venue for dinner, Miles contacted Mike Williams at the airport hotel. "Have an extra hour in bed tomorrow," he said, "we'll take-off for Algiers at 10.00 hours."

About seven miles out of Tunis, a few hundred yards to the north of the Medjerda road, there is a thriving agrarian community. In this pleasing spot an enterprising chef had converted an old stone building into a first-class restaurant. By the time Mike and Jasem reached this place, they had agreed to drop formality.

"You know, Miles," said Jasem after they had ordered dinner, "there is an inbuilt, extremely powerful, international inertia which will oppose the specific measures you are determined to initiate."

"But why?" asked Miles.

"Let's take a family that lives in England, or America or in any country that has not experienced famine in modern times," explained Jasem. "You want to go to a supermarket. The competition between the various markets is fierce, and you have to make a choice – which supermarket? When you get there, the shelves are so stuffed with food that the problem is which particular brand to put in your trolley. Buy regularly, and you get a loyalty bonus. Seen from that point of view, how can there be famine? Surely it's only a matter of distribution?"

"But we see the TV news, we listen to the radio, we get reports from organisations like Oxfam and UNO. The information, the facts, are there," Miles argued.

"Politicians," said Jasem, "do not win votes by alerting people to disasters. They would lose votes if they proposed to give five per cent of GNP to an international disaster fund. I am, of course exaggerating, they would lose votes if they proposed to give *one* per cent! A few hundred miles south of where we sit, millions have died of starvation in recent years. Millions survived as refugees. But who wants them?"

Miles said, "I think perhaps I underestimated the strength of what might be called the Pontius Pilate syndrome."

"We must consider carefully each land reclamation scheme. The drive for short term gain has often had disastrous consequences simply because all the parameters were not considered. If I had my way," said Jasem, "Rachel Carson would be compulsory reading for all students and politicians – *Silent Spring*, and *The Sea Around Us*."

"You, Jasem, have studied all these matters, I haven't. Of course I've heard about the destruction of rain forests, the loss of soil when the trees are gone, the silting up of rivers, and global warming. I am not interested in short-term gain of land which turns into a long-term, perhaps irreversible loss." Miles thanked God that he had listened to Ahmed Rahman and added, "That's why I want your guidance and involvement, and that of other experts."

"I am not trying to discourage you. I wanted to make the point that our main enemy will not be Mother Nature. It will be man. The kind of people who reduced vast areas of the Aral Sea to salt flats and desert by taking water from its two main feeder rivers, the Amu Darya and the Syr Darya, for hopeless irrigation purposes. The kind of people who dump atomic waste from power stations into the sea. All developed nations, including the UK, do it. The kind who destroyed the rain forests of North-West America and made the infamous dust bowl in many of the plains states of America by ploughing up the prairie against the advice of Native Americans. It's a stubborn greed and ignorance that leads to so many examples of industrial and agricultural pollution of rivers, lakes and seas, the consequent destruction of wildlife – and we are brainwashed into thinking that's progress so long as this year's GNP is up on last year."

Miles Poundmore retired to his hotel room realising that his grass roots initiative would bring him into conflict with established and powerful cartels in which he had been a leading player. He was encouraged that Jasem Al-Mana appeared to be firmly on his side.

Three More Days?

"Sheila," said Laurie Colgate, "Phaeton is attracting more than its fair share of attention. People are fascinated almost to the point of paralysis by it. Maybe they think we'll escape unscathed if they will it to land in the Pacific, or Siberia or Yucatan? Our attention is diverted from the problems that we actually face, here and now, on earth. There is a hypnotic dread, a nightmarish quality in the prospect of this visitor from outer space. Or do you think it's just a form of escapism?"

"It's probably because no guilt is attached to it," said Sheila. "It's nobody's fault, there's no one to blame, not even the government. We can truly share the excitement, the dread, the experience with our neighbours whatever their nationality, colour or creed. Jim and I were talking about this last night. We think that in the south a lot of people feel guilty because we didn't do more to help people in the north when the first blizzards struck. The storms were so sudden, the cold was numbing. The snow brought everything to a standstill, except for people with sledges, snowshoes or skis. And we all thought it would be cold for a few days and then relent, as our weather always does."

"What I meant," said Laurie, "was that ice, snow, and frost are nothing new. We are familiar with them. We get them most winters. I heard an old man say, 'We had snow in July once and nobody panicked.' But the scale of our arctic weather now has a kind of cold inexorability about it. It freezes people's wills before it freezes their bodies. When that happens, they lay down and die. So many people up north refused to move. Will the same happen if the Arctic temperatures and the blizzards move south? Look! I've got an idea, hold the fort for a while, I'm going to see Douglas White at Climap. If anything urgent comes up, give me a buzz. I need half-an-hour with Douglas. I want to discuss yet again the remote possibility of global warming, induced by human activity, triggering an advance of Ice Age conditions earlier than it would otherwise have happened from purely natural causes."

Laurie Colgate, Senior Astrophysicist at the Royal Greenwich Observatory, and Douglas White, Director of Climap UK, had met on numerous occasions over the years, usually at conferences or seminars. In the late 1980s the Green Movement and Friends of the earth had invited them to present papers. Early in the twenty-first century it had become more widely recognized that man was inflicting serious, if not fatal, damage on the only planet in our galaxy that could sustain human life, and their advice was again much in demand.

Douglas White's secretary showed Laurie into the large, panelled office with its wide window overlooking Big Ben and the Houses of Parliament on the opposite bank of the river.

"What a pleasant surprise," Douglas White greeted his visitor with outstretched hand and a wide smile, "is it getting too hot for you at Church House?"

"Douglas, you know Church House isn't a hot place, even if it emulates one at times. Actually I have something on my mind. If you could spare time to talk shop for half an hour you'd be doing me a favour."

"It's coffee time, shall we adjourn to the cafeteria or stay here?"

"We shall need to consult your globe and computer models, let's stay here," replied Laurie.

"My globe and computer models? It's not Phaeton that's on your mind?" queried Douglas.

"No. It's ice. That's closer than Phaeton and, at present, poses a more immediate threat. I've heard from a colleague that the US President wants to pin the experts down. He called them all to a meeting at The White House and told them he wanted no more theories. He said he'd had dust particles in space theory, Arctic sea-ice theory, ice-sheet surge theory, volcanic theory, the Milankovitch astronomic theory when what we really had was a big freeze. He then said he didn't want any more theories about it but only wanted to know if it was going to get worse or go away."

"I don't see how he can pin the experts down," said Douglas.

"The present weather doesn't quite fit any of the theories or patterns we have gleaned from research into past cold spells, or little or big Ice Ages. It would be comforting to think that the astronomical theory gives a firm basis for forecasting future climatic changes; it certainly helps, but then there are so many other variables. For instance, whilst the precession cycle is now warming the climate, tilt and eccentricity changes are cooling it!"

"Apparently the President wants his experts to give him the forecasts he feels entitled to expect from experts," Laurie explained. "He reminded them that, according to the experts themselves, the last ice age arrived with dramatic suddenness.

"All of us who live north of – say latitude forty-five, share his problem, and bearing in mind that glacial ice sheets three kilometres thick have, on five known occasions, reached as far south as New York, you can understand his worrying. Should he tell American citizens in states north of latitude fifty to move south now? And that would only be the start of the great migration – or should he advise them to stay put?"

"As far as our research shows," Douglas responded, "there have been up to fifty glacial periods on earth – ten of them major ice ages lasting about 100,000 years. The last one ended between 7,000 and 10,000 years ago. We shouldn't be due for another major freeze-up yet. But Laurie, what specifically did you want to talk about?"

"I actually want to test an idea, it's not a theory, it's based on intuition rather than scientific data – that's why I wanted a private chat about it. Stop me if I go wrong. During past ice ages mean global temperatures dropped by only five degrees Celsius. We know that where plant life and shrubs and trees grow, sunlight is absorbed and the earth is warmed. Where there is no vegetation, light is reflected back into space causing cooling of the earth's surface. Right so far?" Douglas nodded in agreement.

"The destruction of large areas of the Amazon rain forest, drought in the vast Sahel region of Africa, the dust bowl states of the USA, the developing desert in the Caucasus region of the USSR, the accidental draining of the Aral Sea, erosion of the Nile delta, the vast amounts of concrete and tarmac that cover so much of the earth in all the advanced nations of the world, soil erosion and flooding in India and the Himalayas, the loss of arable land in Australia due to intensive farming methods – I could go on, Douglas, but you get the point?"

"Yes, I do. Alarming, isn't it? Then we have CFCs, fossil fuels, motor cars, aeroplanes, and the Ozone Layer?" he suggested.

"Right," said Laurie. "Now here is the important point – you meteorologists say that a slight increase of the sun's heat output is necessary to trigger an ice age. You say that a slight increase in temperature would cause cloud cover to extend in the polar regions. This would raise winter temperatures slightly by preventing heat radiation, and decrease values in summer by reflecting the sun's rays back into space. Now, crucially, higher temperatures and the consequent expansion of oceanic waters mean that more moisture is swept up from the sea to be dumped as snow on the land. Put simply, snow and ice fall out of the sky to make the glaciers grow and spread. I want to suggest that human activity has played a part in creating the conditions that have, in fact, caused the present increase in cloud over polar regions. I think that the advance of the ice sheets is, in a minor way, the result of what we, the human race, have done to our environment."

"I see what you're driving at," said Douglas.

"We've looked at the records held in the ice sheets of Antarctica and Greenland. We've studied microfossils in the varying levels of old seabeds. We've examined rocks and fossilized pollen, and so we've got a startling picture of the last ice age," Laurie said. Encouraged by Douglas's interest he continued, "Not only did the last ice age arrive suddenly, but it was heralded by wildly fluctuating climatic changes, such as we have experienced recently. Then followed increasing rain and snow, stronger winds and an overall fall in world temperatures, such as, again, we have experienced recently. For prolonged ice age conditions we require a sustained lowering of temperatures in the order of five degrees Celsius, to which we may, or may not, be heading now. And, of course, in the ice ages surface temperature of the seas fell too, anything from two to six degrees Celsius, which reduced local air temperatures even more."

"The balance is precarious," commented Douglas. "When you think that, during an inter-glacial period about three-quarters of the earth's surface is under water, about one-seventh of the remaining quarter is desert, or is so inhospitable that it's uninhabitable. If then the human race, through overpopulation, and consequent and growing demand for food, housing and water, continues to degrade even more land, there must be big trouble ahead."

"If world population growth continues to accelerate as it is presently doing – one billion in 1830, two billion in 1930, four billion in 1975, five billion in 1987 and still rising dramatically driving the demand for resources far beyond earth's capacity to supply," said Laurie, "then massive areas of productive agricultural land covered with ice could only cause food production to decrease."

"Agreed," said Douglas.

"My reason for trying to find new ways of looking at the present ice problem is this – if we understand its cause, can we get a better idea of its extent and duration? In other words, what answer should the experts give to the US President and our own Prime Minister?"

They had continued their discussion over lunch. When he returned to his office Laurie had a clearer idea of which indicators he should focus on in his search for clues as to the extent and duration of the ice advance.

*

As he prepared to leave Tunisia, Miles did not expect, on this trip, to see Jasem Al-Mana again, but Jasem was at the airport to see him off.

"I have spoken to my friend, Mohammed Ramzi in Algiers, and I look forward to a joint meeting as soon as it can be arranged," said Jasem. As Miles shook hands before boarding *Ariadne*, Jasem gave him an envelope, "These are unofficial reports, which I wrote after visits to other countries, including USA and Australia. On those visits I met Native Americans and Aboriginals and I learned new lessons in humility. Careful, painstaking research, catalogued in our modern way, should always be balanced by sensitivity, the affinity which mankind must have with the earth, if we are to be truly human. You talked about grass roots projects, I hope you find these encouraging," he said.

*

Mike Williams brought Ariadne in to land at Algiers International Airport a few minutes before eleven o'clock. If there were no hitches in his talks with Ramzi, Miles hoped to take-off for the six-hundred mile flight to Rabat no later than 4 p.m. There were no hitches. Mohammed Ramzi was a much travelled, well-read man. At one point in their conversation he suggested that, provided suitable replacement planting took place, rain forest depletion, which was a contentious subject in so many parts of the world, was not always harmful – but soil erosion almost invariably was. His main problems in Algeria were caused by poor scrubland, low rainfall – or none at all in some areas – and industrial development. Miles thought it odd that Ramzi did not see the desert as a problem.

"For some of our people," Mohammed said, "the Sahara is a way of life. Understand it, learn and abide by its rules, and it will teach you a good way of life. Ignore its lessons and it will kill you."

On arrival in Morocco, Captain Williams was talking to the servicing engineer when Miles interrupted. "I'm off now, Mike," he said, "you and the crew take Tuesday off. Have a look round Rabat, or drive down to Casablanca, it's always worth a visit. My meeting tomorrow begins at 10.30 a.m., I should finish business no later than tea time, I'll leave a message at hotel reception confirming take-off time on Wednesday – I hope to bring it forward to ten."

Miles Poundmore's travelling wardrobe was transferred from *Ariadne* and placed in the car which drove him to the International Hotel. His room on the fifth floor overlooked the sea. He told the hotel porter who brought up the large case containing clothes, and the small toiletry item, to open the door to the veranda. Miles showered, changed into casual clothes, moved a comfortable chair on to the veranda, picked up Jasem Al-Mana's report and sat down. Before reading the report he watched the enormous red sun sink behind a low fringe of glowing, multicoloured stratus cloud that illuminated the sky where it met the darkening blue Atlantic.

He switched on the veranda light. The red glow of sunset diminished as blackness spread outwards over the sea and the western horizon. He opened the Al-Mana report.

The first page contained few words: An unofficial report of observations made during official visits to several African countries, and to America, Australia and India. Jasem had visited a number of countries, or states, in each continent. Probably for diplomatic reasons, there were two distinct strands to each report. For example a footnote on the Kenya page read, "For my comments on visits in Kenya arranged by government officers in Nairobi, see official report."

In Jasem's unofficial report Miles read that the Baringo initiative was a long term success because, eventually, officials and experts listened to the wisdom of the locals, the people who for generations had lived on, and loved, their land.

The story was repeated in differing situations in the USA, Brazil, Australia, India and Nepal. Each unofficial report occupied little more than one A4 sheet of paper, which appealed to Miles. They illustrated that the notion power equals wisdom was not only arrogant but often foolish too. The last page of the report was a statement: "The true scientist, whatever his particular discipline, is filled with awe at the beauty of the world he observes, not as something other, but as that of which he is part."

Thoughts about Europe's Common Agricultural Policy surged through Miles's mind as he looked out over the vast waters of the Atlantic Ocean. The bureaucracy that gave an official in some central city office the power to dictate what a farmer should grow, regardless of the fact that neither the official nor his superiors knew anything about the nature of that farmer's land, was arrogant. The idiotic view that artificial fertilizers, and generous dollops of pesticides would allow any kind of crop to be grown anywhere was equally naive. Jasem Al-Mana had made a greater impression on Miles than he had at first realised. As he thought of him, some of his words echoed in

Three More Days?

his mind: "Mammon is the God of the Nations"; "Am I my brother's keeper?"; "There are no short cuts in good husbandry"; "Our enemy is not nature – but ourselves"; "Rachel Carson should be compulsory reading".

Strange, he thought, *when Victoria tried to get me to read,* The Sea Around Us, *I hadn't time. When I get home, I'll read it, and* Silent Spring *too.* Had he become involved in this because of the ice? Or was it profits – or Phaeton? His first reaction as the threat of the latter drew nearer had been to escape with his wife, family and friends. Now he wondered if that was cowardice: running from the enemy.

On the table beside his bed there was a copy of the Koran, and a copy of the Bible. He opened the Koran, which was an English translation. After reading two suras, he turned to the Bible. Vicky had tried to get him to read it with her, but he hadn't time. Since those days he had read the New Testament from cover to cover. He pondered on the authenticity of human religious traditions and St Paul's warning about hollow and deceptive philosophy.

After breakfast at nine the next morning, which for him was late, Miles walked round the hotel gardens. As soon as he stepped out of the air-conditioned interior of the hotel, the humidity was apparent. The Riff mountains to the north, and the Great Atlas mountains to the west held Atlantic moisture in the basin they created. Was his philosophy "hollow and deceptive"? From what he could remember of Christian teaching it criticized neither success nor riches, but the arrogance, lust for power, or greed that could so easily accompany them. Jasem had said, "Mammon is the God of the nations". That remark had hit home. "You cannot serve God and Mammon".

After ten Miles waited at the reception desk, something he had never done before. A man of medium build asked the receptionist to let Mr Poundmore know that Hassen Osman had arrived. Miles introduced himself. Hassen Osman was impressed that such an important man should have the courtesy to greet him in the hotel foyer.

"I have spoken to my good friend, Jasem Al-Mana," said Osman. "Much of my country is mountainous, but agriculture employs seventy per cent of our workers and is an important part of our export trade. We constantly seek to improve it by methods that can be sustained."

Miles considered this opening remark carefully. Why mention mountains? No room for refugees? He was glad he had read Jasem's unofficial report. He said, "Recent events, that could affect mankind on a global scale, have opened my eyes to problems that most of us have been only too happy to leave to politicians and bureaucrats. Quite often decisions which affect people, agricultural communities for example, are made by some remote body which has little or no understanding of the way of life of the local people, the village community."

"Our system of agriculture listens to, and takes note of, the local community within an overall national policy," said Hassen Osman.

"Yours is the kind of experience we need to guide our efforts," responded Miles. "I don't want to replace one bureaucracy with another. I want to help to spread the grass roots movement that, for example, started years ago in the Baringo district of Kenya, in the great plains of the USA, in Nepal, India and Australia. I believe that personal fulfilment should be part of the production process, so we must work at the grass roots. That's why I represent no one but myself. I have no political influence nor power of any kind. I want to put the right tools in the right hands to tackle food production in the best way. We can only do that with the assistance and goodwill of people whose life work is with soil."

Eventually Hassen Osman agreed to commend the project to his Minister, but not with the enthusiasm that Miles had hoped for. When *Ariadne* left Rabat International Airport at 10.00 hours on Wednesday, bound for London Docklands Airport, Miles seated himself at his electronic console. He had set himself three tasks: first to check the regular progress reports from each of PI's national headquarters; second to arrange the first meeting of his Grass Roots Initiative Group; and third to check progress reports on ice and Phaeton.

★

Three More Days?

Victoria Poundmore returned to London on Wednesday. She had mixed feelings about Covent Garden and Il *Seraglio* the following evening, but she knew Eileen was looking forward to it. Meanwhile, she thought about the uncertainty and fragility of existence. What if Phaeton destroyed mankind? She wondered about the purpose of human life. She wondered if in November Phaeton didn't put an end to all, would they all be saying, "They shall grow not old as we that are left grow old." Death is inevitable, but it shouldn't be senseless, that makes a mockery of it. Perhaps physical death, being inevitable, is inconsequential, not to be taken too seriously? But try telling a grieving mother that. No, she decided, physical death is not to be taken lightly, otherwise He would not have said, "Greater love has no one than this, that they lay down their life for their friends." The Resurrection was the answer she thought, but trying to understand how it was the answer was beyond her. That's what faith was about, she decided. She must speak to Miles, yet again, about faith. She had it firmly fixed in her mind that when Miles returned from his "unnecessary" trip to Italy and Egypt, she would have only three more days in which to convince him that faith was essential.

A Trip Up North

From her office in Church House, Westminster, Sheila Maclaren continued to track and plot Phaeton's progress towards earth. Her computer, linked to the Observatory's system, gave the most accurate and immediate information available. She used this to prepare daily briefing notes for various ministers, and other people, on a need to know basis.

Laurie Colgate followed up his idea on global warming by speaking to colleagues who covered the disciplines that impinged on climate and weather. In addition to meteorologists these included a geophysicist, an archaeologist, an astronomer and an oceanologist. He was particularly interested in what the latter had to say: according to him, ocean currents generally conformed to the 100,000 year climatic cycle. Following their morning's work Laurie and Sheila adjourned for lunch in the Church House cafeteria.

"Scientists, people like you and me, tend to think in what, for the layman, are unrealistic categories," said Laurie.

"But we're soon brought down to earth when we go home and talk to our families," Sheila replied.

"I wonder about that. We talk objectively of ice ages in terms of a hundred thousand years. If we suffered arctic winters for ten or twenty years, scientists would probably call it a 'blip'. But it is more than a blip to the people who have to live through it."

"Relativity again," suggested Sheila. Laurie continued, "One of my friends reminded me this morning of a dramatic change in climate that took place a few thousand years ago. I don't think we know what triggered it, but we do know that a sudden failure of the Gulf Stream obliterated the Atlantic Drift. Warm water was no longer pumped from the hot regions of the southern hemisphere, via the west coast of Scotland, to the very cold seas around Greenland and Iceland. The whole circulation process came to a standstill and icy weather displaced our temperate climate. Did

A Trip Up North

that cause the freezing winds, or were the winds the trigger that switched the Gulf Stream off? It's an equation where the variables are the atmosphere, the oceans, the land masses, the sun's energy output, and winds and water vapour on a global scale."

"Yes, I recently attended a lecture on that mini ice age," said Sheila. "Europe had been warming up nicely, but suddenly it was back in ice age conditions, the North Atlantic froze over. But that was quite recently, in the 1780s. And yet, at the same time, the rest of the world was warming up."

"I'd like to go to Greenland to see for myself what's going on around that narrow band of glacier-free civilisation down the west coast."

"Ho Ho! I don't think the travel budget would run to *that*," responded Sheila. "Let's get back to Phaeton. He is still a very big meteor, still coming straight for us and still very scary. If he hits us, the damage will be incalculable." They discussed the News headlines, the wide variety of articles, and the bookmakers' odds against a hit by Phaeton. "Prepare to meet thy doom" placards and religious tracts were again much in vogue.

Half an hour after they returned to the office the phone rang. Sheila answered it. Their phone number was known to a select few – ministers, scientists, and Laurie and Sheila's spouses only. Laurie heard Sheila ask, "How did you get our telephone number?" Evidently she was not satisfied with the reply, "No, I'm afraid you can't speak to Dr Colgate." A long pause, then, "Very well, I will ask him." She put her hand over the mouthpiece and said, "A chap called Miles Poundmore says he must speak to you. He says a Minister, whose name he would rather not mention, gave him our number."

Laurie took the phone. "Colgate," he said. Then, "No, I'm sorry. I cannot possibly leave my office." He listened again, "Very well, but I must tell you that I am extremely busy at present." He put the phone down with a deep sigh.

"The publicity-shy head of PI is coming to see us, Sheila," he said.

"What's PI? Something to do with Intelligence?" she asked.

"No, Poundmore International is one of the world's biggest conglomerates. I bought shares in it years ago – as many as I

74

could afford. Miles Poundmore is caricatured as a faceless, ruthless tycoon who eschews publicity. He refuses to be photographed or interviewed. We are about to join the privileged few who know what he looks like. He said to me, 'I won't waste your time and I'm not prepared to waste my own.' He asked *me* to go to *his* office. Right away, he said! But he's coming here in ten minutes!"

The security system at Church House worked well – as did Miles Poundmore's. He refused to give his name to the security officer at the reception desk, "Tell Mr Colgate it's the man from PI," he said.

The security officer escorted the "man from PI" to the office on the first floor. He knocked on the door. Sheila called, "Come in," the door opened and "The man from PI," announced the security officer in tones weighted with sarcasm.

Miles wore a dark blue, lightweight suit. Laurie had expected an older man. He knew that Poundmore had been at the top of the tree for almost thirty years. The years had served him well. He looked younger than his fifty-two years.

Laurie rose to greet him, "Good afternoon, Mr Poundmore, I'm Laurie Colgate, this is my assistant, Mrs Maclaren. How can we help?"

"I watched your Phaeton Press briefing last Monday. Nothing we can do about the meteor, my concern is the ice. I have just returned from visits to Italy, Egypt, Tunisia, Algeria and Morocco. Can we talk in confidence?" he asked, looking at Sheila.

Laurie motioned him to a chair and said, "Nothing you say will be repeated outside this office without your prior agreement."

"I went to those countries because I foresee, if the blizzards and ice continue and spread, food shortages and famine on a colossal scale. At first I saw it as a straight business opportunity. I sent our stocks of fridges and freezers south of the equator and bought up all the non-perishable food I could lay hands on. I also increased our agricultural and heavy engineering businesses and our snow and ice transport and clothing interests. Whilst I am sure we must continue to be businesslike, I now see the whole thing in a wider context."

"I'm an astrophysicist, Mr Poundmore, I don't see a connection between my work and what you are doing," said Laurie. Sheila Maclaren returned to her computer console.

"The connection needs to be made. Whether the ice is here for one year, ten years or a thousand years is irrelevant. People can freeze to death in a few hours, they can starve to death in less than a month – quicker if there's no water to drink. However, we could make better plans for our own people if we had some idea whether this will be a long or short freeze. That's where I hope you will help."

"I can explain why it is at present impossible to say how long the ice will persist. We don't yet have a positive, scientifically agreed view on what caused this very cold weather." Laurie then explained, as briefly and simply as possible, the various factors that governed climate and climatic changes. Using his globe he explained precession, eccentricity and tilt, the vital part the sun played, the winds, the atmosphere, clouds, and seas, especially the currents. Some currents, he said, brought warm water, on the surface or at relatively shallow depths, from the southern oceans to the north, and exchanged it for cold water, which travelled in the opposite direction at much deeper levels.

"Since we are speaking confidentially," Laurie added, "I will tell you that I do have an idea about what may have triggered the ice advance. I can't call it a theory, it hasn't been scientifically tested."

"How long would it take to test your idea – to turn it into a theory?" asked Miles.

"Too long. At present I don't have the time to write either the necessary papers or conduct experiments. Also, I need to take a trip up north – *that* might just settle the questions in my mind."

"How could a trip up north do that?" asked Miles.

"For nearly two years now there has been a persistent band of thick cloud in the region of the North Pole. That has resulted in relatively cold summers due to the cloud reflecting the sun's heat back into space. Consequently there has been little or no ice melts in those regions in the last two summers. In the winter this cloud has produced more precipitation, more snow, more ice – lower temperatures, more ice, more heat loss from reflection into the atmosphere. I need to see for myself if there are indications of causes, other than the cloud, for the present extension of polar weather. I want to see what the west coast of Scotland and the west coast of Greenland have to show in the way of change, if any. I need to talk to observers on the ground in those regions. Then I might just be in a position to make a balanced judgment on what is, for the moment, nothing more than a tenuous hypothesis."

"Why don't you go and see for yourself then?" queried Miles.

"In Government-funded scientific work you don't present your superiors with hunches. You put up papers which argue your case. In due course these are considered by higher authority. After that your project is funded, or it isn't," replied Laurie.

"Could you find the time to go up north if someone provided travel facilities?" asked Miles.

"Provided my head of department approved, yes," Laurie answered. Miles enquired further about global patterns of energy, weather, winds and ocean currents. He said, "A marvellous integrated system. A global interdependency, I'm beginning to realise, which operates throughout the universe."

Laurie said, "Whether we are tracking weather or a meteoroid we must take into account all the influences that might affect its nature and its course, including the effects of human activity."

"Time is short," said Miles, "I will telephone you about flying to Scotland and Greenland within an hour. I assume Prestwick would be OK, and possibly Nuuk?"

"Yes, both would do well, but I'm not sure about the airfield at Nuuk. How fast is your plane? I can't be away for more than two days at the most."

"From Prestwick we can reach the southwest coast of Greenland in two and a half hours, and only two hours for the return journey with the help of the jet wind. Thanks for seeing me. Hope your boss approves your flight."

Laurie accompanied Miles to reception, negotiating the security officer who, whilst noting in his log the exit time of the "man from PI," stared impassively as they passed his desk. On returning to his office Laurie smiled broadly and said, "It's as well to have a 'head of department' up one's sleeve. In this case I approve my trip, Sheila. If, that is, Mr Poundmore manages to arrange it."

A Trip Up North

Miles telephoned the PI office at London Docklands Airport, "Mr Poundmore speaking, put me through to Captain Williams please."

"I'm sorry, sir, Captain Williams is not in the office today." Miles remembered that Mike Williams was on leave in Brantome. "Is Mr Simpson there?" he asked.

"He's airborne in *Ariadne*, sir, doing a calibration test on the navigation and instrument landing systems."

"What time is he due to land?"

"He said he'd be about an hour, he took off forty-five minutes ago, so he should be down at 15.45 hours, sir."

"Ask him to telephone the minute he gets down," said Miles. He was getting involved in detail, which he didn't like. It was distracting, but it had a bearing on his business interests. Phaeton could write off his empire, and there was nothing he, or anyone else, could do about that. The ice was different. That was an enormous challenge which could, and must, be faced. He was now aware of, and wanted to understand, the intricate details of glaciation in its global context.

When the phone rang, Miles answered it before Eileen could pick up her receiver – "Poundmore," he said.

"Simpson here, sir, I understand you want to speak to me?"

"Yes, I have an urgent flight in mind. You're a member of the British Airline Pilots' Association aren't you? Does that mean you've got your captain's ticket?"

"Membership of BALPA doesn't mean that, sir. But I am fully licenced, have an instrument rating, and am qualified as instructor and as captain on multi-engined jet and piston aircraft."

"I want a flight to Prestwick tonight. Greenland tomorrow, back to London the following day. Two passengers, are you happy to do that?"

"Certainly, sir." Harry Simpson was glad of the opportunity to demonstrate his considerable experience and talent. When he joined PI, he had a total of 6,000 hours flying with the RAF and BA; many of those hours as an aircraft captain. In the six months he had been with PI he had flown 500 hours, but for only forty of them had he been in command – and then only for short, unimportant trips.

"Would we land at Nuuk?" Miles asked.

"I think not, sir. Better to fly up Søndre Strømfjord to Kangerlussuaq, but I will check that out. If the trip is urgent, I suggest I file a flight plan for Prestwick as soon as possible."

"Get all the preliminaries done," said Miles, "we won't need a stewardess. Dr Laurie Colgate and I will be the passengers. I will telephone again shortly to give a take-off time."

Harry Simpson drew up flight plans to Prestwick and Kangerlussuaq, noting the frequencies of appropriate navigation beacons, he said to *Ariadne*'s Electronics Officer, "We timed that air test just right. We're off to Prestwick tonight, Greenland tomorrow, and back to London the following day. Sorry it mucks up your wife's supper party – the boss says it's urgent." It was part of their contract of employment as aircrew with PI that, occasionally, flights would have to be undertaken at short notice.

The dark-blue Rolls drove through the archway into Dean's Yard, Church House, Westminster. After parking, Giles climbed the steps to the main entrance. At that moment Laurie Colgate came through the swing door and, seeing the Rolls and the uniformed chauffer, he said, "You must be Giles."

Giles took Laurie's overnight bag, opened the passenger door and said, "After picking up Mr Poundmore we are heading straight for Docklands Airport, sir." He put Laurie's bag beside him on the front passenger seat. Negotiating the traffic in Horse Guards, the Mall and two minor roads, the Rolls arrived at the PI office in Pall Mall five minutes later.

Miles stepped into the car, "Away we go, Giles," he said. He turned to Laurie, "Let's do away with formality," he proposed, "my name's Miles, and I must say I'm looking forward to learning more about ice caps and glaciers."

"My name's Laurie. I have this hunch, and that's all it is at present, that this cold spell will be severe, with ice age temperatures, but it will be of short duration, perhaps less than three months. Analyses of ice cores taken from the Greenland Ice Sheet tell us that regional temperatures can change much more rapidly than had been thought prior to recent research. That's why I agree with you about connections being made."

A Trip Up North

He explained, "In the past 4,000 years major volcanic eruptions in various parts of the world have caused dramatic climatic changes. Historians and scientists have noted that the dates of these changes sometimes coincide with mass migrations, or even the disappearance of whole peoples, the Minoans for example. Eruptions nowadays tend to be less violent, but they can still affect our weather."

The rush-hour traffic slowed down their progress to the Docklands Airport, but conversation fully occupied their minds. "What's your plan for Prestwick?" asked Miles.

"The Atlantic Drift warms the sea, including coastal areas north and west of Scotland. If that warm water drift had been diverted away from Scotland, there should by now be some indication of it. My father, a sprightly seventy-nine-year-old, lives at Ayr, which, so far this year has escaped heavy snow. As an ex-aviator, he appreciates climatic changes. He has kept his own amateur weather station for many years, he also knows which plants give early warning of changes. I shall go straight to his house, read his records tonight, and check his garden, especially some of the shrubs, at first light tomorrow," Laurie replied.

"If we take off at nine tomorrow morning we can be at Kangerlussuaq by 11.30 a.m. Simpson has filed for clearance at 25,000 feet – below the strongest head winds, and reckons we can make it in two and a quarter hours. Tonight I'm booked in at the airport hotel, but I would very much like to meet your father, see his records and listen to your discussion," said Miles.

Giles drove into London Docklands Airport, formalities were completed in ten minutes and *Ariadne* was airborne just after 6 p.m. Laurie was impressed by the comfort and luxury of what Miles called a small jet job. They reached their cruising altitude of 25,000 feet in five minutes.

"Have a gin and tonic," said Miles. "After that we can enjoy a light supper. It's odd to think that a massive ball of rock and iron, thirty miles in diameter is, at this very moment, heading straight for us at 25,000 mph. We carry on as if it doesn't exist, but if you're like me, it's in the back of your mind all the time. An image of a cold, impersonal, missile that can destroy life on this planet. What's the latest on Phaeton?"

"Nothing new. It travels 600,000 miles a day. When we first spotted it, it was about 18,000,000 miles away. We invariably track such objects, and soon realised that we were directly in its orbital line of flight round the sun."

"Suppose it lands in the Pacific, would we get away with less damage?"

"There might be less immediate impact damage, but its explosive arrival would certainly trigger volcanic activity on a scale we haven't experienced for ages. The resulting tsunamis would cause flooding, destruction and chaos worldwide. Climatic changes would follow and they would, I think, be serious, if not catastrophic," replied Laurie.

"I read somewhere that widespread volcanic dust could cause a real ice age – you know – a hundred thousand year effort. And here we are, optimistically planning for a three or four-months cold spell that could make life very difficult indeed. How long before we can be certain of a Phaeton hit or miss?"

"Unless it miraculously changes course, not until the last few seconds, as it enters the three lower layers of earth's atmosphere. The highest of these layers is the mesosphere, at a height of about fifty miles. It will then be seven seconds from impact. The lowest level, which enables us to breathe, the troposphere, goes up to a height of about seven miles. This, and the stratosphere directly above it, extend upwards some thirty miles."

Harry Simpson reported, "Prestwick in fifteen minutes, gentlemen."

"So you don't know whether it will hit or miss?" persisted Miles.

"It is generally agreed by scientific observers around the world that Phaeton is approaching at a shallow angle. As it is lined up now, it would hit the surface of the earth at an angle of less than ten degrees. It would bounce and skip for thousands of miles, breaking up, spreading devastation, fire, and enormous dust clouds for thousands of miles either side of its path. We reckon that, on impact, it will be between twelve and fifteen miles in diameter, what we call an oblate spheroid, half as big again as the Yucatan asteroid," replied Laurie.

"Not very encouraging. Do you think it might miss us?"

A Trip Up North

"I mentioned that its shallow approach angle could cause it to skip when it hits earth's surface. That gives reasonable grounds for hope," said Laurie as the "Fasten seat belts" sign lit up.

The Value Of Boring Records

"I last flew to Søndre Strømfjord in 1991, when it was still a United States Air Force Base," Harry Simpson said to his employer, as they watched groundcrew at Prestwick fill *Ariadne*'s fuel tanks, check engine oil levels, and service de-icing equipment. "Then the Cold War ended and Greenland established home rule. The airfield is still operational, but on a much reduced scale. It's now known as Kangerlussuaq. It is the best place for us because the weather at the capital, Nuuk, is awful. The further south you go, the more likely you are to encounter fog. Kangerlussuaq is 200 miles north of Nuuk, and I think it will better suit Dr Colgate's purposes."

"I hope our stay there will be short," said Miles, "are you suggesting we might run into problems?"

"When I was last at Kangerlussuaq the USAF had about a thousand personnel – down from a wartime peak of more than 8,000. Now the airfield has less than 300 local staff to handle a relatively small amount of traffic. Since fog can be a problem, diversion is a possibility, but at this time of year we should be OK. I mention that in case you and Dr Colgate are arranging for someone to meet you."

"Right," said Miles, who considered Greenland to be almost off the edge of the world. He was impressed by the young pilot's knowledge and experience. "Is there anything else we ought to know?" he asked.

"You probably know this, but even in summer, which is just about ended there, it is advisable to have thermal underwear and a Sidcot flying suit or something like that. Also a waterproof jacket, trousers, boots and headgear. We have four sets of suitable outer clothing on board, plus insect repellent. Mosquitoes should be finished for the year, but if there are any about, they're absolute murder," said Harry.

"What sort of temperature can we expect?" asked Miles.

The Value of Boring Records

"Kangerlussuaq is inside the Arctic Circle, so by now it should be well below freezing," replied Harry.

Miles and Laurie hired a taxi at Prestwick airport for the short drive to Colgate senior's house, which was situated on the coast a mile or two south of Ayr. After introductions, Joanne Colgate invited their visitor to stay for dinner and, since her husband, Hugh, observed that they had much to talk about, Miles accepted. He told the taxi driver to return at 10 p.m.

"You have forty-five minutes before dinner," said Joanne, "why don't you take Laurie and Miles to your study, Hugh, give them a drink and show them your electronic weather station?"

Hugh poured a sherry for his wife, after which he led the way up to a spacious first floor room, the windows of which looked over the Firth of Clyde towards the Isle of Arran. Miles was impressed by the computers, the wall maps, a large, illuminated globe of the world and an array of instruments, some of which he recognised as recorders of pressures and temperatures.

"Anything unusual in temperature or pressure readings, Dad?" asked Laurie.

"Nothing significant. Since we last spoke, I've compared present sea temperatures at my bit of coastline with those of the past ten years. There's nothing out of the ordinary. As you would expect, given the recent weather, air temperatures are down," replied Hugh.

"What about barometric pressure readings here?" he asked.

"For the last two years they have been a little above average," Hugh answered, "and, if you look at this graph," he showed them a poster-sized graph on the wall, alongside what he called his "graph" computer, "this traces wind direction and strength, red line for direction, blue for strength. You can see that, about two years ago, our prevailing winds gradually changed from south-westerly and, more noticeably in the past nine months, easterlies have predominated."

The graph had weeks, months and years as the horizontal co-ordinate, and the main eight points of the compass as the vertical, beginning with "N" and ending with "NW". "It's very basic," said Hugh to Miles, adding, as he pointed at Laurie, "these scientists take much more detailed readings."

"It is impressive. I use computers to keep myself informed about my business interests, yours help to give you a global picture of weather patterns," said Miles, as he scrutinised the charts and computer print outs that adorned the walls of Hugh's study.

"In spite of our worldwide network of readings – perhaps because of them – we cannot agree upon the causes of the northern hemisphere's extreme weather. I sympathise with the US President. There are too many theories flying about. What we need is an answer to two questions, What caused it and how long will it last? Have you any ideas, Dad?" asked Laurie.

Miles watched as son and father faced each other. Here was one of the country's leading astrophysicists asking his aged father for ideas.

"Yes, but rather simplistic ones. Scientists look at the whole picture – astronomy, oceanology, geophysical, atmospheric – how all the various forces interact. I observe the changing wind pattern and link it with global warming. At this stage I think it's a short term phenomenon, but that's more of an intuitive judgment than a scientific one," said Hugh.

"You don't think the Atlantic Drift has moved westwards?" asked Laurie.

"I know it hasn't, at least not in my part of the world," replied Hugh firmly. He pointed to his Ayr coastal sea temperature chart, "If it had moved away, it would be indicated by lower readings on that."

"Interesting," said Laurie, "so far, your readings, and your intuition, support my own uncorroborated views."

"I don't want to bore you," said Hugh, turning to Miles.

"I'm far from bored," responded Miles, "in fact I wanted to ask if you think that human activity has much effect on global warming? Or is that story alarmist propaganda?"

"I think there has been media concentration on CFC gases to the exclusion of other, vital, and to my mind, disastrous human activities. For example, the winds pass over the land picking up moisture which is swept up into the atmosphere. The moisture is then cleansed and deposited as rain. As we know, in many areas around the world the winds now pick up industrial pollution, mix

The Value of Boring Records

it with the moisture and drop it as acid rain. Add to that overuse of artificial fertilizers, which leach into rivers, lakes, ponds and underground aquifers, and you begin to understand the terrifying way in which mankind is not only poisoning and killing fauna, flora and trees, but himself too." Hugh looked at Laurie, "Am I talking too much?" he asked.

Laurie shook his head, "No. Your views are helpful, and Miles has more than a passing interest in all this."

"Then I'll make one more point," said Hugh, "which would be adequately covered if I merely said, read *The Sea Around Us* by Rachel Carson."

Miles interposed, "That is precisely what Jasem Al-Mana said to me in Tunis."

"We pour all kinds of waste, including atomic waste, into the seas and oceans of the world. That is another way in which we introduce poison into the food chain. If you want a fairly detailed description of that process, read Jeffrey Levington's Afterword to a later edition of *The Sea Around Us*. Using our oceans as dumps for waste also has an effect on Global Warming. When ocean temperatures rise, the billions of minute plants known as plankton release a chemical which acts as an agent, causing cloud cover in that area. The cloud reflects the sun's heat energy, and the result is a drop in temperature." Hugh looked at Laurie, and added, "Suppose the waste we dump into ocean and sea kills the plankton?"

"We lose a natural cooling process and produce more global warming," responded Laurie.

Hugh's intercom unit buzzed. "Dinner time," he said.

After dinner, during which ice was not mentioned at all, Miles spoke to Joanne, "We had a most comprehensive discussion in Hugh's study. I can't imagine why he and Laurie should wish to be out at the crack of dawn. What clues to future global temperatures will they find in your garden?"

"Because of the widespread anxiety about global warming, and the extremely cold weather conditions we have experienced recently, Hugh examines our trees and shrubs regularly," Joanne replied. "He thinks that certain species of trees and shrubs will give early warning of long-term climatic changes. Perhaps Laurie will tell you exactly what Hugh is looking for tomorrow."

"If the world's remaining ice caps were to continue to melt," said Hugh, "ocean levels could rise dramatically, by as much as thirty feet, and there would be no option other than evacuation to higher ground for millions of people around the world. Bangladesh is one example. The Netherlands and Florida are others. But almost any low-lying coastal land in the world would be at risk."

"I find this confusing. At the same time that we prepare for what could be either a mini ice age, or an all-out centuries long ice age, which incidentally would reduce sea levels, we persist in our worries about global warming. Don't we know which it's going to be?" asked Miles.

"That is precisely the position," said Hugh, "it's like a finely balanced seesaw. The boy at one end and the girl at the other are of equal weight. Neither touches the ground. They're both alive and kicking, waving their arms about, trying to induce their end to go down. The winner will be the one who hoists the other into the air. But it's deadlock. They sit quietly for a while, then one of them drops a pin. That insignificant item is the trigger. The one who drops the pin loses the battle."

"If you look at that as a long term analogy, you can see how the variables could affect the outcome," suggested Laurie. "Suppose, instead of a pin being dropped, the boy and girl agree to have their lunch on the seesaw? Each one's energy intake will have a bearing on the outcome. Suppose it were to rain or snow, with one wearing clothing that absorbs water, and the other clothing which allows rain to run off? And the seesaw itself – the boy or the girl might cover more wood at one end. If so, one end could absorb more snow or rain than the other. Then, if the sun shone, its heat might melt snow faster at one end of the seesaw than the other."

"I see," said Miles. "In that analogy the variables make the outcome unpredictable. Unless, of course, a definite trend indicated how the balance was being disturbed." He looked at Hugh and asked, "Do you have any firm views as to which way world climate is heading?"

"You must remember, Miles, that I am an amateur," said Hugh with a smile. "But I do have a view, which is that the

The Value of Boring Records

seesaw will fluctuate vigorously for some time. Neither side will gain a clear victory for about ten years. Then I think the boy's end of the seesaw will hit the ground."

"And the boy represents ice?" asked Miles. Hugh nodded agreement. The doorbell rang. Miles glanced at his watch, it was five minutes past ten. He thanked Joanne for her hospitality, "I have enjoyed a delicious dinner, a warm and pleasant evening in good company," he said, "and it's been instructive too." As he put his overcoat on, he said, "Laurie, I should have mentioned that we have Arctic clothing on board *Ariadne*. Young Simpson has practical experience of Greenland. He's also brought insect repellent, just in case mosquitoes are still around."

The moment Miles got to his hotel bedroom he picked up the telephone and dialled his home number. "Vicky, darling," he said, "I hope Eileen let you know that I had to fly up north at short notice?"

"She did!" replied Victoria.

"I'm sorry I didn't get home after my trip round the Med. You'll be interested in our potential development there. I'll be able to tell you all about it in a couple of days. I shall come straight home when we get back from Greenland."

"Greenland, the land of ice and a handful of Eskimos. What interest can PI possibly have in that place?"

"You'll be surprised. I'll tell you when I get back, Vicky, I need your help. It's possible that electrical storms will prevent me from telephoning Eileen whilst airborne in *Ariadne* tomorrow. Would you tell her to email Geoffrey Wenock, please?"

"I will," said Victoria, "what's the message?"

Miles said, "Remind Eileen that *Andromeda* is anchored off Naples." Then, speaking slowly, he said, "Message to read, Proceed Tunis stop. To arrive 3 October at zero eight hundred hours stop. MP boards ten hundred hours. Capelli, Rahman and three guests board noon stop. Message ends. Have you got that, Vicky?" Before she could reply Miles added, "I do hope you'll come with me. It will be an interesting development – one that you will fully approve of."

Victoria did not commit herself to flying to Tunis. She said, "Let's talk about it when you get home; and put your thermal

The Value of Boring Records

underwear on for your Arctic trip. And Miles, you must think about faith. Good night, darling." She put the phone down, convinced that Miles was embarking on yet one more scheme to enhance PI's profitability. There had been hundreds of them – all successful. But now that Phaeton threatened humanity with extinction Miles might have only three days in which to find his faith in God.

Hills to the north and east of Hugh Colgate's house sheltered it from the east and north winds which frequently blew at gale force, with bitterly low temperatures in the prevailing weather patterns. The house, on sloping ground north of the Heads of Ayr cliffs, looked across the choppy, grey waters of the Firth towards Arran and the long peninsular of Kintyre. Before first light Hugh and Laurie drove to a sandy beach where they walked and talked, whilst checking water temperature at a number of points. Afterwards they looked at trees and shrubs, noting the normal early indications of next year's growth.

Miles arrived early at the airport, to find that Harry Simpson and the Electronics Officer were already there.

"Harry," said Miles, "I need to do some work on the PI computers, is *Ariadne* plugged into an external power supply?"

"The power supply is available, the EO will come with you to make sure it's connected. I'm visiting the Met Office and Flight Planning, I'll join you in half an hour," said Harry.

Once the computers were working Miles emailed Eileen. The message set out the details of the meeting to be held on *Andromeda* on 3 October. She was to ensure that a copy of the message was transmitted to all PI branches on the secure network, and a formal note of the meeting was to go to Jasem Al-Mana, Mohamed Ramzi and Hassen Osman as confirmation of the arrangements that Miles had previously discussed with them. Next, he carried out his normal check of PI's international performance statistics.

At a quarter to nine Harry Simpson and Laurie Colgate boarded the aircraft together. Miles switched off the PI computers and joined them in the cabin. He looked at Simpson, "Ready to go?" he asked.

"I'm delaying take-off for fifteen minutes," replied Harry. "Northern Greenland is covered with cloud and mist, and the south and west coastal areas are fogbound. The Met Office reckons the north should be clear by noon. I've decided to play safe, we'll follow the Great Circle route, begin our descent off Cape Farewell at noon, then head north up the Davis Strait, continuing to let down well clear of Greenland's icy mountains.' That will bring us nicely up the coast. We can get a fix from Nuuk, check on the weather at Kangerlussuaq, and, if all goes well, we shall head up the Søndre Strømfjord in the clear. That's the best and safest approach to the airfield."

At 9.15 a.m. *Ariadne* lifted off the Prestwick runway and climbed northwest for a few minutes before turning west to follow the Great Circle route to the southern tip of Greenland. At 22,000 feet Harry levelled off, trimming *Ariadne* to fly about 1,000 feet above the undulating layer of altostratus cloud which shimmered in the pale sunlight. At this lower altitude the headwind was less severe. Some ninety-five minutes later the layer of stratus gave way to clumps of cumulous cloud which thinned enough for them to catch glimpses of the coast of Iceland far to the north of their track. Gradually visibility improved until *Ariadne*'s crew and passengers could see beyond the low banks of mist and fog that eddied and swirled around the mountains of Greenland's east coast.

About fifteen minutes later Simpson pointed to their starboard side where, due west of Iceland, a peak rose clear of the clouds and mist, "That's why I prefer to approach Kangerlussuaq via the west coast. That's Mount Forel, 11,100 feet. There are plenty more like it."

Gaps in the low cloud and fog were sufficient to give a clear view of Greenland's icebound southeast coast and glimpses of the vast ice field stretching inland. As they passed a few miles south of Cape Farewell Harry began a slow descent, at the same time turning gently starboard until they were heading northwest. He spoke to the EO again. "By the time we turn north for 'Kangers' this low cloud and fog will have disappeared. We shall see the southern stretch of the Davis Strait – it usually remains ice free throughout the year. North of 'Kangers' it's frozen most of the year. The first half of the Søndre Strømfjord, you see," he pointed to the map which lay on the console between them, "lies south of the Arctic Circle. The rest, including the airfield and town, is inside the circle. You'll know it when we land!"

Laurie Colgate was using binoculars to make the most of the opportunity to see the great glacier from the air. Miles suggested, "You'd see a lot more from the cockpit – let's go up front."

The EO gave up his seat. The fog had cleared, and in every direction remnants of the last ice age spread out below them. Harry turned *Ariadne* until she was heading North. The rugged coastal cliffs showed streaks of black banded by huge flows of ice and, topping it all, the dazzling white of the famous icecap. As they approached Nuuk, the landscape increased in grandeur. Here the mountains had been formed from rocks nearly four billion years old. In places massive flows of ice spilled out, their weight and grinding pressure cleaving steep canyons through which the glacier tumbled, casting gigantic icebergs over cliff edges into the sea. Laurie made notes, then turned his binoculars to the east. There the waters of Davis Strait carried a good deal of ice. The pilot caught Laurie's attention, pointed ahead, and said, "The entrance to Søndre Strømfjord."

North of the fjord, the binoculars showed the icy waters of Davis Strait stretching up through Baffin Bay and beyond to Polar regions. "It's about 140 miles from the fjord's entrance to the airfield. You run out of superlatives when you try to describe the scenery en route," said Harry. The final approach to Kangerlussuaq airfield was no less spectacular, with a panoramic fairyland of white mountains, blue waters and the glistening expanse of the glacier in the distance. An exquisite welcome to Greenland. Laurie Colgate spent five hours with a Danish colleague, a geophysicist, whose helicopter enabled them to cover far more ground than would otherwise have been possible. He also met an Inuit Eskimo who gave him important information about the Baffin Bay population of Bowhead whales. Miles accompanied them on their mission during which various readings of temperatures, sea and ice levels, and winds were recorded; movements of wildlife were also noted. On returning to Kangerlussuaq they compared their findings with the boring records of previous years, decades and centuries.

Victoria Is Three Days Early

Today, some time, she neither knew nor cared when as long as she spoke to Miles before it happened, Phaeton would hit or miss planet earth. Today, Miles must find his faith in God. Vicky attended morning prayer at her church off the East India Dock Road. Afterwards she spoke to the young priest who had taken the service.

"I have a problem," she said.

He smiled encouragingly, "Shall we sit down?" He led her to a seat away from the areas open to the public. The vicar had introduced him to Mrs Poundmore soon after his recent appointment as curate at All Saints. He knew that her husband was the Chairman and Chief Executive of the well-known conglomerate, Poundmore International.

"My husband has no faith," she blurted out. This was not at all what she wanted to say. She had intended to ask a question about prayer. But time was short. The main problem must be dealt with.

The priest looked thoughtful. Their eyes made contact. Hers sought reassurance, his acknowledged the anguish which lay behind her blunt statement. Wisely, the young man waited. Seven years ago, as a physics graduate, he had known all the answers about faith. But that, he learned later, was because he had not permitted the real questions, and his doubts, to surface. There had been no problem whilst he maintained a strict dividing line between his religious life and his scientific studies. It seemed right that his spiritual life as a practising, working class, evangelical Christian, in a Church which he had thought of as God's revelation of heaven to a hungry world, should be kept separate from his secular work.

His work dealt with the physical aspects of reality, which had nothing to do with his spiritual life. That way there were no questions because there were no doubts. The Church itself had cleared away all doubt by clarifying what was to be believed in the precise statements of The Apostles' Creed. Put simply, faith at that time was, for him, an absence of doubt. Don't question Mother Church's teaching or you'll end up confused and in trouble.

Suddenly, he had experienced hell. The certainties had evaporated in a blinding, searing light which persisted in illuminating a statement, sometimes in his head and at other times before his eyes, in which the key word was "Truth". For a time, which had seemed an age, he had lost his inherited belief. Doggedly he continued to attend church services, although they had become empty, meaningless rituals in which the "saved" prayed for the "others", of whom he was now one, including the poor, the sick and the starving of both kinds.

"Can one person's prayer help another to find faith?" she asked.

"Before I answer your question, let us first make sure that we are talking about the same thing. That word, 'faith', means different things to different people, even people of the same religious persuasion. When you say your husband has no faith, do you mean he doesn't come to church?" asked the priest. He knew very well that Mr Poundmore did not come to church – certainly not to this one.

"He comes with me to the Abbey twice a year. But it's deeper and more personal than that. I love him and I don't want him to die before he finds faith in God. He's furious with God at the moment. He said that a loving God wouldn't sling a bloody great meteor at something he loved," Victoria answered.

"A man doesn't usually get furious with someone he doesn't believe in," observed the priest, "and I can understand his anger. A long time ago a man named Job was angry with God, and, although the circumstances were different, the principle was the same."

"But Job had great faith in God," Victoria objected.

"How can you be sure that your husband hasn't?" asked the priest. "The Bible reminds us that faith is not professing, not simply uttering the words, 'Lord, Lord,' but doing God's will. A positive alignment of our will on the side of good and truth, which, in time, reveals the peace and beauty of the reign of God to those who diligently seek it. And you know where Jesus told us to look for it."

She smiled. His short address that morning had been about the meaning of those words from the New Testament: "The kingdom of God never comes by watching for it. Men cannot say, Look, here it is, or there it is, for the reign of God is inside you."

The priest recalled the words emblazoned in his mind by the blinding light which had exposed the darkness of his despair: "I am the Truth." It was curious that he was unable to remember how those words came to him. They were not spoken or written. Yet he had "heard" and "seen" them. He had wondered why the other words from that saying, "The Way and The Life", were missing from the experience. In time he realised that, in his quest for the way and the life, none of his preconceptions had gone unquestioned. He had tried to follow the way and the life with every fibre of his being, spiritually and materially. There had been no separation. Body and spirit were united in those aspects of his quest. He had failed to seek the truth with equal integrity.

"Surely my husband would be closer to the Church if he had a religious faith?"

"That would depend upon his perception of the Church and of religion," answered the priest.

"Are you saying that faith is not dependent upon the Church and religion?" asked Victoria, involuntarily raising her eyebrows.

"The only true and meaningful answer to that question must come from your own, personal, experience," said the priest. "In my experience, faith depends on God. We can only speak from our own experience. Church and religion were, for me, a kind of preparation. But I had to meet God on my own, I had to understand those words: 'God's reign is inside you.' We must look inside ourselves for our answers, because, if God doesn't reign there he doesn't reign anywhere. You asked if your prayers can help your husband to find faith. Your prayers can support him, but only he can open his mind and heart to God."

"I see," said Victoria uncertainly.

"Were you, as I was, taught to think in pairs of opposites?" asked the priest.

"Do you mean good and bad, black and white, that sort of thing?" she asked.

"Yes, that's what I mean. You see, culture, religion and upbringing condition our minds to accept uncritically some concepts which have become sacrosanct by tradition. This can happen in all fields of human experience. For instance, I was taught to think about life and religion in pairs of opposites. You know good and evil, truth and lies male and female. Even, mistakenly as I now know, spiritual and material which, like some of the others are not actual opposites. Indeed, one emanates from the creative power of the other."

"You think my husband may be more critical than I am?"

"As I said, that depends upon his understanding of religion. Western religion tends to be paternalistic. God is Father, male and good. Many people today find that concept limiting. It leads to an interpretation of the Garden of Eden myth in which woman is cast in the role of temptress. We consciously think of God in human terms, but, since God transcends all thought, in trying to conceptualise him at all we get wrong ideas. We need moments of stillness, of listening, of waiting upon the One who alone brings awareness of the eternal within us. Listening is the prayer of the seeker."

Victoria thanked him, said she hoped they might talk again, then made her way home in a thoughtful mood. If faith was not dependent upon church or religion, but on God, she wanted to remember when she first became aware of him. Her experience of God seemed now to permeate every aspect of her life. And a surprising experience in this East End church had taught her that riches could separate you from real people – if you let riches get in the way. And if you were separated from real people, then you were separated from God. That East End experience had brought an awareness of spiritual power into her life which had broken down many conventional boundaries that had previously dimmed, or obstructed her belief.

★

An oil leak in the port engine delayed take-off from Kangerlussuaq for an hour and it was not until 10.00 hours the

Victoria Is Three Days Early

following day that Harry Simpson lifted *Ariadne* off the icy, windswept runway. Both Miles and Laurie were anxious to get to London as soon as possible. After a brief stop at Prestwick, they flew on to the London Docklands Airport, arriving at 15.30 hours. Miles, as promised, drove straight home to see Victoria.

Laurie took a taxi to his Emergency office at Church House, Westminster. There he found Sheila plotting key temperatures on her worldwide chart. Every day she transferred these figures to her computer which would then give her daily, weekly, monthly, quarterly and annual average temperatures at key points around the world.

"Useful trip?" she asked.

"Very useful. When I've written out my notes and made the necessary cross-references, we should find the '*Ariadne* thread'," he replied. "Any panics while I've been away?"

"Just the usual round of phone calls, and a visit from the PM's PPS. I have put a note on your desk about that – nothing urgent. No action required, other than your briefing notes for the PM," answered Sheila.

Laurie worked late that night, transforming his notes into an official report on "Present effects of the Atlantic Drift in Icelandic and Arctic Regions" 30 September 2010. When he arrived home at 10 p.m. he was tired, but happy about the outcome of the Greenland venture.

For Victoria and Miles it was one of those rare, priceless evenings spent together without interruption. After supper, as they sat on a two-seater sofa in the drawing room, Vicky, in a circuitous way, raised the question of faith that dominated her mind. "Darling," she said, "let's not even think about Phaeton."

"I quite agree," replied Miles, "there are much more important things to talk about."

"Not PI's new found interests in Greenland, I hope? Another cracking business scheme to swell profits and..." She suppressed further negative comment about PI and added, "Let's talk seriously about spiritual matters."

"All right, but not in an airy fairy way. You can't separate spiritual and material matters, they're interdependent, aren't they?" suggested Miles. "It so happens that the Greenland trip had nothing directly to do with PI, yet I believe it will, in some way, have an influence on PI's future."

Vicky decided to head off the possibility of a vague philosophical discussion by asking a direct question, "Do you believe in the power of prayer?"

To her surprise Miles replied, "It's funny you should mention that. I've been reading 'The Letter of James', you know, the one who was supposed to be the brother of Jesus. I agree with him where he says, 'What's the use of praying for someone who is hungry and cold if you don't give them something to eat, and clothes to wear?' Now that, to me, puts prayer in its correct context for life on earth. Spiritual influence in an earthly environment. Incidentally, that's a description of the human race as God intended it – earth inhabited by heaven. When your mind is open to that, you're praying."

Victoria hid her surprise. If Miles was reading the New Testament, that must be an answer to prayer, even if he misquoted it. "Yes," she said, "that's where James says, 'faith without deeds is dead.' So you do have faith?"

"I don't think I could have built up and run PI without it," Miles replied. "You see, I believe that the whole of creation depends upon faith – God keeping faith with life that he created. Take the scientist who came with me to Greenland, now he understands the physical laws of the universe, an interesting man. He said that the real mystery was the power of the word. We've discovered the secret of atomic structure and particles in the universe, but not the secret of the sustaining power behind them. I've never known time spent on board *Ariadne* to fly so quickly. It's unbelievable that, in less than three days, life in our tiny bit of the universe might be extinguished by Phaeton. I admit I find it difficult to understand how the source of love can allow, or even contemplate, such a catastrophe."

"What do you mean, 'in three days'? Phaeton's due to hit or miss any minute now," said Vicky, looking up at the ceiling as if expecting the meteor to crash into the room.

Miles turned so that he looked directly at Victoria. "Which newspaper have you been reading?" he asked. He looked at his watch, picked up the remote control unit from the low table beside the sofa, and switched on the television. "Let's hear the headlines," he said, "we're just in time for the ten o'clock news."

The headlines included notice of government announcements:

"Under the emergency regulations, special instructions have been issued to Local Authorities to deal with possible damage which Phaeton the meteor may cause should it collide with earth or pass by within earth's atmosphere. During the next three days appropriate instructions will be disseminated by means of television, radio and press releases. The police and armed forces will mount security patrols in clearly identified armoured vehicles. They will exercise special powers to enforce a three-hour curfew to take place on the third day after this government announcement, that is, on Sunday, 3 October 2010. The purpose of the curfew is to ensure that all members of the public are under cover during the crucial final moments of the meteor's approach towards earth."

Miles switched the television off. "You have three days in which to make your peace, Vicky. I don't know what's bothering you, but clearly you've got something on your mind."

She gave a happy, carefree laugh. Miles did have faith in God. He might not express it in conventional religious terms, but to hear him say that the whole creation depended on faith! How wonderful to hear him say that he could not have built up and run PI without faith. She murmured, "The priest said, 'In my own experience, faith depends on God.' That's what you have found Miles, isn't it?"

"Well of course. It must come from him. What a funny mood you're in Vicky. Which priest are you talking about?"

"Oh, it was the curate at All Saints. When I asked him a question about faith, he told me it didn't depend upon church or religion, and that surprised me," said Vicky.

"Laurie Colgate, the chap who came with me to Greenland, said that love is the creative power of the universe. It's impossible to describe it in human terms. He speaks of it as a kind of amalgam of faith, hope and charity and all the virtues, multiplied by an unknown quantity not less than infinity. It's strange how these things go in threes – you know – 'The Way, the Truth and the Life.' He said that when you open yourself to this power, this love, it's like an eternal radar signal that's reflected back, and increased by every reflective contact it makes. As you receive this power, this love from God, so must you transmit it to others, or the power dies in you."

"I can understand that," said Vicky, frowning in deep concentration. "Yes, I read recently that you should not mistake your ideas about God for God himself, because that inevitably leads to arrogance, idolatry and self aggrandisement. We naturally have ideas, but we mustn't let them become images."

"It means that man can never directly speak for God. God speaks for himself through his people. I know that we can speak to God and that he – speaks is the wrong word – *communicates* with us," said Miles.

"How long have you been reading the New Testament?" enquired Vicky, who could not recall seeing him open a Bible in the whole of their married life.

"If you count school, almost from the days when I first learned to read. There was a bit of a gap when I left school," he said.

"How big a gap?" persisted Vicky.

Miles turned in his seat again, fixing his eyes on Vicky's, "A gap of about thirty years," he said. "I've been reading a modern translation on all my travels for the last eighteen months. When I started to connect the gospel with my everyday work, it began to make sense. It is not anti-business. It is anti-crookedness, anti-evil, anti-sharp practice. I discovered that it is pro-good, pro-honest business, pro-fair dealing and pro-compassion. It brought a new dimension to the world around me. I experienced it in the sandy expanses of North Africa, and the people I met there, and again in the stark and icy beauty of Greenland, and the very different people I met there. But so far, it's not an experience I get in church."

"This young priest talked this morning about the reign of God being inside you. In his address he said that when you open your heart and mind to the reign of God you are given power to assimilate deep truths which, as you grow in faith, sharpen your perceptions and increase your love in a kind of balance. I think that's what he meant. I suppose the balance is a check on our human leanings towards idolatry and arrogance. That's really what you are saying in a different kind of way." Vicky looked at Miles, "I love you," she said, putting her arm round his shoulder.

Her love was tested when Miles said, "I'm flying to Tunis on Sunday, 3 October."

"But you said that's the day Phaeton arrives! You can't leave me on *that* day!" Vicky's voice broke with emotion.

"Of course not," said Miles, "you must come with me. You need some warm sunshine and a change of air."

"Miles! You know very well I can't leave on that day!" Victoria went to her desk and retrieved a piece of paper. "Here's the time of your meeting as passed on to Eileen – MP boards *Andromeda* Tunis 10 a.m., 3 October. Capelli, Rahman and three or four guests board noon.' To get to Tunis by ten you don't need to leave London before five that morning."

"I *do* need time to make preparations for a crucial meeting when I get there," said Miles impatiently. "I tell you what, Vicky, I'll have a word with Laurie Colgate. He'll give me the latest prediction on Phaeton, and then we can agree a timetable."

Laurie told Miles that a general press and media release had already gone out. The salient points of this stated that the latest scientific opinion was that Phaeton would be at its lowest altitude of approximately seventeen miles at eighteen hundred hours on 3 October. It would then be east of the Ural Mountains on a course that would take it far to the south of Moscow, over the Mediterranean, across Morocco or southern Spain and out over the Atlantic. It should, relative to earth, be gaining altitude before crossing the Moroccan or Spanish coast, and shortly afterwards it should pass out of earth's atmosphere.

Miles had caught Laurie just before he left for a briefing meeting with senior ministers. There was not enough time for him to put his question about the likely effect the meteoroid would have on the Mediterranean area. He was perturbed. A mass of iron and rock, thirty miles in diameter, travelling at 25,000 mph, with a white-hot temperature of something like 3,000 degrees centigrade, passing only seventeen miles away! For the first time since the meteor was sighted, he was afraid. Not so

Victoria Is Three Days Early

much for himself, but for Vicky, for the family, for friends, colleagues and employees in the Middle East.

"Let's make a compromise, Vicky," he suggested. "I'll come to the Service in the Abbey, then we'll follow Government orders and take cover. When Phaeton's disappeared, we'll celebrate. After that, early the next morning, let's fly to Tunis together."

"You think Phaeton will disappear? Oh! Yes, we'll go to the Service together, then we'll celebrate and fly to Tunis," agreed Vicky. She was happy now that she and Miles would be together at the time of Phaeton's crucial brush with earth.

★

Winnie Smith, the PM, and four of her senior ministers were seated round one end of the long table in the Cabinet Office when Laurie Colgate, and Douglas White from Climap UK were invited to join them. The PM said they would first discuss Phaeton, and, whilst thankful that the latest forecast of its path indicated that a major, global catastrophe might be avoided, she said it must not be assumed that widespread damage would not occur. The UK, she said, would give immediate and substantial aid as part of an all-out UN aid package which was now being assembled at strategic locations. Laurie answered questions about Phaeton's shallow trajectory, confirming that, when the meteoroid encountered earth's denser atmospheric levels, it would skip and obtain lift, as a stone skimmed in a flat trajectory bounces on water.

"There was," Laurie said, "a real danger at this point that sizeable pieces would separate from the main body. Such pieces might crash on earth if, as was likely, they were blasted with explosive force from the underside of Phaeton. However," he continued, "all the major scientific authorities confirm my own findings which are that Phaeton will gain lift from its contact with earth's atmosphere causing it to accelerate away from our planet's gravitational field, and so to continue on its orbit of the sun. The bad news is that considerable damage is likely from its flight through our atmosphere. First, we must expect violent winds, storms, tsunamis and changes in weather patterns: second, we expect the main body of the meteoroid to be within thirty miles of earth's surface for two point four minutes. During this time it will travel more than 1,000 miles and we must be prepared for devastation along its track. Third, any major pieces breaking away and striking earth's surface could inflict major, catastrophic damage."

After discussions about the meteoroid's track, during which ministers asked questions about the nature and scope of damage, the PM asked for Douglas White's weather predictions. Heavy snow had again fallen in eastern Scotland and north-east England – and there was more to come. Following the presentation of their reports Douglas and Laurie retired from the Cabinet Room. The ministers remained, huddled round one corner of the great table, trying to find solutions to insoluble problems.

The Countdown Begins

For many years Victoria had attended a midweek service at All Saints, off the East India Dock Road, where she had made many friends. An elderly, aristocratic lady, whom she had met at the Abbey, had persuaded her to accompany her saying, "You will meet real people there, my dear, unvarnished people."

The church stood in a parish which was less than half a mile north of the Thames. During the war most of the men of this area had earned a living at the adjacent London docks, or as crew members in the merchant vessels which sailed from them. Heavy bombing of the parish and its church in WWII, had led members of the Abbey's congregation to form an ad hoc group to support the battered church and its people. After the war there had been long, difficult – sometimes bitter – days before rebuilding was completed.

On that first visit Victoria had avidly observed the phenomenon: her elderly, titled companion, considered to be a trifle starchy at the Abbey, was on Christian name terms with the All Saints people. She loved and trusted them – and they reciprocated. After the old lady's death, Victoria maintained her contact with the church throughout times of great social and political change in the dockland parishes. Her first effort to involve Miles had also been the last, "Not my cup of tea, Vicky. And don't go in the Rolls, they'll vandalise it."

"Blind prejudice," Vicky retorted, "and don't worry, I'd rather walk than take your precious Rolls."

The thought of Vicky walking unaccompanied in dockland had alarmed Miles, "Buy a small car," he suggested.

"A good idea," she said, and much to his annoyance, promptly bought a Citroën 2CV.

"Victoria!" he complained, "You know we have a British manufacturer in the PI Group. I could have bought you a Mini at trade price."

"I know," she responded, "but my friends at All Saints might vandalise a Mini. And in any case," she added, "I wanted a 2CV."

"Oh well, there's one consolation. A 2CV looks as if it's been vandalised before it leaves the factory," Miles retorted.

That was in the days of the old Miles, she thought. The one who, on Christmas Day and Easter Day, attended a service at the Abbey wearing a dark suit and a long-suffering expression. At first she thought that the change in Miles would be nothing more than a flash in the pan; the threat posed by Phaeton had given him a new, but temporary, focal point to distract him from his fanatical devotion to PI.

As she thought about the change in her husband, whom she had loved when he was poor, whom she still loved now that he was rich, whom she loved "for better or for worse", Victoria realised that it was not due solely to the threats posed by Phaeton and the ice. Two people and two events had recently made deep impressions on Miles: the first she was aware of from brief comments, made by him, in reference to the wisdom of an Arab named Jasem Al-Mana at a meeting in Tunis. The second was a scientist named Laurie Colgate who had accompanied him on a visit to Greenland. The Greenland trip had nothing directly to do with PI, but, Miles had said, it might in some mysterious way influence PI's future. Those two journeys involved real people; neither would have taken place but for Phaeton and the ice. It was time for Miles to meet more real, "unvarnished", people.

She imagined the new Miles driving with her, in her now ancient 2CV, to All Saints, just off the East India Dock Road. After Phaeton, even though globe-threatening disasters might be left in its wake, thanksgiving services would be held in almost every church in the country. There would be one at the Abbey. There would certainly be one at All Saints.

*

Laurie Colgate and Douglas White were working together on two papers in the latter's office. The first paper, which Douglas referred to as the "Putting Phaeton to Bed" analysis, was almost complete.

"Have we missed anything out of our appreciation of the situation?" asked Laurie.

"I think it's all there," Douglas replied, "but we shall have to meet the PM's Emergency Committee again. Some of the technical terms might need explanation, after which ministers should be able to amend their orders to local authorities."

"The Home Secretary requires us to specify those aspects of Phaeton's contact with earth, or passage through earth's atmosphere, which might cause injury to persons or property," said Laurie. "Some day we must revise our paper on, 'Safety Precautions'. Phaeton itself, the whole meteor, isn't going to strike. I'm almost sure of that now." He paused, looked thoughtful, and asked, "How do we give an honest picture that presents the truth, without creating panic?"

"We can only give the facts as we see them," said Douglas. "Then, if invited to do so, we can suggest dissemination in such a way that members of the public are encouraged to take sensible precautions."

"So!" said Laurie, "we await the arrival of a massive ball of incandescent rock, mineral and metal, about the size of the Isle of Wight, hurtling past at an uncertain height. It radiates terrific heat. It creates the air-tearing, ear-splitting noise of a thousand thunderstorms rolled into one. It generates hurricane force winds, tornadoes and cyclones, with tsunamis as a non-negotiable extra. There is also the possibility of fragmentation. A lump or lumps weighing, perhaps, a million tons could be exploded from the main body of the meteorite in any direction. It's a similar problem to the one your people have in tracking and predicting the course of a hurricane, but on a bigger scale, with friction-heat and fragmentation factors thrown in."

"Let's get down to the nitty-gritty then. If we run the disc with your models on, we can review our specification of the aspects, agree or revise them, and then detail, under each head, the methods by which damage or injury can be avoided or limited." Douglas slotted Laurie's compact disc into the computer.

The first model showed earth and its atmosphere, the rarest parts of which extended some 1,500 miles above earth's surface. Laurie's model emphasised the troposphere, the lower seven to ten miles of air which contains three quarters of the total atmospheric mass and most of its moisture. Above that, in order of decreasing density, ascended the stratosphere, the mesosphere and the thermosphere, their combined layers reaching an altitude of about 300 miles.

These four layers of atmosphere would significantly and progressively increase friction heat on Phaeton as it closed with earth's surface and as atmospheric density increased. Because the meteor's approach angle was shallow, it would take fractionally more time to pass through each atmospheric layer, thus generating more heat. However, the scientists believed this adverse effect would be more than compensated for by the skid/lift effect as the meteoroid approached earth's denser, lower levels of air. These essential facts were noted alongside each of Laurie's diagrammatic presentations.

The most optimistic diagram showed Phaeton's approach angle reducing to zero as it encountered the mesosphere at a height of some fifty miles. The most pessimistic showed it reducing to zero as it entered the troposphere at a height of only seven or eight miles. The former case represented a miraculous escape with possibly no more to endure than unusual weather patterns, extra storms and the possibility of fragmentation rock strikes. Both cases were beyond mankind's recorded experience, but the latter promised mayhem. Scientists believed that it threatened fire, storm, flood and destruction. But where, and on what scale, it was impossible to forecast with certainty. They had made their computer models as accurate as possible, their interpretation of them had been checked and re-checked, but at best they could give only an indication of what might happen. They decided to include a footnote: "The above predictions assume that Phaeton continues on its present course, and that it does not explode."

By 3 p.m. they had sent their detailed analysis, with supporting diagrams, to the Home Secretary, saying also that they held themselves ready to attend on her should elucidation be required. As far as they were professionally concerned, Phaeton had been "put to bed", not to sleep but to doze fitfully, whilst his watchers began the countdown which would not end until the nightmare was over.

The Countdown Begins

The two men next turned their attention to the immediate, more ponderous, and infinitely more frigid threat of ice and snow.

★

Miles Poundmore reclined in his comfortable leather swivel-chair, legs stretched out on the matching inlaid leather surface of his large desk, which, apart from the intercom and his feet, had nothing on it. His eyes were fixed unseeingly on the facades of famous London clubs on the other side of Pall Mall.

Eileen was worried. On his arrival over an hour ago he had neither spared a glance at his indispensable computer console, nor switched on the visual display unit. There had been no questions, no incisive telephone calls. Normally, when he had been away from the office for more than twenty-four hours, he breezed in shouting, "What's the latest buzz in the city, Eileen?" Next, without waiting for an answer, "Get that good-for-nothing Capelli or some other unfortunate director on the line."

"Where am I lunching today? Who with?" The stillness and the silence were uncanny. Only once before had she seen him bereft of his natural ebullience, and that was thirty years ago.

They had been sitting in a tiny cellar office in Park Place, off St James's Street. He was about to tell his private and confidential secretary, twenty-year-old Eileen, about two extravagant, and financially insupportable propositions to which he had committed Poundmore Entrepreneurial Services.

In those days they shared one small office; essential facilities were shared with occupants of other cellars – euphemistically described as 'basement suites'. After a wordless two hours, twenty-two-year-old Miles had said, "I've asked Victoria to marry me."

Eileen gasped. Victoria's father had achieved high rank and a knighthood in one of the armed services. He was not rich, but he had picked up a couple of directorships which, with his service pension, made life comfortable. He didn't employ a chauffer, but one was available when required. His lady wife employed a housekeeper-cook and a maid. He would expect

The Countdown Begins

Miles to maintain at least equivalent standards for his beloved daughter.

Before Eileen had recovered from that shock announcement Miles had said, in an equally flat, expressionless voice, "I've arranged a one-hundred percent mortgage on my father's house as part collateral for that property company."

Eileen had screamed, "We're ruined! A block of decrepit buildings off Cannon Street, a few mouldy houses in Kensington and, star of the portfolio, the dregs of a wine bar in the city! You're mad."

But it had worked. Eileen's father had shown such faith in Miles that he too had raised a mortgage to encourage the new company, to be called Poundmore International, in its early days. Eileen would not admit that she was married to PI, but it had become a way of life for her. She would never entertain any other suitor.

On this occasion there was nothing dramatic about Miles's unaccustomed silence. He had decided to take time out to listen. His only words to Eileen had been, "Morning, Eileen. No phone calls please."

He had no idea what he expected to hear. In fact he decided not to "expect" anything. That would be presumption. What eventually happened was that, at first, a few statements popped up in his mind. It is a miraculous fact, he thought, that each human being is unique. Phaeton, he realised, was forcing him to face death as a fact of life: like a change of direction for good, and not evil. You go through a one-way door. You had to have the trust of a child. But you can't become, or achieve, what you don't believe in – can you? Something to do with faith. Praying for the starving is useless if you don't have the will to do something about it. Whether Phaeton destroys human life now, or whether we last another ten million years makes no difference when you have glimpsed, if only for a fraction of a second, the Eternal. It was strange how, since Phaeton had first been spotted, the days had raced by. That is – until the countdown began. Now the minutes were like hours and the hours dragged like days. Some words of Goethe ran through his mind: "If you wish the blossom of the early and fruit of the late years, wish what is charming and exciting, as well as nourishing and substantial. Wish to capture in one name heaven and earth."

He thought of Vicky's words last night: "When you open your heart and mind to God's reign, you receive power to assimilate deep truths which, as you grow in faith and spirituality, sharpen your perceptions and increase your love." To know, inside yourself, heaven and earth. Sharpen your perceptions and increase your love? No! Increase your love and sharpen your perceptions: "The blossom of the early and fruit of the late years." Unless you knew and trusted God, you might ask, "What late years?" You could become cynical and unbelieving. You could put all your eggs in one earthly basket – yourself. You alone are the truth the way and the life. You could die knowing, and believing, that there is no one there.

That was it! Sometimes you forget that God might speak to you through other people like Vicky or Jasem Al-Mana. Like Laurie Colgate and his father. Like Eileen. He flicked the switch on the intercom, "Eileen, let's have coffee – now, in here, I want to talk to you."

Eileen acknowledged the order in her dutiful, secretarial voice. Five minutes later she opened the door to Miles's office, without knocking. He had told her not to knock unless there was someone with him, it wasted time. She poured coffee into a cup and took it to his desk.

"No, Eileen," he said, "we'll sit in the easy chairs at the coffee table." Raised eyebrows were the only indication of her surprise.

"You may think I'm trying to emulate Scrooge at Christmas," said Miles, "you know – better late than never."

"Well, it is the first time since we left Park Place that we've wasted – er – had coffee without – well, we always carry on working during our coffee break."

"Oh, I don't mean the coffee. We'll carry on working as usual," said Miles. "You and Vicky are the only two people who have grown up with PI right from the start. If I disappeared, you are the only person who could put up a 'business as usual' sign. I'm offering you the job of Company Secretary."

"But I already am," said Eileen.

The Countdown Begins

"You do the work," Miles agreed, "but our legal adviser's chief clerk signs as Company Secretary. That's how it began thirty years ago – it gave authority and panache to the accounts – and I've never bothered to change it. His signature probably costs us ten thousand a year these days."

"I can see that it would be an economy if I signed," Eileen said drily.

"Oh, it's not that – ten thousand is neither here nor there – I think it's time you had recognition and status in the group. The Company Secretary could also be an executive director. With a seat on the main board you would, in theory, have more authority. I can't honestly say that it would be more than you exercise already."

"I would want to continue as your Private and Confidential Secretary. If I can do that, I accept the title and responsibilities of Company Secretary. If not, I decline them." Eileen spoke with a hint of that asperity which endeared her to Miles who thought, *If I can't get the better of her, she's the right person to look after my interests*.

He chuckled to himself as he realised that she thought he was trying to pull a fast one. "My dear Eileen, if you had put that the other way round, I would have withdrawn the offer. There is no one who could possibly replace you. By the way, how is your assistant coming on?"

The ever-tactless Miles, she thought. "As long as that's understood, I accept with thanks. Do I get an increase in salary?"

"One thing at a time," he said. "Your assistant?"

"The agency vetted her extremely carefully. She's a bright girl, well up to her job and learning mine too. She has a sharp commercial instinct and enjoys the worldwide scenario. But I've told her that if she doesn't break one unacceptable habit she'll have to leave."

"Oh, and what's that?" asked Miles. "Swearing and blaspheming was an habitual part of her language. I told her it must stop. She said it was inbred, inherited from her mother."

"Is she staying or leaving?" queried Miles.

"I've not heard one blasphemous outburst, or any 'f' or 'b' words for two weeks. She stays," replied Eileen.

"Your pay is already in line with a junior director's, so no salary increase. You will get a thousand a year director's fee. You already have a company car. You can have a bigger one if you wish."

"I just wanted to see what you'd say," responded Eileen. "I'd have been worried if PI hadn't made a profit on the deal. You mustn't lose your cutting edge. Business could be fraught with financial problems from Phaeton, and ice and snow in the coming months. I'm glad to see that our insurance arm has spread a lot of risk in the past month through its reinsurance strategy. It probably means there'll be a period of lower profits from insurance, but it's a timely hedge."

"Yes," said Miles shortly. "I'm cutting lunch today, switch my computer on, Eileen. I need a couple of hours alone. After that I want a word about the embryo North African Agricultural Trust."

Eileen continued her round-up of statistics on the PI network until Miles buzzed on the intercom. "Get on to Martin at PI car factors. Tell him to change my Rolls for a Jaguar. I want the usual fittings – he knows what they are – and I expect a substantial saving for PI. Tell him to phone me if he has any doubts about which model I should have."

On receiving the signal ordering *Andromeda* to standby at Tunis at 08.00 hours on 4 October, Captain Geoffrey Wenock told his "Jimmy the One" to arrange for ali crew members to board by 05.00 hours on 3 October. She would sail at 06.00 hours, and, steaming at an economical twelve knots, she would make Tunis by 06.30 hours the following morning. He ordered the duty officer to check all navigation equipment, fuel, water, and safety gear including lifeboats, rafts, and all stores. He said he would carry out a full inspection at 5.15 hours on the third.

He was somewhat concerned that they would be about halfway to Tunis at the time that the meteorite was supposed to pass over – almost directly over – Sicily. They might have to take shelter in the lea of Sicily, or even make for Palermo Harbour. He asked his wife to invite Jack and Rosie up for a drink – a gin and French – whilst they sat on the veranda talking about the unsettled weather to the north, and the blizzards that were moving down from Scotland to hit northeast England.

The Countdown Begins

"Are you well up in physics, Jack?" asked Geoffrey.

"My degree is in engineering, Geoffrey. We touched on atomic structure and electromagnetism, but then I got hooked on the oceans, navigation, astronomy, ships and the Navy," he replied.

"I wondered what you thought about Phaeton. How can an enormous, island-sized chunk of metal and rock weighing billions of tons screech through space at 25,000 miles an hour?"

"Probably the result of an interstellar explosion millions of years ago. Earth orbits the sun at a speed of nearly 70,000 miles per hour. Suppose in earth's formative years one of our volcanoes erupted and exploded a piece of rock at such speed and force that it slipped out of earth's gravity. That kind of thing happened often millions of years ago," said Jack.

"The Admiralty has issued a fleet order about Phaeton. I'm not sure whether it's wise to be at sea. If it passes seven miles overhead would we hear or see it, do you think?"

"You've heard the supersonic bang made by a jet travelling at 700 miles per hour. Imagine something as big as the Isle of Wight flashing by at 25,000 miles an hour just seventeen miles away from you! I think the noise and the shock wave will be devastating. Picture the build-up of a massive bow wave of pressurised air, the intense heat, the vast vacuum in Phaeton's wake, the incredible, overwhelming noise." They moved away from the veranda, the baby, and their wives.

"It's not a time I would volunteer to be at sea. But orders are orders," said Jack, with a grin.

The Original Phaeton

After long and tedious hours of work on mathematical formulas, graphs, specifications, computer models, appreciations and papers for records and for VIPs, Laurie Colgate and Douglas White completed their labours and predictions on the twin phenomena of Phaeton and the Ice.

"I'm having my first 'Phaeton' day off tomorrow," said Laurie.

"I shall have one after the curtain falls on this drama," Douglas responded. "In any case I haven't been so involved, or so exposed to the media's guns as you have. I hope you'll enjoy a nice quiet day. You've chosen a good one, tomorrow should actually be a couple of degrees warmer, with light and variable winds. The calm before the storm. London is due for its first significant September snow in living memory on the following day. Tell Sheila I'll be happy for her to ring me if any problems crop up."

★

Laurie went home to the Baker Street flat which he occupied during the working week. Usually he left London for his home in East Anglia as early as possible every Friday, but this weekend Angela had joined him at the flat for the final days of the Phaeton countdown. That evening they discussed the number of people he had met, whose paths, in the ordinary course of events, he would not have crossed.

"There are the VIPs who required 'Phaeton Information Briefings', especially those who have made personal contact. The Prime Minister for example, and most of the senior cabinet ministers," said Angela. "Are they random meetings, in the same category as Phaeton's brush with earth?"

"Looking at your question as an astronomer," said Laurie, "I think of Immanuel Kant's statement that the laws of space are known to the mind because they are of the mind. Wherever

113

Phaeton began his journey, he is subject to the laws of space. Earth began its life in the same way, part of a galaxy born in primordial space. We are of the earth, and therefore of space.

"But our mind, our being, our spirit, I think of as 'other' – not random. If you ask, what other? I can only say, the mind beyond. That which informs the individual and collective unconscious. That which we ignore at our peril. The 'marriage of true minds' is not accidental."

"Do you mean God arranges them?" asked Angela.

"I mean the One whose creative love makes everything. Who sees order, beauty and artistry in an infinite diversity of form, magnitude and colour," answered Laurie.

"Well, you do mean God, don't you?"

"The trouble with that word is its association with institutional religions, with conquest, power, division. With a god who, apparently, sets man against man. A god who backs one religion and rejects others," said Laurie.

"But some religions have got it wrong, haven't they? We ought not to change God's name because some religions mess things up," objected Angela.

"The trouble is that all religions mess things up. The God of love and creation remains silently in the background, in the deep space of our minds, when the god of religion, institutional power and intolerance takes over."

"That's a lesson in humility, the bedrock of love," said Angela. "What shall we do tomorrow?"

"The forecast says a dry, warm day. What about a leisurely breakfast at the Chiltern, followed by a stroll round Hyde Park? After which we shall repair to a place of your choice for a madly expensive lunch."

"You really are off duty? I can't believe that Sheila or Douglas or someone from the PM's office won't phone you. OK then," she said decisively, "that's the plan for tomorrow, away from the phone. It might be the last day off that we spend together."

"Sheila's standing in for me, with Douglas as back-up if required. Between the Observatory Staff and all the other stargazers we've worked out what we think Phaeton will do. The countdown will continue, unaffected by my absence from the

The Original Phaeton

office for twenty-four hours. At the end of that period, Phaeton, whose speed has increased a little, will be 650,000 miles closer. What an attention seeker he is, and blessed are the ignorant who don't know he's there," said Laurie.

After the promised leisurely breakfast the following morning, Sheila and Laurie strolled along Bayswater Road in the warm sunshine.

At Lancaster Gate they turned south onto the path by the Serpentine.

"It's an age since I first walked in Hyde Park," said Angela. "It was before I met you, when I was still at school. For a treat after exams our music teacher took six of us to Covent Garden, after we'd spent the day sightseeing. Do you know any Serpentine verses?"

"I can't believe that you and I haven't walked in Hyde Park before. I've neglected you. No, I don't know any Serpentine verses, what are they?"

"I'll repeat the one our music teacher told us. See if you can tell how it gets its name, it goes 'Greater grows the love of money, as money itself grows greater.'"

"It begins and ends with the same word. Is that it?" he asked.

"Trust you to get it! There were six of us and not one of us guessed the answer."

"I think it follows from a mythological story about the serpent with its tail in its mouth, you know – the beginning is the end. Now look at that boy," said Laurie, pointing to a small boy standing by the lake.

The boy stood with right arm drawn back, head and body bent to the right. As they watched, he brought his arm sharply forward in a horizontal arc. A stone shot out of his hand, flying at a shallow angle to skip on the glassy surface of the water three times before sinking.

As they came up to the youngster, Laurie said, "Well done, that was a good skimmer."

"I'm trying to get four skips," said the boy. "My dad said the stone must be flat and the water calm to do that." He took another stone out of his pocket and showed it to Laurie.

"That's a good one, flat, with smooth edges and a slightly

convex bottom," said Laurie. "If you get the same speed and angle as last time, I reckon you'll get four skips."

They noticed the care with which the boy took his stance. Again he bent to the right, his head horizontal, left arm outstretched to give balance, his right arm swinging back and forward to work up speed. A picture of concentration. Then the major effort: the stone sped out of his hand in a flat trajectory, his arm following through, as in a well-executed tennis drive. The convex bottom of the stone touched the water lightly. The skip was about three yards. Another touch, a skip of a shorter distance, and two more skips before the stone sank on its fifth contact with the water.

They congratulated the boy and continued their walk. Angela said, "I know what you're thinking, don't dare mention it."

"It was a good exercise," Laurie observed, "and informative too. If that stone had been travelling at 27,000 mph, the lift it got from its first touch on the water would have propelled it out of earth's gravity."

★

Miles Poundmore was frustrated. His attempts to talk to Laurie Colgate had failed. Mrs Maclaren, Colgate's assistant, said that Mr Colgate would not be in the office at all that day. She was unable to give him her bosses home telephone number; instead she gave him Douglas White's. White had been helpful, but not helpful enough to disclose the vital phone number. However, following his talk with White, Miles made several international telephone calls. The first was to Jasem Al-Mana.

"Jasem, in view of Phaeton the meteor's passage close to Mediterranean countries on the third of October, would you think it sensible to postpone our meeting at Tunis until the seventh?" They discussed the fact that, according to expert opinion, very rough weather would develop in the meteor's wake. "It would be unwise," said Miles, "to send *Andromeda* and her crew to sea on the third. It would be advisable to postpone sailing for a few days."

Jasem agreed to postponement of the meeting until 7 October

The Original Phaeton

2010, so Miles spoke next to Mohamed Ramzi, Algiers and Hassen Osman, Morocco both of whom agreed. He told Eileen to inform Angelo Capelli in Rome, Ahmed Rahman in Cairo and Captain Geoffrey Wenock in Naples of the change of date for the meeting from noon on 3 October to noon on 7 October. A further instruction to Captain Wenock was that accommodation should be prepared for up to five more guests aboard *Andromeda*.

Miles gave up trying to contact Laurie. Instead, he telephoned Vicky. "Would you be able to come here for lunch today?" he asked.

"I'm sorry, Miles. I'm having lunch with Penelope Tudor."

"Could you come here for coffee after lunch?" he persisted.

"Not really. She asked me ages ago and I accepted. I could come for tea, say half past three?"

Miles settled for that, and wondered if he, as Eileen almost implied, was losing his cutting edge? A few days ago Victoria had said that he was out of touch with ordinary people. She alleged that he lived in a world of big business, Rolls Royces, yachts and jet aeroplanes, whilst most people, like the millions who made up PI's customers around the world, lived in semi-detached houses, rode bicycles, paddled canoes and flew model aeroplanes. "You are out of touch with your markets, Miles," she had said, "but I love you."

Miles instructed PI's property manager to buy a property in an Oxfordshire village, a community of some 1,500 people, with a good pub, which he had frequented whilst reading Economics at Oxford. The property included a modest, stone-built cottage with a living room, dining room and kitchen – also central heating, three small bedrooms, a bathroom and two toilets. It had a garage, and the shed in the garden was big enough to accommodate two bicycles and a canoe.

After a spate of phone calls and talks to a number of PI directors and managers, Miles sat at his desk ruminating. If I was out of touch with my markets, and losing my cutting edge, he thought, PI would be going broke. But it wasn't: its UK capital asset base alone was enormous, with three people owning sixty-eight per cent of the shares. Its turnover was still increasing, though there were one or two holdings in Australia and North

America which should be pruned or disposed of. That might be what Eileen had in mind. Authority, he had been taught, should be matched with responsibility: he was allowing his Australian and American directors a little extra time to exercise their responsibility. That did not mean he had lost his cutting edge.

He decided that PI's cutting edge should be extended. There would have to be safeguards, of course.

Eileen brought in the latest PI computer print out. The Australasian divisions were leading the field, well ahead of the Americas, and, to his surprise, the anticipated decline in Europe was very slight – at present. "Eileen," he said, "Vicky's coming to tea at 3.30 p.m. I want you to join us."

"Certainly, sir," said Eileen.

The snow in northern England and Scotland lay deep: so deep that the weight of the upper layers had compressed the lower levels converting them into ice. In many areas of higher ground in these regions, snow from the previous winter remained on shaded northwest and north facing slopes. This old snow was now ice. It too lay compressed under successive heavy falls in a month which, for most of the past hundred and forty years, had ushered in the pleasant, balmy season of autumn.

At a meeting of the Cabinet, the Prime Minister was subjected to veiled criticism from the Home Secretary. This was because the PM had taken note of, and acted on, expert advice to the effect that general evacuation from snowbound areas should be delayed until the Phaeton emergency was over. The start of the evacuation, originally scheduled for Sunday, 26 September had been delayed until Monday, 4 October. The expert advice had come from Mr Laurie Colgate and Mr Douglas White, observed the Home Secretary, who was peeved at the interference with her plans. As far as she was concerned, the incident made her look as if she didn't know her own mind.

"Heather," said the PM to the Home Secretary, "I understood from your report that evacuation of the sick, the aged and infirm, mothers and babies, and anyone in immediate danger is going ahead with only minor hitches. Your report also states that the evacuation of Cumbria is proceeding according to plan. Apart from politically motivated exceptions the general tone of the media today, both here in London and in reports from the worst-hit areas, is that we've got it right."

There were murmurs of "Here, here," and, from Mick Taylor, "It's going very well 'eather, don't let 'eadline-loving reporters fash thee, lass." Mick invariably accentuated his northern accent at Cabinet meetings.

The Cabinet's siding with the PM annoyed Heather, increasing her resentment at what she considered to be unwarranted meddling in the running of her department.

★

The Duty Officer on board the yacht *Andromeda* in Naples harbour received the signal from PI headquarters with glee. In addition to the Captain there were three other officers. The Captain did not do a duty officer stint so, when in harbour, each officer spent one week in three on board. Granted it was comfortable and you could have your wife aboard, if you were married, or have guests of suitable standing! But it was boring with only a duty seaman, who also acted as engineer, for company. Now he would get a few days ashore before they sailed to Tunis.

He telephoned Captain Wenock saying, "Signal from PI, sir."

The Captain assumed his "on board" taciturnity, and said, "Read and file copy in my signal's folder." The duty officer read out the signal and the Captain thanked him.

To his wife he said, "The best of news, our trip to Tunis is postponed for five days. Common sense prevailed. It would have been suicide to deliberately sail under a rogue meteor the size of Phaeton. Who knows what seas will be blown up by such an enormous object, travelling at such tremendous speed? My dear, I'm going below to tell young Jack. I must have a word with him about safety measures for *Andromeda* during the Phaeton countdown."

★

The madly expensive lunch which Angela and Laurie enjoyed was followed, three hours later, by afternoon tea in the peaceful, club-like atmosphere of the same hotel in Park Lane.

"You've never told me whether the panic trip to Greenland was worth all the effort," Angela said.

"It was a wonderful opportunity to see how nature qualifies our painstaking statistics. It was the same in Prestwick. Dad said that he'd kept his opinions to himself for two reasons. One, although he kept track of global statistics, his environmental observations were local, and two, because he felt that he should not voice his intuitive views on the ice phenomenon unless asked to do so."

"That's a typical example of your father's modesty," said Angela. "He said there was no evidence that the warming influence of the Gulf Stream was drifting westwards away from the Perthshire coast. He has, however, recorded the predominantly easterly winds up in those parts during the past two years. The last nine months were particularly interesting. There, as in northeast England and in Scotland, these winds carried snow which remained for longer periods on the north and west faces of the higher hills. In those areas, which the sun doesn't touch for long if at all, snow remained throughout the summer, keeping local temperatures lower than usual."

"What about Greenland?"

"That was, literally, the icing on the cake," said Laurie. "We approached Kangerlussuaq airfield via the Søndre Strømfjord, which is about 150 miles long. It's a majestic combination of mountain, ice and water."

"I had always thought of Greenland as a forbidding sort of place, where a handful of Eskimos exist in perpetual blizzards, with occasional glimpses of the midnight sun. Don't they live in igloos and catch fish through holes in the ice?" she asked.

"Some of that's still true for a handful of hardy folk who wish to preserve the old ways. Very few Greenlanders want any commercial development – they have a marvellous, seemingly unpolluted environment, which they don't wish anyone to spoil," replied Laurie.

"I'm sorry. I interrupted your description of the fjord."

"The airfield and town are at the inland end of the fjord where it's virtually ice-free. Even so, in the winter months, the temperature in Kangerlussuaq is in the minus forty to fifty Celsius range. Flying up the fjord near the mouth, you see icy cliffs tumbling down to the blue water. The blue is tinged with a kind of milky quality – as if it might turn into ice at any minute. In spite of that, my Danish colleague at Kangerlussuaq said that the immediate area was ice-free, even though it's north of the Arctic circle. More importantly from my point of view, he regularly compares notes with researchers stationed on Baffin Island. Their particular interest is in Bowhead Whales."

"I thought your concern was the atrocious weather we are getting in the UK. What on earth have whales got to do with that?"

"Food," replied Laurie. "Bowheads feed on a tiny crustacean about half the size of a garden pea. If the circulating currents of water were not operating, and, to a lesser extent the seasonal northerly gales, the masses of crustacea, or copepods, on which the Bowheads feed, would not be there. No food, no whales. Beluga whales have also been spotted, moving south, off the west coast of Greenland, as expected at this time in a normal year. Also, no unusual changes in the habits of flora or fauna were reported from any of the observers in Greenland's enormous territory. Any global changes in weather are almost certain to affect Arctic regions. It happened one year in the eighties. Climatic changes in the Pacific produced lower temperatures around Greenland. Result? More ice, fewer crustacea and few, if any, Bowheads in that year."

"And is that all the evidence you have to support the advice you gave the PM about the Arctic weather we are getting?" asked Angela.

"Not quite. We've made computer models based on statistics from previous cold spells, and there have been quite a few in the last two hundred years or so. I'm in daily touch with colleagues in the USA and Canada who are in much the same position as we are. When the evidence is there, we have to believe it, interpret it, and present our findings. Having done that, Douglas and I are trying to trace the *Ariadne* thread that would lead us to the source of these cold, easterly winds."

"It's a global nightmare," said Angela. "Although I believe you

The Original Phaeton

when you say that Phaeton will miss planet earth, there is this picture in the back of my mind. It's one of a flaming furnace, the size of the Isle of Wight. It's heading straight for us at 27,000 miles an hour. We're trying to run away from it as fast as we can. But we make no headway. The earth spins round under our feet. There's no end to the nightmare because Phaeton gets no nearer. It hangs there, threatening, like the fourth Horseman of the Apocalypse."

"I can understand the nightmare, but I can't explain it. If you come to the office tomorrow, Sheila could show you the computer pictures forecasting Phaeton passing out of earth's atmosphere. I believe that the meteorite will inflict widespread damage, but if we're sensible, loss of life should not be high. We should not suffer on the scale caused by Apollo's son, the original Phaeton. He created havoc."

The Ice Advances

At 3.45 p.m. Victoria took a taxi to PI's Pall Mall office. She suspected that Miles's postponement of his trip to Tunis had upset his work schedule. The invitation to tea filled a gap in his day.

Eileen's assistant greeted her, "Good afternoon, Mrs Poundmore," she said as she walked to the connecting door to Miles's office and opened it for Victoria.

Victoria smiled, said, "Thank you," put her hat and coat on the stand and walked into Miles's office.

Miles rose to greet her, "Vicky darling, it's a kind of working tea. I know it must be a bit of a surprise, but I do need your help and Eileen's too – in some urgent reorganisation."

"Eileen," said Vicky, "I hope you know more about this than I do. Are you referring to reorganising PI, Miles? If so, I'll join you for a cup of tea, then I'll leave you to it. The last time I helped out, Eileen was the only person who showed any appreciation."

"This time it's different," said Miles. "It involves both of you personally. Rather more than you might think. You've probably forgotten, but you are both major shareholders in PI, and, since only thirty-two per cent of PI's UK shares are held by staff and the public, the other sixty-eight per cent remain in private hands. They are held by you two ladies and me. Would you be mother and pour the tea, Vicky?"

"After more than thirty years, why bother about shares at this particular time?" asked Vicky, as she put milk in their cups.

"For some time PI's lawyers have been pressing me to regularise our share register. There's nothing illegal about it, shares owned by other companies, members of staff and the public, are properly registered and dealt with by our Company Secretary," he smiled at Eileen.

"Well, let's leave it at that then," said Vicky, pointedly looking at her watch.

The Ice Advances

"Eileen, as Company Secretary, do you have any idea of the value of your holdings in PI UK?" asked Miles.

"Not an up-to-date one," replied Eileen, "but a couple of years ago they were worth about fifty million pounds."

Vicky gasped, "Are you really a multimillionaire, Eileen? If so, why on earth do you continue to work here?"

Miles concealed his surprise at Eileen's knowledge of her "paper fortune". It indicated yet another instance of both her loyalty to PI and her integrity.

"PI UK's asset value is well over a billion pounds, so a conservative estimate of the value of a sixty-eight per cent holding would be 680 millions. The current value of your ten per cent, Eileen, is 100 million. Your thirty per cent, Vicky, is valued at 300 million and my twenty-eight per cent at 280 million."

He and Victoria had not discussed their assets in money terms for years. He watched her with amusement – which turned to concern.

"Three hundred million! And I budget down to the last penny." She glared at Miles, which was not the reaction he had expected.

"It's only paper money, Vicky," said Eileen. "The real money is needed to finance PI's day-to-day business. You could sell your percentage, but control of PI would then pass out of your family's hands. You might not enjoy that."

"*His* hands," retorted Vicky, pointing an accusing finger at Miles. She recalled her father's anger when she had confessed that the splendid house he had given her as a wedding present had been mortgaged for nearly half a million pounds. That money had been swallowed up by PI. Now, thirty years later, 300 million must represent a good return. And she still had the house, unencumbered by debt. Miles had repaid the half million long ago, besides surprising her with gifts of great generosity. And now another surprise, something he had never mentioned – she held the greatest number of shares. She was wealthier than she had ever dreamed possible. It could ruin her life. Then she calmed down. Nothing had changed.

"The capital value of our shares is not the main point. Thirty years ago, when you, Eileen, and you, Vicky, put your money on me and PI, you risked losing it, and your homes too. I put my shirt on the venture. At that time I exuded confidence partly because I'd nothing else to exude, but also because I'd done my homework."

"Miles dear, what is the main point?" enquired Vicky. She did not want him, at this moment, to admit to anything covered by a businessman's seal of confession.

Eileen smiled at Vicky, then looked at Miles. "Dividends?" she asked.

"You two and my father mortgaged properties for a million pounds to invest in PI. Shares were allocated in line with the amount invested. As agreed, I held the shares so that I could use them as collateral if required. I also classified them as 'ineligible for dividend' because, in those early days, PI needed every penny it could get to finance expansion. When we began to perform really well, I repaid your capital in cash or in kind, but forgot to lift the dividend embargo on our shares. That is what our lawyer-accountant advises us to deal with, and, at the same time, to invite major shareholders to take their seats on the Board. Incidentally," he added, "if one of us should decide to sell shares, they must first be offered to one or both of the other major holders."

"So that's why I'm Company Secretary," said Eileen. "What about the dividend payments?"

"The Company Secretary ought to put that on the agenda for the next board meeting," replied Miles, with a grin. He turned to Vicky, "We need a fresh, unprejudiced eye to look at PI's property portfolio and perks, Vicky. First in the UK, and subsequently in the major overseas divisions." Catching Eileen's eye, he added, "Eileen keeps this portfolio in order, but taking on the secretaryship means she can't continue to do it. Would you take that on, please, Vicky?"

"I don't know that much about business," protested Vicky.

"You can't possibly be serious?"

"You run three houses in a most efficient manner. Your experience, applied to PI's domestic inventory, would be invaluable. No doubt Eileen would tell you how to make a start. You'll soon get the hang of it."

The Ice Advances

★

Refreshed by his day off, Laurie went to his office in Church House at eight o'clock the next morning expecting the business of the day to centre around Phaeton. After all, there were only approximately thirty-four hours – 2,040 minutes – to zero hour. It was not yet possible to be precise about the time of Phaeton's passage through earth's atmosphere because varying temperatures and pressures affected the meteor's speed. Changes in gravitational fields also affected its acceleration, making it unwise, as yet, to announce the crucial time precisely.

The Home Secretary's instructions on the action to be taken by all citizens during the emergency had been passed down the line, in writing, to local authorities for dissemination to the public; local and national radio and television also broadcast them, calmly, but frequently and insistently. One hour and twenty minutes before Phaeton's entry into earth's atmosphere, warning sirens would sound. This was the signal for the opening of all doors and windows in every building in the land. One hour later the whole population would seek the protection of the best cover available to them. No one, other than the security forces, was permitted to be outside. Extra security cameras had been positioned to deter those who might be tempted to take advantage of open doors. Security forces were to patrol, mainly in armoured vehicles, to give protection to colleagues engaged on what was called external duty. Any person, other than members of the security forces, found out of doors during the curfew would be arrested. Special underground shelters had been provided adjacent to areas of high population. These were to be occupied by the medical arm of the security forces twenty minutes before zero hour.

Advice on the wearing of ear protectors, sunglasses and protective clothing had been followed by instructions for the servicing of fire equipment, the provision of first aid stations and the manning of hospital accident units. All possible safety precautions had been carried out in a spirit of unity and cooperation not experienced since World War II. A commentator in a west midlands city noted that: "Factions, rivalries and feuds –

political, religious, and ethnic – have been put aside, if not forever, then at least until it is considered safe, physically and morally, to reintroduce them."

In another city, Christians from mainstream churches and others representing most denominations, worked alongside people from a variety of religions and no religion – Buddhists, Hindus, Jews, Muslims, Sikhs, atheists and others. An exuberant priest, interviewed on television News, said, with unconscious irony, "It is marvellous to see how people are pulling together for the common good in these critical days. Caring for the aged and infirm, for the weak and needy, in fellowship, fun and compassion, as if there were one faith, one world and one God."

However, banner headlines on the front page of a much-favoured and respected daily newspaper declared thus: "SNOW and ICE are the real enemies. Phaeton should not be allowed to distract our attention from the Ice Age conditions in the north, and the government should understand that no further delay in evacuation is acceptable." The front page article continued, "More heavy snow last night. Temperatures down to minus twenty-two Celsius. For many of those who were not evacuated yesterday, today is too late. Snow ploughs are unable to get through to many towns and villages marooned by the latest blizzards. And the forecast? More heavy snow for northern England and for Scotland."

Food supplies, however, were now being delivered by air. Communities were showing remarkable resilience in improvising ways of keeping people warm, fed and watered. Skis and snow-shoes were in great demand, with competent skiers acting as messengers in some counties.

Ingenious methods for keeping communication lines open had been devised. Electronic communication via computers was being restored as people accustomed themselves, and their technology, to the conditions. The challenges involved were now being tackled.

Late editions of many papers took up political stances in the saga, "Does the Government have a policy?" asked one. Another took a more philosophical, non-judgemental line: "With regard to evacuation from the regions which the blizzards have hit hardest, those who would exercise authority without any responsibility are, like the Etruscans, advising their leaders to go in both directions at once."

A cartoon depicted Winnie, the PM, as a helmeted Horatius holding the bridge, with the caption: But those behind cried Forward! And those before cried Back!

The article continued. "The government's policy to evacuate those most at risk is proceeding according to plan. Supplies are now regularly delivered to special dropping centres in all regions isolated by snow. Prime Minister Winnie Smith said that her government's policies during the present emergency are based on the best professional advice. Irresponsible comment is unhelpful to those most affected by the weather, and also to the services and volunteer organisations mobilised to render assistance."

Heather Moor, the Home Secretary, had scanned the news headlines. She read the main leading articles before the morning meeting of the Cabinet. During the meeting, Heather, who was extremely sensitive to adverse media comment, launched a bitter attack on the Cabinet's chief policy adviser on the Arctic weather conditions. She carefully avoided mentioning names, but everyone knew she meant Laurie Colgate.

"He advises us that, although there may be more snow, this abnormal weather is likely to continue for only a few more weeks. He asserts that none of the indicators which would lead us to expect prolonged Arctic conditions are present. His theories and advice are absolutely contrary to what is, at this very moment, actually happening in our northern counties and Scotland." She turned her gaze on the PM. "I would like it to be minuted that I favour full evacuation forthwith. But I shall, of course, accede to Cabinet's decision."

The Prime Minister said she regretted that her Cabinet colleagues were not of one mind on this matter of national importance. In fact Heather, the Home Secretary, was the only member not in agreement with government policy on the snow crisis. It was an odd situation since hers was the responsible, co-ordinating department of State in the crisis. Her husband was friendly with someone who held a senior position in the Meteorological Service. This man had confided to Heather's husband, "Off the record, old boy, I can find nothing on the charts to indicate any let up in this weather. Quite the contrary, I expect it to spread south. But that's only my opinion you understand." Heather had contemplated resignation. But it would be foolish to resign: it might spell the end of her very successful political career. As the Cabinet ended its discussions, the Prime Minister reminded members that, in the interests of public morale, a united front must be presented to the country and, especially, to the media. The Cabinet must be seen to be of one mind.

★

Laurie Colgate, Sheila Maclaren and Douglas White concentrated their efforts on tracking Phaeton. He was now less than one million miles away – 952,000 to be exact. They were puzzled, not so much by the slight decrease in his mass, but by the increase in his speed which was now 28,000 mph. They checked and re-checked sighting positions and information from colleagues around the world: their calculations were confirmed.

"If Phaeton is accelerating, it could be good news," said Sheila.

"I can't see that it will make much difference. In fact it might be bad news," Douglas responded. "If he's going faster it means more heat, more compression, more noise, and therefore greater damage from fire, pressure waves, wind, decibels and tsunamis when he hits our atmosphere."

"I see Sheila's point. If Phaeton enters earth's atmosphere earlier than we at first anticipated, the sun will be higher over the western horizon. That *must* be good news. It would mean that earth's rim is now less of an obstruction in Phaeton's path to the sun. It could even mean that the meteor will not penetrate the mesosphere – that it will not approach closer to earth than fifty miles. The downside is, as you say Douglas, more speed, more heat, and greater danger of an explosion when, or if, the meteor enters a denser atmosphere."

Of the many interruptions to their work that day, few had anything to do with Phaeton. Snow and ice, having captured the morning headlines, continued to dominate news bulletins throughout the day.

The Ice Advances

★

At half-past five on that Saturday evening, 2 October 2010, twenty four and a half hours and 686,000 miles before Phaeton's tangle with earth, the Home Secretary called on the Prime Minister at her office in Number 10. Winnie was not pleased.

"Prime Minister—" said the Home Secretary.

"Just a minute, Heather, if this is to be official, we'd better switch on." Winnie switched on the video camera and sound recorder.

"Now, Home Secretary," she said, "what's on your mind?"

Heather realised that she had started on the wrong foot. She should have said, Winnie, not "Prime Minister". She should have kept it off the record, at least for the first few minutes.

"Prime Minister, I am deeply concerned about the heavy snow, the further heavy snow, today. The press, television and radio are having a field day about what they label 'A Frozen Government.' There is a particularly obnoxious cartoon in one of the evening papers. It shows me sitting with my feet in a snow drift, and with a forefinger stuck in each ear. The caption is libellous – it says – 'Not only cold feet, but she's deaf to the cries of the suffering.' Please let me give the order for evacuation to begin forthwith."

Both Heather Moor and Winnie Smith knew that this could not be done without the consent of the Cabinet, which was not scheduled to meet until the next morning. The PM also knew that anything looking like panic action would be unwise and counterproductive. It would put an enormous question mark against her leadership and her reputation for steadfastness, under fire from the media.

"Home Secretary," she said, "would you like me to assume responsibility for the Cabinet's Snow Policy?" Adroitly, she put the ball in the Home Secretary's court.

"No, Prime Minister," replied Heather, conscious of that damned recording machine. "I am well able to handle it. Thank you for allowing me to voice my deep concern about…" her voice tailed off. She had intended to finish with, "the government's perceived inaction". She stopped herself. That remark would have been recorded for posterity and, perhaps, the snide comments of her colleagues.

The Prime Minister switched off the recorder. She knew that Heather had swallowed an indiscretion. "Good night, Heather, we are passing through stormy weather, literally and metaphorically, but I believe our policies will be vindicated."

★

Sheila Maclaren raised her eyes from the computer keyboard, turned to Laurie and Douglas and said, "On my model, with no data entered for today, and speed unchanged at 28,000 miles per hour I read, 17.45 hours, 679,000 miles to contact with earth's atmosphere within the troposphere, angle zero at an altitude of roughly seven miles. So, unless the figures change, it will play the very devil with life on earth – and probably with earth itself."

"Thanks, Sheila," said Laurie, "we've got a read off at exactly the same time, we'll compare in a jiffy, after we've confirmed our data." The two men cross-checked every entry on their separate computers and screens, ensuring that no wrong keys had been pressed.

"Twelve hours back, Phaeton achieved a speed of 29,320 mph," said Laurie. "The figures I'm calling have been cross-checked with Douglas. Speed constant for twelve hours. It may show a slight decrease due to drag when it enters the exosphere at a height of 500 miles. At 17.45 hours today I read, 677,680 miles to contact with earth's atmosphere, angle zero. It will penetrate the stratosphere down to an altitude of roughly seven miles at 16.45 hours, zero-hour tomorrow. Phaeton will pass approximately 1,500 miles south of our plotted track – that's because of acceleration and a now un-eclipsed exposure to the pull of the sun's gravity."

"It might not be a Yucatan! I'll phone the PM and tell her the chances are now better for a near miss."

After listening to the latest figures for Phaeton the Prime Minister said, "It sounds like good news to me, Dr Colgate. Is it?"

Laurie answered cautiously, "On the face of it, yes, almost miraculously good news. But my professional instinct is to stress

The Ice Advances

that we are by no means out of the wood. Phaeton at present is set to pass through earth's atmosphere at a height of seven miles. There will be catastrophic consequences, but probably not total annihilation of life on earth. Our hope must be that earth's outer atmosphere provides that extra bit of lift which would cause it to accelerate away from us at a higher altitude."

"Thank you, Mr Colgate, apart from releasing the new timing and track, we will, as far as Phaeton is concerned, leave our security arrangements intact. Now, tell me, does media coverage of the blizzards bother you?"

"It does, Prime Minister, though not professionally, because I stand by my advice to the government," replied Laurie.

"Let's weather the trial by media then, and, at the key moment, don't be surprised if I ask you to give the public the benefit of your expertise on television. Thank you for your help, Dr Colgate."

★

Miles persuaded Vicky, as PI's new director of Property and Perks, to accompany him on a visit to a recent PI acquisition. Giles, already briefed about their destination, drove the car round to PI's front entrance in Pall Mall.

"What's happened to the Rolls?" asked Vicky, as she ducked into the back seat of the dark blue Jaguar.

"Wrong image," replied Miles shortly.

Giles chuckled to himself as he eased the powerful Jaguar smoothly through the London traffic and onto the M4, heading for Newbury.

PI Hits Headlines

"What do you mean, the 'wrong image'?" asked Victoria, as she tried to settle into the back seat of the strange, new car.

"It's possible that my image, as Chairman and Chief Executive of PI, gives an impression of someone out of touch," replied Miles. Quoting Victoria's own words, he said, "For the last twenty years I've lived in a world of big business, Rolls Royces, yachts and jet aeroplanes. It's time I got back in touch, otherwise, I might lose my cutting edge."

The dark-blue Jaguar purred effortlessly, at a steady 75 mph, along the M4 motorway towards Newbury. Victoria wriggled in her seat. She was comfortable, but not quite as contented and relaxed as usual. Giles looked big, too big, in the driving seat. His dark blue, peaked cap almost touched the roof. In the Rolls she had sometimes wondered if he was still there: the high back of his seat and the tinted screen partition had given her, and him, the soothing feeling of privacy. She had loved the sense of unassailable and voluptuous security, which she had experienced as the soft, warm upholstery of the Rolls embraced her body. There was a difference, she acknowledged, between comfort and luxury. Miles, too, in these less sumptuous seats, seemed bigger and closer than usual. And the words he had just uttered pinched a nerve, adding further to her indefinable sense of unease.

"Is the Rolls in for servicing?" she asked.

"No, darling. I traded it in for this," he replied.

She shuffled in her seat. The Rolls had accustomed her to more headroom, a little more leg room, wider elbow supports. She turned towards Miles, "Let's have a drink," she suggested.

"Oh, I'm sorry," he said, "this isn't fitted with a drink's cabinet. Giles might have a flask." He raised his voice, as the Jag was not fitted with an intercom system either. "Giles, do you by any chance have a flask of gin?"

Giles passed the flask of gin, the bottle of warm tonic water and two plastic beakers, all of which Miles had given him, to the rear. Miles unfolded Vicky's table, carefully poured two drinks, looked at her, raised his plastic beaker and said, "Good health, darling. Sorry we can't have ice and lemon, this car doesn't have a fridge. But it does run well, doesn't it?"

"Cheers," said Victoria, in a weak voice. She detested drinking gin and tonic out of a plastic beaker.

At junction 14, Giles turned north up the A338 heading towards Wantage. For about twenty minutes they drove through the rolling Berkshire downs where racing stables and stud farms flourished amidst prime arable land. The car turned left onto a minor road. Vicky glimpsed a sign post which said "Letcombe…" but she couldn't make the rest out. Trees lined both sides of the narrow lane, arching overhead to form a gloomy tunnel which pressed in on the car. As the sun set behind the hills, the car's lights were the only sign of movement in the valley. They were in a remote part of the country.

"Why on earth would PI own property in such a wilderness?" she asked.

Before Miles could reply, the car slowed down. Giles turned the Jaguar off the lane and parked in front of a public house in a tiny hamlet.

"Let's have a proper drink here," said Miles.

The man behind the bar smiled, "Good evening, Mr More, good evening madam," he said. "What would you like to drink?"

Victoria said, "I'd like a proper gin and tonic in a proper glass, please."

"One proper G and T and one dry sherry, Jim, and can we have the menu please," said Miles.

"You obviously know this place," observed Victoria, "how long have you been coming here?"

"Only since PI acquired property down here. But it's a place that grows on you. I knew it well in my student days. This pub has a good chef. You'll enjoy dinner. As usual in such places," he said, lowering his voice, "I drop the 'Pound' and pay cash!"

"OK, Mr More. But I'll never understand your fear of publicity."

"As I've said before, it's not fear, my love, it's strategy. There is a time for everything under the sun. A time to be named, and a time to be incognito, a time to use a credit card, and a time to pay cash. Can you imagine the fuss if the press found out that the boss of PI had sold his Rolls? They'd put two and two together, make three, and publicise their adverse, misinformed comment. PI shares would take a dive. Markets, like rattlesnakes, are nervous creatures."

"Where's Giles having supper?" asked Vicky, fishing for information.

"He's staying the night in this pub. I expect he'll eat here," replied Miles.

"Oh! So we're not going home tonight? Are we staying here too?"

"We're staying at PI's new property. That'll give you a chance to assess its merits," he answered. PI, he had decided, should try the experience of a semi-detached affinity with its customers. It would be interesting to see if a little relative hardship sharpened or blunted cutting edges.

After supper they returned to the bar, she to enjoy a Cointreau, he a Cognac. The barman switched a radio on for the nine o'clock news from London. Snow was falling in the capital. The announcer said, "Many experienced observers believe that the government's chief adviser, Dr Laurie Colgate, has misread the weather indicators. Delay in evacuating people from the frozen north could prove to be a fatal error. Journalists on the spot continue to urge the Home Secretary to begin total evacuation at once."

"Poor Laurie," said Miles, "I wouldn't want his job while Phaeton and the ice are hanging around."

The announcer next gave the latest news of the meteor. "Our own experts, using the latest scientific equipment, report that Phaeton accelerated, some twelve hours ago, to a speed of 29,320 mph. They calculated that, at 21.00 hours, that is, at the start of this news bulletin, Phaeton was 582,390 miles from earth. Our experts say that Phaeton will pass through earth's atmosphere earlier than had previously been stated. The meteorite's closest proximity to us will be at 16.45 hours tomorrow, 3 October 2010.

There are now 1,365 minutes of Phaeton's countdown to go. Another item of news is that one of Britain's largest companies has offered to finance an initiative to improve world agricultural output. We hope to have more details of this in a later bulletin."

"I don't like the sound of that! I wonder if someone's got wind of PI's plans? And I bet their 'experts' used Laurie's figures for the news of Phaeton," said Miles. "Yet they're implying that previous statements were in error. There's an hysterical media witch hunt at the moment – I wonder who started it, and why?"

"Is Giles taking us to the PI building?" asked Victoria.

"No, we're walking. It's only a hundred yards away. Are you tired?" he asked solicitously.

"Tired, and curious," she admitted.

"Goodnight, Jim, see you again," said Miles, as they left the inn and made their way to "Dunroamin", the desirable country cottage which he had snapped up for PI. The other half of the property was occupied by a shepherd, a gnarled and wise old countryman with whom Miles had made friends on his previous visits.

Victoria's suspicions had been aroused by Miles's attitude. She couldn't put her finger on any one thing, but there were too many coincidences: the sudden invitation to tea in the office, the shares, the revelation of her surprising wealth, the property portfolio – the loss of the Rolls – this trip to the depths of the Oxfordshire countryside. Her "antenna" twitched nervously as she strained her eyes in the darkness for her first glimpse of the new PI property. This would be a maiden inspection of a building in what was now "her" PI portfolio. A porch light winked faintly ahead. It was, she saw, the front door of a semi-detached house. She continued onwards. Miles turned into the short driveway.

"This is it, darling," he said.

★

The Prime Minister sat with her husband, Leo, in the sitting room of their private apartment.

"Winnie, I want to ask a question which springs from curiosity, not criticism," said Leo.

The PM put a marker in her book and placed it on the table. She had sensed that Leo was unsettled. "Ask, you have my full attention," she said.

"Why are you so sure that Dr Colgate is right about Phaeton and the snow in the face of widespread opinion to the contrary, some of it well informed?" asked Leo, trying to conceal his agitation. He was unable to control the nervous twisting of interlocked fingers, a sure sign that he was worried. Winnie knew that attacks on her administration, her leadership, her policies, upset Leo. He was aware of the Home Secretary's disquiet about Cabinet policy on the snow crisis, and he knew that a number of newspapers backed the Home Secretary's line.

"Laurie Colgate, and Douglas White of Climap, with the input from their own scientific and professional departments, are the best informed and most balanced advisers available to me. They check their findings and opinions constantly with colleagues worldwide. I know that Dr Colgate's opinion is under fire from sections of the press. If I followed their advice instead of his, we wouldn't have a policy at all."

"But suppose he's wrong?" asked Leo. "Where does that leave you?"

"Suppose he's right, and I had given way to irresponsible newspaper pressure? Can you imagine the headlines in those papers? 'Millions needlessly forced to leave their homes, Prime Minister Panics.' Who foots the bill? Believe me, Leo, I weighed the evidence carefully, and my policy is based on the best advice."

At ten fifteen that night, Laurie Colgate's phone rang. Angela answered, intending to fend off any further intrusive calls.

"Mrs Colgate?" said a woman's voice.

"Yes," replied Angela shortly, suspecting a female journalist.

"Mrs Smith, the Prime Minister, speaking. I'm sorry to telephone when I know what a busy day you and your husband have had, but I would appreciate a word with him. Is that possible?"

"Yes, Mrs Smith, I'll get him at once. I'm sorry, I thought you might be another reporter," said Angela.

"I understand. Some of us pay a high price for freedom of speech," said the PM cheerfully.

"Prime Minister?" said Laurie.

"Mr Colgate, I hope the media's continuing attacks are not upsetting your wife. I'm sure that you regard them as no more than a nuisance – an occupational hazard. My situation is much the same. I often repeat to myself the words of a famous predecessor – 'In war resolution', and it is a kind of war, a war of words. Now, I know it is short notice, but I wonder if you and your wife could come here to lunch at one o'clock tomorrow? There will be no one else. It will be a private lunch in our apartment."

Laurie said that he and his wife would be delighted to accept the invitation to lunch the following day – Phaeton Day. He explained to the PM that he would have to return to his office by 2 p.m.

★

Miles opened the front door of "Dunroamin". "Our neighbour kindly switched the heating on," he said. "I asked him to get us some milk, eggs and bread too. Cosy, isn't it darling?"

Victoria surveyed the cramped entrance hall, the narrow staircase, the primrose-coloured, distempered walls, the three plain white doors with brass handles and the electricity meter on the wall behind the front door.

"Why does PI need a property like this, in a benighted village like this?"

Opening the door to the living room Miles answered, "It's a very attractive, stone-built cottage. It used to be the home of the cowman at Newman's farm, a mixed farm in the area." He entered the small sitting room, "Look, Vicky, wall-to-wall carpeting, a three-piece suite, television, a corner cupboard for drinks, and a fire basket that will take logs."

"But why?" persisted Vicky.

Miles switched on the television, "I decided that some of PI's senior people are out of touch with their markets. That's undesirable. It could influence their commercial judgment. If I remember correctly, you said more or less the same thing yourself, Vicky. As the new PI Property and Perks Director I thought you would like to assess this place. We could use it as a 'keeping in touch with our market' cottage, in which senior people can spend a few days when they need to be brought down to earth. That is if you agree?"

He pointed to the television, "Did you hear that?" he looked at his watch. "The ten o'clock news headlines mentioned PI – we must listen."

The room was small, much smaller than those to which Victoria was accustomed. It was airless, but she felt too tired to do anything about it. She slumped into, or more precisely onto, one of the easy chairs; the seat and back were designed to ensure that one did not slump.

After a protracted tour around the regions worst hit by snow, the television newscaster arrived at the item about PI, "Poundmore International, the well-known British conglomerate with worldwide interests, is now advancing its interest in agricultural machinery to agriculture itself. Our sources reveal that Miles Poundmore, the shy and elusive chairman of PI, is personally behind an international grass roots initiative to make wastelands bloom. He is said to deplore the fact that millions of people starve in a world of plenty. Mr Poundmore himself was not available for comment."

Miles, pale with anger, switched off the television. "Who did they get that from, Vicky?" he asked accusingly.

Victoria did not answer. She was tired, and, although she loved the countryside, she did not warm to the particular bit of it in which PI had chosen to acquire an inadequate cottage in which senior people could be brought down to earth.

Miles knew that his half jocular, half serious country cottage scheme was in danger of backfiring. He also knew that the unwanted, untimely publicity given to his agricultural ideas could jeopardise all the careful plans he had discussed with his Egyptian, Tunisian, Algerian and Moroccan contacts. To make matters worse, none of his instant communications systems were to hand. Except the telephone.

"Vicky," he said, "you look tired out. Let me show you your bedroom. It's small but warm and comfortable. All the things you will need are either in your wardrobe or on the dressing table." He thanked his lucky stars that he had followed his usual practice of equipping the new PI property with wardrobe and toilet necessities. Leading the way up the narrow staircase, he showed her the bathroom and her bedroom, "Would you like a hot drink or a water bottle?"

She shook her head and said, "I just want to sleep."

Whilst Victoria prepared herself for bed, Miles checked his own bedroom: all was in order. But, overall, things had not turned out as he had planned them here. And, to make matters worse, his "make deserts bloom" project was in danger of turning sour. He heard Vicky leave the bathroom and return to her bedroom. Leaving his own bedroom light on, he went into her room.

"Sleep well, darling," he said, kissing her.

"Goodnight," she said, "put the light out please."

Miles hurried down to the living room, picked up the telephone and dialled Eileen's number. The ringing tone sounded for a long time, he was about to replace the receiver when a sleepy voice said, "Hello."

"Eileen, Miles here. Sorry if I've disturbed your sleep. Did you—?"

"I saw it!" she interrupted. "I wondered if you'd watched the ten o'clock news. There was a kind of warning shot in an earlier bulletin. For the first time in PI's history we have a mole in the garden."

"We can sort that out tomorrow, the real danger is that our overseas partners in the venture might think we are pulling a publicity stunt. If they think that, they'll abandon ship. The whole scheme will fail, and then we'll get the kind of adverse publicity that we've never had before. What I'd like you to do—"

"Miles," Eileen interrupted again, "I have spoken to Mr Al-Mana. He heard that programme and was glad that no specific wastelands were mentioned. He will speak to the other people and he expects the meeting to go ahead as planned."

"Oh, Eileen, what would I do without you? Let's hope that Phaeton and the snow will combine to make PI's farming business un-newsworthy. Who can the mole be? How can we flush him out?"

"I've thought about that and I have some ideas, but first, have you mentioned the grass roots agricultural plan to anyone outside PI?"

"No," Miles answered without hesitation.

"And Capelli and Rahman are the only PI staff who know about it. Would the Algerian or Moroccan talk about it?" asked Eileen.

"No, they wouldn't. That kind of publicity would only cause them trouble. It can't be our computer network, that's secure. Our CDs are always locked up unless in use, aren't they?"

"Yes, but before you phoned, I had narrowed my search for the mole down to the CD safe. Leave it with me. We might nip this one in the bud before any real damage is done."

"OK, Eileen, see you about mid-morning. Thanks for all your efforts tonight."

*

Laurie and Angela discussed their important social engagement: "The PM is sending a car for us at twelve fifteen tomorrow. She said it was primarily a simple social lunch. She and her husband, Leo, want to meet you. She's not inviting anyone else so no one can make wrong guesses about the purpose of our being there. I asked her to tell the driver to pick us up here. I'll get back from the office by noon. The driver will take us to the back entrance to number ten."

"Sounds a bit cloak and dagger. I must decide what to wear now, so that I'm not rushed in the morning. I'd better give my hair a quick rinse. Don't worry," she said, "I won't breathe a word about where we're going to lunch."

*

Around the world that night scientists and astronomers, professionals and amateurs tried to keep in touch with Phaeton's progress. Many of them would not see him again unless – or until, said the optimists – he gained altitude once more after passing through earth's atmosphere. Some people continued to believe, and some papers with a particular religious slant continued to print, that Phaeton would slam into the earth. They said they believed "experts", confirmed this view, "but sinful men still refused to face the truth".

Snow fell on London that night, only a thin covering, but enough to sharpen the pens of the "Evacuate now" scribes.

Colgate Advises

Miles retired that night with a feeling he had not experienced for years – an acute and disturbing sense of contrition. Usually, when his head touched the pillow he went to sleep. That was why one went to bed: to sleep. The next morning would then bring refreshment and vigour, a readiness for the new day's work. Tonight, Saturday, 2 October 2010 he tossed and turned in his bed. His semi-detached strategy had backfired. The idea had been to illustrate, in a humorous way, that one's pursuit of excellence should be wholehearted. Settling for something less was not a virtue. It betrayed either mock humility or laziness.

The last thing he had intended was to upset Vicky. He loved her completely. Her attractiveness, her courage, her honesty, her compassion. His tired, but restless mind momentarily ran out of superlatives in his attempt to do justice to his beloved. After tossing and turning for an hour, he opened his eyes, got out of bed, stumbled to the window and drew back the curtain. The twinkling stars added to the moon's pale illumination of the rural scene. Inspired by the silhouetted landscape, he continued to catalogue Vicky's attributes... her fighting spirit, her resolution, her refusal to let friends down. The cold drove him back to bed. He closed his eyes, seeking sleep. Above all, her, what was the word? Her integrity! He raised himself on his right elbow and thumped the pillow with his left fist: her int... *thump*... eg... *thump*... rity... *thump*.

He willed himself to sleep, but her words echoed in his head: "A world of big business, Rolls Royces, yachts and jet aeroplanes... out of touch... customers... semi-detached... bicycles... canoes... model aeroplanes" – the words projected a colourful kaleidoscope on a panoramic screen in his head. His mind refused to give way to sleep.

And then... "I don't want you to lose your cutting edge," Eileen had said. Well, he wouldn't lose his cutting edge! He

Colgate Advises

would jolly well extend it. That was the idea. So far, he'd run PI as an autocracy. Now he wanted Vicky and Eileen to become equal partners in a... "triocracy". Was there such a word, he wondered? If there wasn't... there is now. At last he slept. It was 3 a.m. on Sunday, 3 October – Phaeton Day. At that moment Phaeton streaked earthwards at 29,320 mph, now only 394,354 miles from the planet.

Victoria had fallen asleep as soon as her head touched the pillow. The air, the stillness, the deeper quality of the countryside silence and darkness, the different car, the pub, Mr More, the PI property, all had combined to exhaust her. Sleep, blessed sleep. She knew it could solve problems overnight, by, apparently, the effortless employment of the unconscious mind.

★

Laurie Colgate arrived at his office in Church House, Westminster at 5.30 a.m. on Sunday, 3 October, Phaeton Day, which had been declared a normal working day until curfew time. He immediately set to work studying the latest computer printouts from around the world, paying special attention to the data from colleagues who had cross-checked their tracking of the meteoroid with positional and photographic information from satellites.

Next he set up the Observatory's equipment so that, at precisely 06.45, he would be able to read off Phaeton's track in relation to earth, its distance from earth, and its speed. At that time there would be ten hours to go to zero hour – the moment of the meteor's closest contact with the planet. He too, would obtain cross checks from satellites, and, he hoped, some graphic drawings which the Prime Minister wanted to see. He jotted down a note to phone the PM's secretary at nine o'clock.

Sheila's main task would be to log the meteor's progress at fifteen minutes to every hour throughout the day, knowing that, if its track and speed were stable, as anticipated, Phaeton's distance from earth would reduce by 29,320 miles every hour. Any noteworthy change in the latter figure, especially if it were a reduction in speed, would imply a change of track and could be of crucial significance. At 6.45 a.m. the two main computers produced statistics, coloured drawings, and cross checks which confirmed the accuracy of Phaeton's predicted plot to date. The meteor's speed was now constant. The "ten hours to zero" countdown had started.

★

Victoria woke up at 7.15 a.m., jumped out of bed, put on her dressing gown, and pulled back the curtains to see what kind of rural paradise lay to the rear of PI's country cottage. She felt refreshed and happy. The sun had already lit up the eastern horizon towards which she looked. Its glowing, pinkish golden light silhouetted a copse of birch trees, which climbed the hill behind and to the right of their garden. *Peace*, she thought. There was not yet enough light to see more than the outline of their patch, but she could see that a hedge ran the length of the garden, between them and their neighbour, a shepherd, Miles had said.

She peeped round the door into Miles's bedroom. He was asleep, but, unusually for him, blankets were all over the place, some on one side of the bed, some the other. He was covered partly by his dressing gown and partly by an eiderdown. She crept downstairs into the small, well-furnished kitchen. An electric kettle, a teapot, in fact all that was needed came easily to hand. Whilst the kettle boiled, she inspected the three ground-floor rooms. Small, but neat, she decided. As the tea brewed, she took the bacon and eggs out of the fridge, and then remembered Phaeton. The gas-fired central heating boiler ignited with a muffled roar – the eggs cracked as they hit the floor. She found a tray, two mugs patterned with a sheep motif, a teaspoon, and a jug into which she poured milk from the bottle she found in the fridge. Neither she nor Miles took sugar, which was just as well, because she couldn't find any. Picking up the tray she went back upstairs, smiled to herself, and knocked on Miles's door. No answer. She knocked again and said, "It's the housemaid, sir, with your morning tea."

"What! Who?" said Miles in a startled, drowsy voice.

Vicky put the tray on the landing window ledge, burst into Miles's room, snatched the pillow from under his head and

Colgate Advises

attacked him vigorously. When he tried to grab her, she darted out of the room, retrieved the tray and said, "Let's have our first ever cup of tea in our very own PI semi-detached cottage. Darling, I had a wonderful sleep. What about you?"

"I had nightmares. The troubled sleep – or lack of it – that goes with an uneasy conscience. I got too hot, then too cold. Then I nearly fell down stairs when I tried to find the loo in the dark. You slept, uncaring, through all my traumas."

"I shall have a bath, then I'll make breakfast, specially scrambled eggs and bacon," she said.

At five minutes to eight they sat down to breakfast at the kitchen table, where there was just room for two. Miles switched on the radio in time for the weather and the news. The forecast was for a few intermittent snow showers in the south and yet more snow, but less heavy falls than of late, in the north.

The news headlines were followed by details of travel restrictions which would be in force throughout the country from 3.45 p.m to 5.45 p.m., that is, from one hour before until one after Phaeton's passage through earth's atmosphere. All civil air traffic would be grounded during this period. Airlines had been given early warning to schedule their flights accordingly. Furthermore, those flights which crossed the meteor's path through earth's atmosphere had been advised to use alternative routes for the twenty-four hours following Phaeton's departure. Information on road and rail traffic restrictions was equally detailed and specific.

Halfway through the bulletin the newscaster said, "The British Company, Poundmore International, had the foresight to buy up all kinds of equipment that is used in Alaska, North America, and countries where heavy falls of snow are normal. Our informant confirms that this equipment is now being supplied to 'UK Eskimos' in Britain's northern counties and in Scotland."

Miles leaped to his feet. "Vicky," he said, "I've asked Giles to pick us up at 8.30 a.m. We must get back as soon as possible to catch that mole."

"Mole, Miles? What on earth are you talking about?" she asked, as she washed up the breakfast dishes. Throwing the tea towel to Miles she added, "Dry these, darling, Giles will be here in two minutes."

Colgate Advises

Whilst Miles performed the "keeping in touch with our markets" task of dish drying, he explained his and Eileen's suspicions about someone in PI whom, they believed, was passing information to the media.

The car stopped in front of "Dunroamin" one minute before 08.30. Vicky heard the toot, and called, "I'll be down in a minute." She looked in the mirror, brushed her hair, applied lipstick and a touch of powder, picked up her handbag, then put it down again. She pulled the bedclothes back so that the bed could "air". This, her mother used to say, was essential domestic hygiene.

Miles called, "Come on, Vicky, we'll be late."

"Be with you in a second," she answered, as she went into his bedroom, picked up the blankets, sheets and pyjamas and draped them over the foot of the bed. She retrieved her handbag, rushed out of the house, and, catching sight of the newly painted nameboard, burst into peals of laughter as she climbed into the car. "Dunroamin! Miles, I bet you had that sign put up. I think this whole trip is a put-up."

Giles closed the rear passenger door, climbed into his seat and drove smoothly away from Letcombe whatever. Suddenly, it registered with Vicky that she was in the Rolls. She decided not to comment.

*

At nine o'clock Laurie Colgate telephoned the PM's secretary. The secretary spoke to the PM who agreed that it would be advantageous to defer lunch until after one. The car would now call for Mr and Mrs Colgate at one o'clock.

*

Earlier that morning, Eileen listened carefully to the news. The only reference to Poundmore International was in connection with the "Eskimos". Phaeton, snow and emergency notices dominated the bulletins. The phrase "To make wastelands bloom", used by the television announcer yesterday was one

Colgate Advises

which she knew had appeared in a confidential letter written by Miles to Jasem Al-Mana. The only office copy was on Miles's special correspondence CD, which was locked in the CD safe when not in use. Paper copies of personal correspondence were made only in exceptional circumstances.

PI's main computer system was never switched off, except for periodical servicing at night or during a weekend. Eileen's assistant had been off work since Thursday, the day before the "leak" was first broadcast, as she had been suffering from a heavy cold. Staff in the general office, on the floor below, rarely visited the Chairman's suite. Eileen switched on her assistant's VDU and selected the edit facility. The option to paste was highlighted. She pressed enter and a copy of Miles's letter to Jasem Al-Mana appeared on the screen.

Eileen grimaced. She selected print and made a copy of the letter, afterwards making a note on it: "Sunday, 3 October 2010. Copy of a letter taken from Assistant Secretary's Computer at 08.30." She signed the note and switched off the VDU.

At nine o'clock, when her assistant arrived, Eileen said, "Switch on your VDU, please." She walked to the console, leaned over and selected paste and the letter appeared on the screen.

The girl said, "It's time PI had some good publicity. I know something about that and the boost it can give to business."

"How did you know what was in the letter?" asked Eileen.

"You were very busy that night, you told me to prepare Mr Poundmore's mail for posting. I read that letter and one to Mr Capelli about skis, snowshoes and snowploughs," said the girl.

"You know the rules about the confidential nature of our work," said Eileen, "you have deliberately breached those rules, which you signed as having understood. Why?"

It became clear that the girl had discussed PI with her boyfriend, a reporter, who saw the possibility of big news, if he could get direct information about the elusive Miles Poundmore.

"You took a confidential CD out of the safe, stole information from it, and sold it to a reporter!" said Eileen accusingly.

"I didn't sell it, my boyfriend did," admitted the girl.

When Miles and Victoria arrived in the office at ten thirty, the mole had gone. Eileen was sad as the girl had shown such promise. Now, with 360 minutes of Phaeton's countdown to go, Victoria had temporarily added the role of Eileen's assistant to that of Property and Perquisites Director.

★

In the office at Church House, Sheila maintained contact with colleagues, cross checking her hourly readings of Phaeton's movements at fifteen minutes to each hour. The meteor's progress remained steady. It was estimated that friction and heat would reduce its bulk by about thirty per cent during its passage through earth's atmosphere. There would be vast amounts of extra dust and debris which, until dissipated, would reflect the sun's heat away from large areas of the planet's surface. Laurie was working with Douglas White on graphs and predictions of weather systems. They shrugged off the morning's press comments which ranged from sarcasm to vindictive personal attack, including one piece of cartoon advice with the caption. "If your charts don't tell you, try looking out of the window."

At 12.40 p.m., Laurie chose the drawing which best illustrated the angle of Phaeton's approach to earth. Sheila provided him with the latest statistics and Douglas White drove him to his flat in Baker Street. He and Angela arrived at Number 10 without attracting press attention.

Angela had expected the Prime Minister and her husband to show signs of strain. The government was not getting a good press during the twin crises. The sharpest criticism came, as one would expect, from a newspaper whose editorial policy embarrassed the parliamentary opposition almost as much as the government: "It is clear that the Prime Minister's adviser is wrong about the snow. He was wrong about it a week ago. This paper warned the government then. He was wrong about it two days ago when a further twelve inches of snow fell in the northeast. He is wrong about it today. Is he wrong about Phaeton too? One thing is certain: the Prime Minister's trust in this man has proved fatal. They should both go."

Mrs Smith, however, seemed more concerned about Angela. She said, "Don't let these people worry you. The worst of them

Colgate Advises

live in what Leo calls a world of 'liesellnews'. Even the best get it wrong sometimes."

For lunch there was salmon cooked in white wine. A working lunch, with only the four of them in the room, during which they talked shop. They made space on the table for the drawing, the main feature of which was a line projected from a dot. The dot represented the meteoroid, the line showed its track towards the perimeter of an enormous circle which represented the sun. The rim of the earth just touched the track line, indicating how close Phaeton would pass.

"This scale of drawing," explained Laurie, "doesn't convey a true picture of the real thing. For example, the earth is scaled down to the size of a table-tennis ball. If we increased it to the size of a large apple, our total atmosphere, drawn to scale, would be represented by a line thinner than the skin of the apple. To indicate the different layers of atmosphere realistically we have taken liberties with scale."

"But it does show why the meteor's shallow angle gives it more time in earth's atmosphere. I find it a very helpful drawing," said Leo Smith. "How long will it take to pass through our air?"

"If everything remains stable, track, speed, bulk etcetera, it will take three point six minutes. If we begin counting from its first contact with the thinnest upper level of air on the entry side, to its exit on the other side, it will travel, at this shallow angle, for some 7,000 miles through our five main atmospheric layers. We can't say, with certainty, that it will penetrate all of earth's three lower atmospheric levels. This is for two reasons, first, the height and thickness of each layer varies, second, as friction and heat cause even relatively minor pieces to break off, this will affect drag and the angle of attack of the main body. Any such fragments represent a threat. There is no certainty at this point, so I can only say that in my opinion, unless Phaeton explodes, it will not penetrate levels below seven miles."

The PM said, "We have to accept the uncertainty attached to this object in space, there's nothing we can do about it. But we can do something about the misinformation being peddled around by irresponsible journalism. Mr Colgate, I would like you to explain the facts about Phaeton to the nation. If you could do that, in the same matter-of-fact way in which you have just explained it to us, people would recognise the voice of authenticity. I have a 'slot' at two-fifteen today. It is intended as a calming talk for those who have been frightened by some of the more lurid accounts of a meteorite strike. I shall first say a few words as an introduction."

"If you think it would help," said Laurie. "I will need a few minutes to jot down notes before going on the air. This chart and these statistics should help to give people a clearer idea of what is happening."

"I have half-an-hour of air time," said the PM, "if you can deal with Phaeton in fifteen minutes, I would like you to follow up with a short analysis of the snow and ice outlook as you have explained it to me."

After lunch Laurie jotted down the headings for his talk. The televised interview was to take place in the Prime Minister's study.

Mrs Smith said, "Dr Colgate, I told the cameramen there would probably be two of us, and that close up shots of documents would be required." She checked the time, "If we go down in ten minutes, that gives us fifteen minutes for whatever rehearsal the television crew want."

Beaten By The Opposition

Captain Geoffrey Wenock surveyed *Andromeda*, and, with a rare smile of satisfaction on his face, said to "Jimmy the One", "I think we've done a good job, Jack. She's as safe as houses – no – safe as the Bank of England."

When *Andromeda*'s trip to Tunis was postponed for five days, the Captain had gone down to Jack's flat to discuss security measures for the yacht.

He knew what damage heavy seas, such as would surely follow Phaeton's passage through earth's atmosphere, could wreak on a ship in the confined space of a harbour. He was determined to do everything in his power to ensure not only the safety of his crew, but that of his vessel too.

With the help of a friend, an Italian harbourmaster, he arranged for *Andromeda* to make an urgent visit to dry dock. And, just in case Miles might be tempted to change his mind and order his yacht to sea, he signalled PI's headquarters: "*Andromeda* in dry dock 2.10 to 5.10.10: will advise when ready to sail."

The two men were in uniform, dressed for duty. They had played important roles in the docking operation. Captain Wenock's long service in the Royal Navy, and especially in the Mediterranean, had built up a mutual respect between him and those Italian port officers who had served in the Italian navy.

His request for a berth in the smallest of the dry docks, to enable a full inspection of *Andromeda*'s hull, at a fair fee of course, had met with immediate action.

"You know, sir, the insurers will classify Phaeton as an 'act of God'. So any resulting loss or damage is unlikely to be covered. The gates of this dock are as massive and strong as any I've seen," Jack pointed to *Andromeda*, "so with any luck, she'll not get so much as a scratch."

After inviting the harbourmaster and the dry dock supervisor aboard for a drink, Captain Wenock and Jack returned to the block of flats to complete plans for the protection of their families on Phaeton day.

★

At PI's London headquarters, Victoria breezed into Miles's office, closing the door behind her, at precisely eleven o'clock. She stood behind his chair, her arms clasped round his neck.

"That girl exposed a terrible weakness in our security arrangements, Vicky. If she'd been a computer buff, she could have duplicated this CD, which has all my private papers on it! I've ordered a new safe to be built into my office. From now on, no members of staff are to be allowed in here on their own, with the exception of you and Eileen."

"A good idea, but don't have nightmares about that girl. It was a simple case of opportunism, not so much hers as her journalist boyfriend's. Darling," she tightened her arms gently round his neck, bent down and kissed him, "I want you to come out with me. Everything in the world will come to a halt at a quarter to four," she exaggerated. "What I have in mind will be a new experience for you. It includes lunch," she added.

In spite of some suspicions, Miles agreed. He knew that, after dropping him at the office, Giles had taken Vicky back home to collect her 2CV, which now graced one of PI's three parking spaces. "What a noisy, smelly, draughty, uncomfortable little brute. It's time you changed it," said Miles. "I think of you as a hardy annual, but only a tough old perennial would drive round in this."

"Just right for nipping in and out of city traffic," replied Vicky, making as fast a time to the East India Dock Road as a London Cabbie.

Miles had a curious feeling that Vicky had balanced the books as she led him into All Saints for the short service at noon. To her surprise he walked meekly into the church, raising no objections. There was a good congregation. Before the service began, Miles whispered to Vicky, "More than usual?"

"Yes, about three times as many."

"Either Phaeton is on the side of the angels, or fear of the unknown drives people to their knees," said Miles. "Funny that a scientifically orientated society should admit limits to its knowledge, but none to its superstitions."

One of the most endearing qualities of the best churches is their recognition that the body, as well as the soul, needs food. Find a church and, in all but a handful of isolated cases, you will find a hostelry nearby. All Saints Church excelled in this respect, with possibilities ranging from riverside inns to pubs sited in the streets which branched off the East India Dock Road.

After the service Vicky drove the 2CV for a short, exciting sprint to The Grapes, an historic Inn on the north bank of the river.

"Mr More, I shall treat you to a pint of ale and a ploughman's lunch, which you may eat whilst gazing at the many vistas offered by Father Thames," Vicky said. "Or, we can watch television and keep up to date with Phaeton." They felt personally involved in the entertainment that ensued, only one part of which had been engineered by Victoria. After the news headlines, the announcer said, "Our extended news bulletin today will be followed, at 2.15 p.m., by an interview with the Prime Minister and the Government's Scientific Adviser, Dr Laurie Colgate, at 10 Downing Street. Before that, we shall hear the views of a well-known journalist who is a forthright critic of government Policy on the present emergencies."

At that moment the curate from All Saints walked into the bar, looked round, caught Victoria's eye, and pushed his way through the throng to join them.

"Mr Gadsby, how nice to see you," said Vicky in a tone intended to convey surprise. Before Mr Gadsby could respond, she said, "This is my husband, Mr More."

The two men shook hands, "Miles More," said Miles.

"Neville Gadsby," responded the curate.

"What can I get you to drink, Mr Gadsby?" asked Victoria, "Oh, and would you like a ploughman's? That's what we're having."

Vicky went to the bar, when she returned with a pint of ale, Miles and Neville Gadsby were deeply involved in a discussion of county and test cricket.

"Thank you, Victoria," said Neville, absent-mindedly. He turned back to Miles, "No county side can stay on top for long. The international game takes their best players."

A sudden hush descended on the bar. The television screen showed an interviewer facing a square jawed, brown-faced man who, in a vehement manner, said: "I repeat what I've written and said before to this government, to the Prime Minister and to the Home Secretary. You have got it wrong. You have got it wrong! Snow, ice and Arctic temperatures are relentlessly creeping south. Far too many lives have already been claimed. And it's only the third of October!"

The interviewer broke in, "The snow hasn't actually advanced any further south this week—"

"We had snow in London, the night before last!"

"Not a very heavy fall. Don't you think Mr Colgate could be right?"

"He's an astronomer and a geophysicist, not a meteorologist. I know that the weather charts don't give any indication at all of an end to this Arctic weather. Laurie Colgate is wrong about the snow and ice. Is he also wrong about Phaeton? For all our sakes, I hope the oracle that advises him about the weather hasn't advised him about the meteor too!"

The interview ended. "There you have it, a blunt attack on the Government's handling of twin emergencies that affect us all. The Home Secretary herself is believed to be unhappy about the stop-and-go dithering of the evacuation. Stay tuned until 2.15 p.m., when the Prime Minister will explain her government's policy of limited evacuation from the frozen north. After that, Dr Laurie Colgate will elucidate the reasoning behind his controversial advice to the government in its dealing with both Phaeton and the Ice."

"My money's on Laurie Colgate," said Miles, "what do you think, Neville?"

"There are few disciplines more rigorous than physics, as I know from my own limited experience. I am sure that Mr Colgate's advice to the government is based on detailed research and careful observation. I read in *The Times* that he regularly consults the director of Climap UK about weather patterns. He's not the kind of man to stake his reputation on astrology or oracles. So I too back him."

Victoria listened, secretly pleased that Miles and Neville were on the same wavelength. She was happy to make an occasional comment, but happier still to concentrate on her ploughman's bread and cheese, whilst they talked.

She heard the announcer remind viewers that all citizens, except security forces, must be under cover by 3.45 p.m., "that is 3.45 p.m.", repeated the female voice. "To minimise the effects of pressure or blast waves, all doors and windows are to be left open…" The announcements continued against the background of renewed conversation in the bar.

Miles drained his glass, and, as he rose to his feet, Vicky heard him say, "But truth, like religion, depends upon culture and the position you occupy in this world, doesn't it, Neville?" He picked up Neville's glass, "Same again?"

"What on earth did Miles mean by that?" asked Victoria.

"He said it in the context of a discussion on religious intolerance, which he says is evil or even blasphemous. I said that it depended on the truth of a religion and what it was being intolerant about."

Miles returned with two pints, and an orange juice for Vicky.

"If your comment about truth is valid, Miles, perhaps evolution has brought us to the stage where modern man can dispense with religion. That is, if the function of religion is, as suggested by Jung, to protect us from a direct and personal experience of God. Cheers," said Neville, lifting his glass. "What a good idea this pub lunch was, Victoria. I'm thoroughly enjoying myself."

Victoria looked sharply at Miles, who raised his glass, smiled, and said, "Quits."

*

Five minutes before the Prime Minister and Laurie Colgate were due to go down to the study in Number 10, the PM's secretary knocked at the dining room door. He gave Mrs Smith a note of the anti-government television interview.

"Anything new in this?" asked the PM.

"No, it's just a bit more vitriolic," replied the secretary, "and, at the end of the programme, the interviewer said that the Home Secretary herself is believed to be unhappy about the government's evacuation policy. I don't know where he got that from, but, coming from the interviewer, I thought it was a bit thick."

"Yes, make a note of it. We'll have words with them later."

In her statement the Prime Minister repeated what she had already told the House and the country. "A precipitous evacuation," she said, "would cause great hardship to thousands of families who would be obliged to leave their homes and possessions, and, in many cases their animals, when there is no firm evidence that a prolonged period of Arctic weather is coming our way."

"The Cabinet," she said, "studied the advice of experts before coming to their decision to limit evacuation to the sick, infirm, and nursing mothers who were advised by their doctors that they should leave on medical grounds. The only total evacuation has taken place from Cumbria. However," she stated, "some people have already received permission to return to certain areas of that county, where, supported by forces with special equipment, they have begun the task of clearing snow from roads and towns in preparation for a general return which, I believe, may soon be possible. It is now my pleasure to introduce Dr Laurie Colgate," she ended, "whose advice I and my colleagues have found invaluable."

Laurie dealt first with Phaeton's journey towards earth. His diagrams illustrated the plane of the meteor's approach path. He showed that a small change in the angle of approach might occur when Phaeton encountered earth's atmosphere. "For us," he said, "this could be good news if the meteor gained lift and passed only through our upper atmosphere as it continues on its journey to the sun." He said that scientists had no previous observation experience of a meteor as big as Phaeton passing so close to earth. He explained the dangers, and the reasons for the government's safety precautions which, he advised, should be carefully followed. He warned that the passage of Phaeton through earth's atmosphere would affect weather patterns at least temporarily. We should be prepared for hurricane-force winds, unusually wide fluctuations in temperature, noise, and, in coastal areas, abnormally rough seas and extreme tidal movements.

"Next we come to the problem of snow and ice," he said. "I understand the concern of those who think we are on the brink of something like another little ice age. They have happened in the past. I understand the worries of those who say this is October, that all the winter months are yet to come. My colleagues and I have, of course, studied past records. Indeed we have had access to research on ice ages both major and minor, long and short, going back for more than 450,000 years. Our observations show clearly that the conditions required to produce even a mini ice age, one lasting three or four months, are not present today. We now know that what we have is an unseasonable and harsher example of the conditions experienced in 1947. Some senior citizens may remember those days, when, although weakened by a long and desperate war, they braved the elements and won. I realise that this kind of weather is doubly exceptional in early October, and it might have been the herald of worse conditions to come. One day, that may well be the case. It is not the case today."

He referred to the prevalence of easterly winds and the presence of more cloud than usual over the Arctic regions. These were temporary phenomena which, he said, were expected to abate in degree over the winter months. "With all the evidence available to me, it would, in my view, have been irresponsible of me to advise the Prime Minister that whole populations should be uprooted from their homes, only to find that, within a month, they were able to return. By staying at home we can keep the pipes defrosted, as our grandparents and parents did in 1947. We can maintain contact with neighbours, and help to keep lines of communication open so that the essential transport of food and other supplies continues. I believe that, in less than a month, we shall wonder why there was so much talk of mass evacuation."

★

"That's told 'em. Perhaps his hysterical critics will stop to think before shooting off their mouths again," said Vicky.

Miles reverted to the subject of faith. "Neville, the people who invented the creeds spoke the truth as they saw it at the time. Were they inspired by love? Or was it fear, or the pursuit of power? And what is the kingdom of God? How can it be within you, me or anyone?"

"I read somewhere that the Garden of Eden, where God walked with Adam and Eve, wasn't a piece of real estate. It was that idyllic land of milk and honey, that haven beyond suffering for which humanity craves. A mythic symbol of transcendence. As for Christ's teaching, it can be taken in two ways. One way concretises the symbol so that you don't see through it – beyond it. That way, you look for a worldly kingdom. But He says, 'My kingdom is not of this world.' The symbol is transparent. To find your own experience of the transcendent, your own eternity, you must look inwards. It's not about earthly prosperity. It's about spiritual awareness. When you accept that God reigns in your heart, not in a narrow, religious way, but over your whole life, then you find the peace of God. The kingdom is now. Seek and you will find."

"But I thought the message of the kingdom was easy to understand? You know, Jesus thanks God for revealing these things to simple people. You need to be a theologian, or a philosopher to make sense of what you've just said," objected Miles.

"I'm a miner's son," said Neville. "I understood what I just said when I was a boy. I was ten years old when my father was made redundant, but not before he had caught the miner's disease. He knew what poverty was, but he was never embittered by it. He encouraged me to work. He studied astronomy with me. My family seldom missed church on Sunday, where my father and I sang in the choir. He said, listen to the church's teaching, but find your own way to God. To do that, you must believe in two things, first that God is, and secondly that it's worth your while to search for him. Those words were my creed. They were based on love. Think of the words, 'love your neighbour as yourself.' Find yourself, know yourself. You are unique. You are part of God's mystery – dependent on him. Begin at the beginning, which for you is yourself."

"I've believed in God from my earliest remembered days," said Miles, "but what do the words, 'try to find him', mean?"

"In the New Testament are the words, 'I will set my laws in their understanding and write them on their hearts... and they shall not teach one another... for all of them shall know me, from small to great.' Your church, the clergy – anyone you trust may point the way; but only you can seek your own eternity, your unique relationship with God in the context of your own life."

"Time, gentlemen," said Victoria. "Much as I would like this conversation to continue, Phaeton is, at this moment, a fact of life."

She pointed to the television as the curfew instructions were announced yet again. "Neville, Miles and I must get back to PI before the curfew, and no doubt you must go to either home or All Saints?"

"You're right, Victoria. I have an appointment in the crypt with a number of people who want to talk about the old days. The parish has changed from a predominant dockland, seafaring place, to a cosmopolitan community. But the heroic memories of World War II, and the bombing which virtually wiped out the parish, linger in the minds of the remnants of a bygone era. They also inspire the imaginations of newcomers. Some of these new parishioners want to hear, first hand, how the oldies survived such hardships."

"Has Phaeton sharpened the newcomers' interest in the church?" asked Victoria.

"An interesting question. An invading meteoroid, thundering in from outer space, has trebled congregations. That is a better response than the God of love can achieve. Fear, on the face of it, produces results quickly, as it has in the past. But does it produce commitment?"

When Time Stood Still

"All these people travelling home to be with their families when Phaeton comes – two hours and 58,600 miles to go," said Miles. He forgot the discomfort of Vicky's 2CV as it sped westwards along Cable Street, heading for Trafalgar Square and Pall Mall. More traffic was on the roads, mostly private cars, than was usual for a Sunday afternoon. "I shall be relieved when this long drawn out drama is ended."

"I shall be glad too. How real do you think the danger is?"

"I've been trying to work that out. You know what it's like if you're standing on a railway platform when an express train rushes through at 70 mph?"

"Yes! That sudden blast of air, the deafening noise, the platform shakes and trembles under your feet. Then comes the aftermath. You feel the suction swirling and pulling at you and your skirt, – or trousers!" replied Vicky.

"Try to imagine an object half as big as the Isle of Wight, the size and weight of ten thousand express trains, travelling more than 400 times faster at 30,000 mph, and passing by only a few miles away," he said.

"I think that's the real reason for these emergency measures. Have you noticed that a lot of the special yellow patrol vehicles are armoured cars? That's not because civil unrest is anticipated, it's to give protection to their crews," observed Victoria.

"Yes, and you can see why Laurie and Sheila, and scientists around the world, say that Phaeton's approach angle is crucial. That governs his distance away from the earth's surface. The flatter the angle, the less the immediate effect of his passage. But what will the aftermath be like? He'll pass us like a flying volcano, like the one on Montserrat, spewing molten metal, rocks and dust everywhere. But in Phaeton's case the whole meteor will be a boiling, vast cauldron, as hot as hell, blasting through our air at more than forty times the speed of sound!"

When Time Stood Still

At 3.25 p.m. Vicky parked the 2CV next to the Rolls in the PI parking space near Pall Mall. As they walked round to the offices, a yellow armoured car moved slowly down the centre of the road. A woman in khaki uniform, wearing a yellow helmet over her long black hair stood in its open hatch. She was turning her head regularly from side to side, checking that all windows and doors were open. On both sides of the vehicle, in large navy blue letters, was painted the word "security". Vicky pointed up the street. About a hundred yards behind the car walked two yellow-uniformed figures, one on each side of the street, double-checking that all doors and windows were open.

As they watched the armoured car, she said, "The curfew is working before it's due to start. Do you realise that, apart from the armoured car crew, we are the only people about in the whole of Pall Mall? Gives you a spooky kind of feeling, doesn't it? Big brother is watching you."

*

First Officer Harry Simpson was disappointed. Since Captain Williams was in Brantome he himself had to find the safest place for *Ariadne* during the crucial few hours following Phaeton's passage through earth's atmosphere. His attempts to find bomb-proof shelter on an RAF airfield where an old friend held the post of Wing Commander Flying had failed. He now had to decide whether to leave PI's aeroplane in her usual hangar, or to park her well away from all buildings. He chose the latter option, taxied *Ariadne* to open ground at the eastern perimeter, locked all control surfaces to protect them against hurricane-force winds, covered her with protective sheeting, and anchored her securely to the ground, doubling, then trebling the normal number of anchorage points and ropes.

Now, on Phaeton day, he decided to spend the curfew hours in the lower ground floor of the airport's control tower.

*

The Prime Minister and her husband remained at Number 10. Leo was plotting Phaeton's latest position on his chart. Soon he would receive the 3.45 p.m. position, when the meteoroid should be less than 30,000 miles away. "It's strange, Winnie, an aspect of relativity I suppose. But suddenly 30,000 miles appears to be uncomfortably close. Yet the next sixty minutes will seem like a lifetime."

Winnie laughed, "It's something to do with equations of eternity. When the mortality of conscious life is emphasised publicly, as it is now, the terms of each individual's life equation change dramatically. All the information I have indicates that intelligent people have changed their thinking, their ideas, in positive ways. In other words, hope, and not fear, has become a dominant factor in their lives. If that kind of thinking is both widespread and sustained, we may find that there is, at last, a genuine and widespread basis for a more just and humane society. If... if."

★

The Home Secretary and her husband were sitting in the well-furnished basement of their private house in London. Heather had tried all the channels on the television, but failed to find one that gave the latest weather report and forecast. The majority of stations focused on Phaeton, which was what she had asked them to do. The others screened films or recordings of sporting events.

"George," said Heather, "see if you can get the weather on Internet, or teletext. I don't want to phone the Met Office again."

George sighed, and tuned into the teletext weather program. This showed them exactly what they had already seen at least six times that day. "There's no doubt about it. The cold winds from the east are abating," he said.

"I can see that. But for how long? Your friend at the Met Office said there was nothing on the charts to indicate any let up in the Arctic weather. I recall precisely his words, George. According to you he said: 'Quite the contrary, I expect it to spread south.'"

"But you don't really want blizzards and snow and ice all over the country, Heather, do you?"

★

Angelo Capelli told Carla to open the windows and doors of his office, as instructed by the government and enforced, if necessary, by the Polizia. Now, through the open window, he gazed across the Via di Santa Pancrazio towards Vatican City.

"Carla, soon we have sheds full of tractors, bulldozers, ploughs and heaters. Soon, we go broke or we make lots of profit, or Phaeton settles our account and we have no more worries. Which do you think?"

"Mr Capelli, I don't know," she glanced at her watch, "but in fifty-nine minutes we shall have one thing less to worry about."

"The Holy Father is praying for the world, and especially for us. The airport has closed down. Everything has stopped, including my watch. It says there are still fifty-nine minutes to go. Tractors from Canada, an ice age in Britain, 'make wastelands bloom', an ice age in America, heating stoves in my warehouses. We are bottom of the PI league. What time is it Carla?"

"There are still fifty-nine minutes to go, Mr Capelli. My watch does not have a second hand. Soon there will be only fifty-eight minutes to go," said Carla.

"Last night I talk to my family about philosophy. Half the members of the human race are murderers, I said, and the other half venerate all life."

"How can you say that, Mr Capelli?" asked Carla.

"Listen, Carla, philosophy is difficult – and long-winded. Half the human race believes in God, the other half in the god of their culture, their religion, their race. Half the human race are adulterers, the other half obey the golden rule. Half the human race are greedy, the other half generous. Half the human race love their neighbour, the other half hate their neighbour."

"Mr Capelli, you can't have more than two halves," said Carla.

"That's what my daughter says, too many halves, papa. My wife says nothing. But my son, he is a bright boy. He says, numbers and time papa. That is the secret, Carla."

"I don't understand. Numbers and time? What does that mean?"

"The number of your years, and the time of your life. There is a time for everything, and a season for every activity under heaven. Think of it like this I say to my children – greed brings an awareness of generosity, and, for a short time, maybe a second, these qualities are of equal strength inside you. They are two halves of an impending impulse. You make your choice! Greed or generosity, adultery or faithfulness. Decisions! It is so with everything."

*

Laurie Colgate returned to his office at 2.30 p.m., his wife Angela accompanied him, having decided that Church House was as good a place as any in which to spend the last hour of Phaeton's countdown. In fact it would be a busy hour, checking data, confirming track, speed and distance – and – keeping the Prime Minister informed.

Douglas White and Sheila had noted the latest information from observers in the far east who had at present the best view of Phaeton. Some satellite pictures had ceased temporarily, as had been anticipated, because earth lay between the meteoroid and many of the satellites.

At 3.45 p.m., Sheila said, "Phaeton will be thirty seconds late reaching his lowest point, which, according to these readings, will occur between the Sea of Okhotsk and the Black Sea at 4.45 p.m. When we get the 3.45 p.m. reading from Greenland we shall be more precise about that position."

Whilst Angela brewed a pot of tea, Laurie, Douglas and Sheila worked at their computers, checking and cross checking the readings of Phaeton's progress. It was a progress that concerned every member of the human race, but there were many who remained blissfully unaware.

*

Ahmed Rahman sat with Selma, his wife, on the sunrise patio in their garden a few miles north of Cairo. Here they had a clear view to the east and to the north.

Pointing to the northeast, towards Syria, Ahmed said, "Phaeton will fly over there, high in the sky. We shall see only a streak, like lightning, because the meteorite is travelling at 500 miles a minute."

"Shouldn't we go indoors, Ahmed, as the President ordered?"

"I want to see all that there is to see – an opportunity that comes perhaps once in a million years. We know Phaeton will be seven miles high, much less dangerous than a direct hit."

"But we *don't* know that," she persisted.

"Unless Phaeton explodes, his actual passage will not be as dangerous as a thunderstorm. You know that lightning travels at a million times the speed of sound, much faster then Phaeton? It heats the air to a temperature of 30,000 degrees Celsius, much hotter than Phaeton. Its heat and speed cause great masses of air to separate and then collide with a velocity and noise that we call thunder. Don't worry. I have thought about it carefully."

"Phaeton is as big as an island," argued Selma, "if a piece of it fell off it could squash you like a jerboa."

"Selma, I tell you, we should worry more about polluted water and diminishing farmland in our country. The dam at Aswan may provide electricity, and irrigation somewhere, but what's happening to our beautiful Delta? Before the dam, sediment from our great rivers enriched the Delta soil every year, but now the Delta is disappearing into the sea. We have more people to feed, and at the same time, less land on which to grow food."

"Phaeton will be here in thirty minutes, I am going indoors, are you coming?"

"No. I would not forgive myself if I missed this opportunity. But next, after Phaeton, the ice. If that goes away too, will we still want to make wastelands bloom? Will we still want to feed refugees and the starving people of the world?"

Selma walked slowly along the winding path to the house.

★

In Tunis, Jasem Al-Mana sat on the high balcony of his house, looking north over the Mediterranean Sea. His family were down in the basement, playing cards, watching television or reading. From time to time he picked up his binoculars, aligning them to the northeast where he judged he might catch sight of Phaeton.

The intercom buzzed, he picked up the handset. "Jasem, you should come down," said his wife, "it is due in thirty minutes and it might be early."

"It will not be early, Mary, perhaps a few seconds – that is all. I will come down as soon as it has passed. Phaeton himself is the calm before the storm." He was not surprised when Mary joined him on the balcony. He smiled, "The real problem is not Phaeton, nor is it the ice. You remember the conversation we had with Miles Poundmore? The real problem is the difference between luxury and comfort."

"I don't follow you, how can that be the real problem?"

"The person who aspires to luxury and an over-abundance of good things in life, becomes blind to the poverty and deprivation suffered by others. A real statesman sees the world as a unity of which he is a citizen. Those who see themselves as citizens of the world are, at heart, statesmen. Their love, and their generosity is not sectarian."

"I don't see the connection between luxury, poverty and statesmanship," said Mary.

"A head of state's vision tends to focus on his own country, beyond that he generally suffers from myopia. A politician sees only his own party, because that is his path to power. That is the way things are, it is the way things work in a modern state. When the slogan expressing political motivation is, let us say, 'prosperity for all', it may well begin with a genuine desire to bring prosperity to all. It ends with luxury for the select, prosperity for the fortunate few, making ends meet for the majority, and starvation for the unfortunate misfits. Do you know why that is?"

Mary, looking at her watch, said, "It's because the nature of politics makes it an essentially short-term business. The short term view, and the fact that power corrupts, will forever equate luxury with the rewards of endeavour, and poverty with sloth. It takes a statesman's long term vision to work with integrity for the abolition of both. The world is short of statesmen because both politics and religion teach leaders to apply, knowingly or unknowingly, the 'divide and rule' principle."

"That's the only way democratic policies work. The majority is always right. Delusion for the people, power for the rulers," said Jasem.

"I can see that might be true about politics. It ought not to be true about religion. Not mine, anyway. There are only twenty minutes to go." Mary placed a chair beside Jasem and sat down.

"If you can't beat 'em, join 'em," she said.

★

Mohamed Ramzi sat, with furrowed brow, in a sheltered cove which boasted a sandy beach near the northeast tip of Majorca. He had retreated from the noise and bustle of Algiers. As Phaeton's approach time drew nearer, that bustle had become frantic, the noise unbearable. That was when he decided to catch the last pre-Phaeton flight to Majorca, to a place which he and his wife knew well. Now, his wife and family were half-an-hour's flight away, the meteor nineteen minutes away, the waters of the Mediterranean a couple of metres away.

Mohamed Ramzi's worry? The powerful people of his country would give neither time nor money to the most important business of improving food production. Political and religious leaders fought a long-running, often subversive battle for power, whilst many of their people lived on the verge of starvation. Industry, they said, was the route to profits and a more prosperous society. Industry needed water just as much as agriculture needed it. Which could produce the quickest boost to GNP? That's where land and water must go.

After a while, about ten minutes Mohamed thought, he looked at his watch. There were still fifteen minutes to zero. All that thinking had taken only four minutes. But he knew that the meeting with Miles Poundmore, Jasem Al-Mana and the others would be important for Algeria. Grass roots agriculture: "Behold, I make old things new," Mohamed misquoted to himself.

★

Hassen Osman was enjoying a few days off work at his holiday home in Casablanca.

He and his wife, Mitzi, were alone as their two teenage children no longer accompanied them on holidays. "What about

When Time Stood Still

the meteor?" Mitzi had asked, in front of the children, before she and Hassen left their home in Rabat.

"Phaeton? What about it? What we do will have no effect on it at all. The experts say it will be many miles up in the sky when it passes over the western Mediterranean. It won't bother about us, we won't bother about it," replied Hassen.

"But papa," said his daughter, a student at Rabat university, "There is a possibility that the meteorite will explode in earth's atmosphere."

"Of course there is, my dear. There is also a possibility that the sun won't rise tomorrow. What will be, will be. Meanwhile, we get on with our lives. I suggest we give Phaeton as much attention as he gives us." Hassen brushed Phaeton aside in an attempt to stop Mitzi worrying.

Now, as they sat on the veranda of their holiday home, all doors and windows opened wide, he looked surreptitiously at his watch. Phaeton was due in ten minutes.

*

"The sound of Newbolt's 'breathless hush in the close' would have shattered this uneasy London stillness," said Douglas, leaning out of one of the open windows in Laurie Colgate's office at Church House.

"Five minutes to go, 2,443 miles away," said Sheila in a tense voice.

"What height have you, Sheila?" asked Douglas.

"Extending the plane to earth, it still reads seven miles," she replied.

Douglas picked up the radio telephone, "Are you there, Laurie?"

"Loud and clear, Douglas. What's new?"

"Four minutes and thirty seconds to go, 2,199 miles. A low of seven miles. Are you staying up top for the fly past?"

"No. Tell Angela I'll be down in half-a-minute. We shall see nothing except on the screen."

Laurie spoke to the PM on the phone at two minutes and ten seconds to zero. "Prime Minister, in ten seconds Phaeton will be

977 miles away – two minutes from his lowest contact with earth's atmosphere when his position will be, approximately, over the Aral Sea at an altitude of about seven miles."

"Thank you, call at one minute ten seconds," said the PM.

★

In All Saints Church, off the East India Dock Road, The Reverend Neville Gadsby gave to the lonely, the timorous and the uncertain the benefit of science and religion combined. As zero hour approached, each minute appeared to lengthen into an infinite number of seconds.

"I've never known anything like it, not even in the war. Time is standing still," said one aged lady.

Neville opened his bible and read from the book of Joshua: " 'The sun stopped in the middle of the sky and delayed going down about a full day.' Now you know how those people felt when time stood still," he said.

The Countdown

"As far as Phaeton is concerned, we are merely observers of spatial mechanics," said Douglas.

"What do you mean by that?" asked Sheila.

"A philosopher's dreams inspire the scientist in his rigorous pursuit of truth. Right up to the moment of truth we like to think that mankind can influence life in the universe. And, of course, we can. Not by exploitation, that leads to death. We influence life by observation of it, and co-operation with it, from the privileged, but limiting, position of an insider. And, of course, by full-blooded identification with it. That's the starting point. 'One who can see inaction in action, and action in inaction, is the wisest among men... his deeds are purified by the fire of wisdom,' says the Bhavagad Gita."

"But surely the fire of wisdom sees that twentieth-century man is as helpless as his so-called primitive ancestors in the face of astral phenomena?" suggested Sheila.

"Yes and no," said Laurie. "From the beginning we wanted, but feared, unbounded life. Most of us are afraid of marching wholeheartedly with the creative spirit of evolution. We choose instead to limit our minds. We confine our God within the boundaries set by the religion – or irreligion – of our own choice, or that of our ancestral culture. And so, in this moment of truth, we put our faith in the laws of mechanics. At the same crucial moment that we accept the laws, we refuse the grace that calls us to venture beyond, to identify with the Being behind the laws."

"Laurie!" shouted Sheila, "A panic call from the American base at Guam! A satellite picture shows that a substantial portion of the meteor has broken away from the main body!"

"Get readings from all master stations, Sheila. Douglas get the run of pictures leading up to the breakaway. Sheila, get a check on Phaeton's speed."

"An increase in speed," called Sheila. "The one minute distance will be 488.666 miles."

Laurie picked up the red telephone. The Prime Minister herself answered immediately, "Dr Colgate," she said.

"Prime Minister, in ten seconds Phaeton will be 489 miles – one minute – from his lowest point in earth's atmosphere. His track will be south of the Sea of Okhotsk and north of the Aral Sea. His lowest point will be over the western tip of the Black Sea. He will cross Italy on a line south of Ancona to the northern tip of Corsica. From that point to southern Spain he will be at his closest to the UK – approximately 650 miles south of Beachy Head. The next crucial moment will be as he gains altitude, passing through the thermosphere on his way out of our atmosphere. He will be over the Atlantic then. Within the last minute a substantial piece has broken away from Phaeton, I will call you when I have information on its line of flight or if Phaeton's track changes."

"Thank you, Mr Colgate, we have recorded that message. I understand that we are now dealing with two missiles. Keep the line open so that I can see and hear essential information as you get it."

Five minutes earlier Sheila had checked that their computer link with the television network was open, ready for the final ten seconds countdown to begin at the precise instant. The Observatory's equipment was accurate to one thousandth of a second. In theory, at this moment, one minute before Phaeton's nearest approach to earth, all citizens of the United Kingdom were indoors, except for the Security Forces. In practice, many people knew that, since Phaeton would pass by more than 600 miles south, and at a height of ten miles, any storms were most likely to come in the aftermath of his passage – and now that of the breakaway as well.

So it was that a few people, equipped with binoculars or telescopes, had taken up vantage points, out of sight of security forces, in the hope of seeing or hearing something. Some looked south, some north, some east and some west. But the great majority of the populace looked at their television screens.

Douglas looked out of the open window, "This must be the most peaceful, the most unpolluted hour that any man has lived since the industrial revolution. London, without the noise and fumes of the internal combustion engine on the ground, and the jet engine in the heavens above."

★

"Isn't it incredible," said Vicky, "only three weeks ago we faced two potential disasters. The first was the frighteningly swift advance of what looked like a new ice age. The second was the possibility of an end to life on earth. Now, in just a minute, the unthinking cause of the second potential disaster, Phaeton, will begin his exit from our part of the universe. Will his exit be as quiet as his entry?"

"I don't think so," Eileen replied. "These security arrangements spell trouble. Practically every government in the world has taken precautions to protect their citizens, not all as thoroughly as ours. But then, countries on the other side of the Globe think they are further away from Phaeton."

"I think that what scientists call the aftermath will be global in its effects," said Miles. "I don't see how a meteorite the size of Phaeton can rip through our atmosphere at 30,000 mph without there being tremendous upheaval. Talking about that, did you send my message to all regional directors, Eileen."

"I did, and all have acknowledged receipt."

"As soon as the countdown starts, we'll go down to the basement," said Miles. "Are all CDs in the safe?"

Eileen switched Miles's VDU off, extracted the CD, put it in the new safe and said, "They are now, sir."

★

After her talk to the Canadian Prime Minister that morning, Mrs Smith said to her husband, "I don't want to get too excited about this, and in any case, I promised to keep it to myself until it has been made public in Canada. Leo, a slow thaw has begun in western Canada, it seems to be moving eastwards from Alberta. They get this kind of thing in a normal winter, so they are not counting their chickens. He thinks this thaw may be different. But the experts don't yet know how or why."

"Pity you can't tell Heather," said Leo. He looked at the clock, "Time to go down to the cellar."

The Prime Minister had sent some members of her staff home, to be with their families for the countdown. Now, with her husband, she joined those on duty as the television announcer said, not entirely accurately, "Once again, as in the twentieth century, monarch and government lead the people to the shelters and cellars of the United Kingdom. This time the threat comes from no human hand, but from a meteorite, a relic from our own solar system's formative turbulence millions of years ago. For the first time in history, in the early years of a new millennium, mankind is able to witness, through the lenses of cameras around the world, the passage of a major meteorite through earth's atmosphere. A meteorite so big that, were it to strike our planet, the consequences for life on earth would be catastrophic. And now, in fifty-nine seconds, the final countdown will begin."

★

"What time is it, Carla?" asked Angelo Capelli.

"Your new clock says there are fifty-five seconds to go, Mr Capelli."

"That last minute was a lifetime. I will tell you when to switch the radio on. Suddenly, Carla, I know that time is an illusion. Every fraction of a second is eternal. You know that, Carla?"

"No, Mr Capelli, I don't know that. It takes sixty seconds to make one little minute, and you tell me a fraction of a second is eternal?"

"Listen, Carla – I tell you. Open your mind and your heart to God for a fraction of a second and it is for ever. That, Carla, is why a fraction of a second is eternal. That is why time is an illusion. How many seconds left?"

Carla sighed, "I gave my whole life to God a long time ago. Thirty-nine seconds to go."

★

The Countdown

Mary Al-Mana, Jasem's Scottish wife, picked up the intercom handset and pressed the button.

"Yes?" said her elder son.

"I want you to talk to me until Phaeton has gone past," said Mary.

"I'm rather concentrating on this game of chess," he grumbled, "but for you I will do that, Mother."

*

"George," said Heather Moor, the Home Secretary, to her husband, "that was David Medden on the phone. He says there are rumours of a thaw in Canada. That's the last thing I need! I'm beginning to think that I have been ill-advised – probably deliberately. A failed ice age could cost me my job at the next cabinet reshuffle."

"Heather, my dear, Phaeton is due in nineteen seconds..."

"To *hell* with Phaeton!"

*

If Selma Rahman had stayed with Ahmed on the sunrise patio of their home, he might not have felt a sudden, unbearable loneliness. He looked around. Not a sign of life. Not a sound. The road to Athribis was deserted. The Damietta River was deserted. Wherever he looked, there was an unnerving absence of movement – of life. The cultivated fields of the delta, and beyond them the distant desert, were deserted. The stillness, the desolation, was menacing in its intensity. Not another human being, not an aeroplane, not a car, not a bird, not an animal, not an insect – not even a fly – to be seen. It was unearthly. The animals, the birds and the insects, they had sensed something, they knew something. They were hiding. Their silence, their absence – was a message, a warning – they were warning him.

Ahmed shifted on his garden chair. The metal legs grated on the pale blue paving stone. The rasping noise violated the awesome silent stillness, and, at the same time, accentuated it. A wave of fear overwhelmed him. Allah was about to speak – to him – Ahmed Rahman.

"Ahmed! Fifteen seconds to go. You should come in!" shrieked Selma.

Ahmed dropped his binoculars and ran along the path to the security of his house.

★

On the northern coast of Majorca, towards the eastern tip, lies a bay with a sandy beach. A few steps east of the bay is a secluded cove: it too has a tiny, sandy beach. On Phaeton day, in the afternoon to be precise, Mohamed Ramzi occupied a deck chair in this cove. He had come here to think. Away from Algiers, and parted from his beloved family for two days, the solitude he sought was enhanced by the stillness. No traffic on the road, no aeroplanes or birds in the air, no ships on the sea. As far as the eye could see – not a sign of life. Mohamed was happy: he had come to a decision.

Whatever the politicians or the religious fundamentalists in Algeria said, he would work with, and for, the people who loved the land. If it cost him his job, or even his life, so be it.

He glanced at his watch. Phaeton was due to reach his lowest point in earth's atmosphere in eighteen seconds. That point was ten miles above the western shore of the Black Sea. The meteor would then be some 1,700 miles east of Majorca. He stood up, adjusted his dark glasses and looked north across the Mediterranean. One hundred miles away lay Barcelona. According to the latest information he had, Phaeton would pass almost overhead of Barcelona. Now he looked to the west, where the hazy brassy orb of the declining sun assumed a blood-red flush. Mohamed watched as the blood seeped from it, like an omen, staining the western sky.

Now he looked northeast, where, out of sight, Corsica bathed in lowering sun and sea. He tried to fix his eyes on a spot 350 miles away, and forty miles above the north Corsican coast. He had worked out that if he could spot Phaeton at that point, the meteor would be visible for one point three one minutes during which time it would cover a distance of 640 miles – unless it exploded.

The Countdown

He switched on his transistor radio in time to hear the announcer say, "As we have previously explained, the official countdown marks Phaeton's lowest point in earth's atmosphere when the meteorite will pass about ten miles above the western shores of the Black Sea. The countdown will begin in five seconds."

Mohamed's eyes were hypnotised by the spot in the sky over Corsica as he waited, holding his breath. Yet he knew that Phaeton would be – at that moment – 1,700 miles east of him.

"Ten... Nine... Eight... Seven... Six... Five... Four... Three...Two... One... ZERO."

There was a long pause, then the announcer said, "That countdown was heard the world over, and it also united the world. Soon, we will bring you eye witness reports from places nearest to Phaeton's historic journey through our planet's atmosphere. Meanwhile everyone should remain in their homes or other places that provide shelter from the hurricane force winds which will follow in Phaeton's wake. Remember," said the announcer in a stern voice, "all doors and windows *must* be left open."

Mohamed switched the radio off. The countdown had been on time at 4.45 GMT. His own countdown, of a little under three-and-a-half minutes, now began. At 4.48 p.m. and a few seconds Phaeton should pass over Corsica.

★

The Reverend Neville Gadsby sat at his desk in the small office. The office was adjacent to the main room in the crypt under All Saints Church. Through the open door he could hear the murmur of conversation from parishioners, and others, who had sought sanctuary in the church during curfew hours. The countdown was over, but the curfew continued. Phaeton was on his way out, the television remained on, and the people wanted to talk. That was good.

Neville thought about the problems of dualism, and the strange definitions we use in our attempts to describe it. As a physicist he thought of the wave-particle duality of matter and energy. As a man he wrestled with good and evil as the products of ultimate first causes. As a Christian he pondered on the divine and human natures of Christ. The telephone interrupted his thought process at that moment of insight when the elusive truth seemed to be on the brink of revealing itself. He ignored the phone. The Parish Secretary ran in and picked up the receiver. "For you, Mr Gadsby," she said, handing the receiver to him.

"Neville Gadsby," he said.

"Miles Poundmore, Neville. If we didn't have a curfew I would, if you had a few minutes, drive down to see you. Can we talk on the phone?"

"Yes, I'll close my office door, then we can talk."

"When we talked in the pub, you mentioned the passage where God says I will put my laws in their heart, And upon their mind also I will write them. You also said something about looking inwards and knowing yourself. That struck me as authentic advice, to seek a direct and personal experience of God, to make that vital inner journey. However, Victoria links these matters with the very things that Jung described as shielding us from a direct experience of God."

"I know she found that difficult. Tell her to go at her own pace. In time, as she thinks it over, it will become clearer. This might help – God knows that love cannot be conveyed by words. It is conveyed by being. Your love for Victoria is inside you – not in your words. You are capable of love because love is in you. Words are symbols and, as such, they have great power, but we must go beyond the symbol to find the power. We must *be*. Love is first and foremost an inward experience," explained Neville.

"I'm beginning to get the idea. I will tell Victoria what you've said."

"If you find that your faith in God has made you spiritually whole, that you have faith, recognise the crutches of religion for what they are," said Neville, "then you'll experience worship in a new way."

Miles, almost a non-churchgoer, struggled with the idea of recognising the "crutches of religion". "Victoria loves her church," he said.

"So do I," said Neville. "Church is not religion. It is prayer, worship, thanksgiving, faith. It should draw together all who love and worship God. The sword of truth neither divides the faithful nor keeps men and women from the Way. It enables men and women – to be transformed."

"Thanks, Neville, I've got that. I'll discuss what you've said with Vicky. She's worried by my lack of religious zeal. We may have further questions, I suspect."

"I will brace myself like a man, you will question me, and I shall answer. Those splendid words, slightly amended to fit the occasion," said Neville.

★

"Sheila, have we photographs, measurements, fixes or any other information on the Phaeton split?" asked Laurie.

"Yes, but no good ones yet. The Australian Tracking Centre reckons there should be better pictures and information from Cambridge, Massachusetts any second now."

"Check direct with Cambridge. Ask them if a general tsunami and hurricane warning has been issued to all Pacific Ocean lands and islands. I'll get on to the Home Secretary, I promised to keep her informed about the ice. Douglas, what have you got on the weather front at the moment?"

"I'm waiting for reports from the Met stations closest to Phaeton's track. I was hoping we would, by now, have some indication of the strength and scope of the pressure wave. The aftermath will cause confusing and widespread disruption of weather patterns. Sorry I can't be more precise."

"Colgate speaking, Home Secretary," said Laurie, "I have no hard news yet about pressure or blast waves resulting from Phaeton's passage. Because of his high speed, there will be a time lag. But if, or when, the disturbance hits us it could be exceptionally violent. I can see from my window that some members of the Security Forces think that now Phaeton is past his lowest altitude, the worst is over."

"Thank you, Mr Colgate, I will speak to the G.O.C. I hear that more snow has fallen in Scotland. What news have you on the weather?"

"At present, Mrs Moor, no news, other than the change in wind direction which I told you about yesterday. There may be more snow, but the wind will gradually shift to the south during the next few days," replied Laurie.

★

"Laurie, information from Australia. Phaeton was some 1,600 miles from earth when the split was observed in the meteorite's left southern face. Gradually the split widened and the meteor appeared to roll slightly. However, dust clouds and vapour made it impossible to see exactly what was happening. A large piece detached from the lower left side. It may have been a collision, perhaps with a GPS satellite, or an explosive separation due to friction, and there was a sudden eruption of smoke, vapour and dust. At the separation, Phaeton's speed increased, his angle of approach to earth lifted. The speed of the breakaway portion decreased slightly as did its angle of approach. More information to follow. Was that what you wanted?" asked Sheila.

Before he answered, Sheila added, "Here it is. The breakaway settled on a track about twenty degrees south of Phaeton's heading. Its plane of descent to earth remained shallow and its speed decreased. It passed over the Philippines and Borneo and was later seen to splash, at a shallow angle, into the southern Indian Ocean north of Kerguelen and the Crozet Islands. Witness report to follow."

"From that report, it seems that the breakaway's contact angle with earth was shallow, they report a splash down, not a plunge," said Laurie. "The major benefit was that Phaeton gained speed and lift and came no nearer to earth than seventy miles. Sheila, ask the Massachusetts Minor Planet Centre, the Australian and French Centres, if they consider the tsunami danger to be more acute in view of the position and direction of the breakaway's touchdown. If you can get one of the centres on the line, I'll have a word. I want to talk over some ideas. Meanwhile, we must try to gauge how Phaeton and his breakaway will affect the world's winds, waters and weather."

Douglas and Laurie studied the computer models of world

weather patterns. They knew very well that the culprits responsible for the cold weather in their normally temperate zone were a series of vast Arctic Low Pressure systems, or cyclones, which had persisted throughout the summer months. Normally these systems would give way to the Atlantic highs alternating with lows which dominate weather over the British Isles from May to October.

Douglas pointed to the screen, "For nearly two years now these cyclones have tracked to the north, so that we got more of the east winds, and when they were further west than usual we got Arctic temperatures too. However, we have noticed that the last two systems have tracked more to the south and east, so that our winds now come from the south. You think that trend will continue?"

"I do. And Phaeton may well speed up the process," answered Laurie.

Phaeton the Scorpion

There was not a breath of wind. In that moment of profound stillness there was nobody in the world but himself. Switching his radio off, Mohamed Ramzi spoke to himself. It was necessary to ask questions, and to hear the answers, so that not one of the vital action points on his list was neglected.

One: set stopwatch. He had listened to the countdown on the radio as Phaeton reached his lowest point in earth's atmosphere about 1,700 miles to the east of the spot at which he stood. His hands trembled as he set his stopwatch to buzz in exactly three minutes. *That gives me a few seconds respite to compose myself before I experience the unknown*, he thought.

Two: place personal belongings, including self, in a secure, sheltered spot. He moved his camera, binoculars, radio, leather holdall and folding chair to a niche behind a giant rock below the escarpment.

Three: check that binoculars, with tinted lenses fitted, are to hand.

Four: set camera ready for instant photography. All this he accomplished in one and a half minutes.

"Will there be a tremendous pressure wave ahead of Phaeton?"

"I think so, but nobody knows for certain," he answered himself.

"I am one hundred miles away from Phaeton's flight path. Will the pressure wave travel that far?"

"I don't know. I shouldn't think so. You will find out." He considered the questions of incandescent heat and light. Heat? At this distance, it dissipated – no action required. Light? Shades fitted on binoculars, sunglasses in pocket. Noise? Ear plugs? He didn't know if they were necessary. *If there's any noise I want to hear it. No ear plugs.* Next he turned towards Mecca and prayed. The stopwatch alarm buzzed. Mohamed stood in his rocky shelter so that he could look towards the spot which he had already fixed

181

upon in the sky. It was 350 miles away to the northeast, over Corsica. "Camera and binoculars to hand," he said.

"Am I composed? No, I am straining my eyes. Pick up binoculars, check dark shades, adjust eyepieces, focus, relax."

Twice he saw specks of light round his spot in the sky, but they were false alarms. Then he saw it. A pinpoint of light surrounded by a halo. White, incandescent. "Yes!" he shouted. A whitish, blue-tinged halo round a reddish, yellow glow. Strange – like a kaleidoscope gone mad. The brilliant, central core pierced through the binoculars, bored into his eyes and out of the back of his head. The whole thing appeared to expand at a fantastic rate over Corsica. It was blowing up, like a balloon; a balloon that must explode if it continued to swell at this rate. It set fire to the sky with a tremendous display of fearsome fireworks. At first the core was circular, like a balloon, but it swiftly elongated into a gigantic sausage shape that fired heavy, flashing artillery. In its wake it left a giant curtain fringed with puffs of smoke, flames and sparks silhouetted against the now blue-black background of sky. Then, like a geometrical exercise, the whole flaming core turned from sausage to circle again. Automatically Mohamed had turned his head from right to left, his feet had shuffled, turning his body rapidly to follow the scorching speed of the meteor.

He stood, open-mouthed as, for a second, Phaeton filled the northern sky high over Barcelona. It dwarfed everything he had ever seen or imagined. A white hot world, enormous and iridescent, firing multicoloured shafts of lightning in every direction. It swamped his brain, dazzled his eyes, stupefied his mind, turned him from man into midget. He had unconsciously traversed through one hundred and eighty degrees. Now he faced the setting sun towards which Phaeton flamed.

Stunned, he put his left hand on the rock to steady himself, whilst lowering his binoculars in his right hand. His eyes hurt. He closed them, reached into his pocket for his dark, wraparound sunglasses. He put them on, cautiously opened his eyes. He could see. Slowly his sight adjusted to the brilliant display of lights set against the black sky. He breathed a sigh of relief, and touched the camera. The opportunity for a unique, once-in-a-lifetime, photograph had gone.

He saw the fan-shaped trail, swirling and eddying out to the west. He took several photographs of it, and left the camera on the rock ready to take more. But there was something he had to do. He couldn't remember what it was, only that it might be a matter of life and death. Phaeton's trail, etched against the black, smoky Mediterranean sky, was now like a blazing, fluffy rainbow. It towered from high in the sky down to sea level and stretched from east to west as far as he could see. A colossal curtain fringed with incandescent dust and flaming debris swirling down the sky. He forced himself to drag his eyes away from it.

He looked at his vital actions list, but couldn't read it. "Sound," he said to himself. The sound of his own voice reassured him. He had to do something about sound.

How long before the sound arrives? That was the question. He had worked out an answer, based on sound travelling at 660 mph, less than one fortieth of Phaeton's speed.

"The answer is forty minutes," he said. "No, forty seconds." He took his sunglasses off – and quickly put them on again. Once more he must wait and see. Some experts said the noise from a meteor as large as the island of Majorca, screaming through the air at 30,000 miles an hour, would be unbearable. Others said the noise would be diffused and muffled by earth's lower, denser atmosphere.

"Sit on the chair, behind the rock in case there is a tremendous vacuum, and wait for it," he told himself. "A tremendous vacuum could suck you up, and Mohamed Ramzi would disappear into thin air!" Later he felt an enormous blast of hot air, accompanied by a deep rumbling and a grating noise that made the ground vibrate, as it does in an earthquake. A hot swirling wind plucked at him as the strange rumbling reverberated and the ground trembled. His camera fell off the rock. He waited apprehensively. The rumbling died away.

"That's it," he said.

As he packed his gear into the borrowed car, the rumbling and shaking returned, this time it was louder and more violent. It shook the whole earth and his car rattled and vibrated as he drove, frightened and dazed, to his friend's house. People in Algiers might not believe it, but he, Mohamed Ramzi, had seen Phaeton.

Phaeton the Scorpion

★

Until today Angelo Capelli had not given much thought to what lay north of Vatican City. Through his office window he looked across the Via di St Pancrazio from the south side, his eyes followed the line of the Via Nuova delle Fornaci up the hill to the city, a little more than a mile away. Today he acknowledged that the north coast of Corsica lay 170 miles beyond, northwest of the Vatican.

"Switch the radio on, Carla, we will listen to the countdown," said Angelo.

Carla looked up from the keyboard of her word processor, "Too late, Mr Capelli," she replied, "the countdown finished five minutes ago."

"Why didn't you tell me? Carla! We have missed a moment in history! Not for millions of years has a Phaeton passed so close – and we ignore it!"

"Mr Capelli, you said you would tell me when to switch the radio on."

"I am a business man, Carla. I buy and sell. When I am buying and selling I am happy, we make a profit. Now we only buy tractors. I supply every house in Vatican City with refrigerators and freezers. Now I have to sell them bulldozers. I must talk to Miles. There is cloud over Corsica. Phaeton is like a bulldozer. He solves no problems."

"Count your blessings, Mr Capelli. Soon the tractors and the ploughs will be working on the land. Your new customers will grow food for the hungry. Mr Poundmore says so, and he knows. You said that there was a time for everything, and the time for ploughing and planting the wastelands has come. The farmers need your tractors to make the wastelands bloom."

★

As she sat with her husband on the veranda of the house in Casablanca, Mitzi said, "You were right, Hassen." There was a hint of admiration in her voice. "How did you know that we would neither see nor hear Phaeton?"

"There are enough scientists around the world wasting their time on a harmless meteor. Sensible people get on with their lives. Between you and me, Mitzi, I am working on plans to improve food production in our country, but at present, that is a secret," said Hassen. He gazed blissfully over the Atlantic towards the rosy sun, which, as usual, smiled on Morocco.

Between the veranda of Hassen's house and the declining sun, indeed between Hassen's eyes and the sun, Phaeton the meteor hurtled blindly onwards. His passage out of earth's atmosphere began at the precise time predicted by the scientists: 16.45 on Sunday, 3 October 2010. Between him and the centre of his orbit there remained a further ninety three million miles of frigid frictionless space at a temperature which hovered around minus 273°C: absolute zero.

*

Miles Poundmore rose early on the morning of Monday, 4 October. A short, brisk walk to the office at four o'clock in the morning was an invigorating prelude to a run through his PI computer disk. He liked to know how colleagues and markets, in the antipodes and the far east, were performing in the crucial minutes before they closed for the day.

Walking down St James's street towards Pall Mall, he felt a dry warmth in the air. Nothing unusual about that. Rejoice, all ye lands, when an Indian summer's day softens the approach of winter. He observed that the stars twinkled normally in the darkness of the pre-dawn sky. In spite of the build up, Phaeton had changed nothing. Unlike his unfortunate, mythical predecessor, he had come nowhere near to setting the world on fire. Doors and windows were now closed again. The security forces had vanished from the streets, normality reigned. The Night Porter let him in saying, "Good morning, sir." For the first time in weeks he had nothing else to say.

The computer statistics from PI, Australasia were good. Miles keyed a note: "Consider inviting Amos Griffin, PI Australia's Managing Director, on to main board: his increased responsibilities could include oversight of PI India."

Having checked that the flow of agricultural machinery to Italy and Egypt included mini tractors and rotavators, Miles turned from his personal computer to the office machine. Switching onto Internet, he scanned swiftly through world news items, stopping when he saw the headline, "Phaeton".

"An Australian Astro research and tracking station has confirmed that a meteorite, thought to be a large breakaway piece from Phaeton, splashed into the sea about six hundred miles west of the remote Kerguelen Archipelago. The main island, about 1,100 square miles in area, once an important whaling station, is still a centre for the fishing industry in the Antarctic Basin. A fishing boat returning to Kerguelen from the tiny islands of Crozet observed an enormous flaming sphere bounce on the sea. However, radio contact with the vessel has broken down. We will bring a further report from our correspondent on the spot as soon as possible."

Following the news, he turned to the weather. The Ice Age prophets were not exactly eating their words, but they were now forecasting unsettled conditions. This was their first step towards admitting that a thaw was about to set in. Whatever the weather, an interest in the production of wholesome food, and responsible grass roots farming of marginal lands, had become part of PI's global planning. Miles made notes in readiness for the meeting to be held on board *Andromeda* in the Bay of Tunis on Thursday, 7 October.

Before walking home for breakfast at eight o'clock, he made further computer notes about financial reorganisation in the UK, Europe, the Americas and Australasia. Next came rationalisation of PI's main and regional boards. Finally, a note to Eileen: "Office computer – please print my notes."

*

David Medden, the Foreign Secretary, talked briefly with the Prime Minister after the morning meeting. "As I see it, Winnie, I must continue fighting our country's corner. I agree that the recent threat to global survival produced an extraordinary sense of unity, but it's no good pretending that human nature has

Phaeton the Scorpion

suddenly turned benign. Given half a chance, there are those of our trading partners who'll pull a fast one. Caveat emptor still applies. Within Europe itself there is again a growing sense of unease, based on a fear that economic muscle might, in the future, accomplish what military might failed to achieve in the past."

"I have heard you quote a famous saying, David – 'A house divided cannot stand,'" said Winnie. "Has it never struck you that we spend our working lives in a divided house? A benign dictatorship may be the only real alternative."

Heather Moor, back from an unsuccessful trip up north, had put on an admirable show at the meeting. "Prudently," she said, "we prepared for the worst. Had the blizzards continued, as indeed our weather men said they would, this government would not have been found wanting. We are fortunate that the armed forces, standing by to evacuate had it proved necessary, are at hand to assist the cities, towns and communities in the north to cope with snow-clearance and the aftermath of Arctic temperatures."

★

There was some doubt about the closing of Laurie Colgate's Observatory emergency office at Church House, Westminster. A close, day-to-day personal liaison between politicians and scientists had produced a number of incidental benefits. Not least of these was a greater sense of global unity achieved through international political and scientific concern during the Phaeton crisis. This challenge, said some, had led to a better understanding of those human aspirations that were common to every race and tribe under the sun. However, the cost of maintaining the office, and who was to bear it, were sensitive political questions.

Meanwhile Laurie arrived at Douglas White's office at 9 a.m. on Monday, 4 October. The two had agreed that, after Phaeton, they would make a further detailed study of worldwide weather patterns.

"I'll tell you what my immediate concern is, Douglas. We've had a long session of unseasonable, cold polar winds and snow hitting us from the east. There were two main factors in this. First the mass of cloud that persisted over Arctic regions. Second the strength of the low pressure systems over Siberia which pushed further south and west than usual. These systems diverted the mild south westerlies from our shores. Is that a reasonable summary?"

"Yes," replied Douglas. "I would add that the Arctic ice caps have increased in volume. Only a small increase in terms of sea level change, but enough to drop the air temperatures of winds blowing down from those regions. Persistent polar cloud provided the moisture for extra precipitation, and the lower temperatures turned it into snow."

"Right. Now here's my concern. I observed no sign of a change in long term criteria for climate in northwest Britain or Greenland. But, before my visit to Greenland, we did see a reduction of that polar cloud and a northward movement of Siberian cyclones. The big question: how will Phaeton's passage, right over the middle of that weakening cyclone, affect world weather?"

"Look at this model," replied Douglas, pointing to the largest of his visual display units, "this shows Phaeton's line through our upper atmosphere. Here, it passes through the southern edge of the north Ferrel wind circulation which produces the westerlies in our latitudes. But as Phaeton advances," Douglas moved the pointer westwards across the screen map, "we see that, in the aftermath, he sucks in tremendous quantities of air from the equatorial regions. This mixes with the Ferrel northwesterlies, strengthens the northward movement and pushes the cold polar air back where it belongs.

"And Phaeton travelled more than a thousand miles on the edge of latitude forty degrees north. Some of the likely weather changes will be hard to predict, especially in equatorial and tropical regions. But this model appears to confirm the end of Britain's Arctic weather – unless Phaeton has a sting in his tail. Could he be a scorpion?"

★

In Cairo, Ahmed Rahman read the signal from PI HQ London:

Phaeton the Scorpion

"Please supply personal details of PI contacts in Tunis, Algiers and Morocco. Subject to your advice suggest each brings wife 7th October."

The wording of that message had caused Miles some problems. At first he had put: "Suggest they bring wives", before changing to "a wife".

Eileen glanced at the message and asked, "How many wives do Muslims have these days?" She did some research on the subject, but could only advise that diplomacy was necessary.

Miles looked for a simple answer, and, after much deliberation he had deleted "a" so that the last line ended, "brings wife, 7th October".

Ahmed smiled. Cultural niceties were an important part of diplomatic training. He understood Miles's difficulty. However, in very few modern Muslim states were women second-class citizens; in most they had gained their birthright of equality. Miles knew that he, Ahmed, had attended Edinburgh University. He would soon know that the other three, Jasem Al-Mana, Mohamed Ramzi and Hassen Osman had been there at the same time. Jasem had met Mary, his wife, at the Edinburgh School of Agriculture in those far-off days. Ahmed reflected that the inspiration to arrange meetings between his influential boss and these three friends had come from Allah.

★

Victoria drove her 2CV to All Saints Church for the short midday service which the Rev Neville Gadsby took. He gave the address, which, as usual, was brief and to the point. He explained that he, as a physicist, did not see Phaeton as an act of God. "The science of astrophysics," he said, "provides an adequate explanation for this particular meteor, and all the others too. The same science could tell us much about our own nature, for we are made of cosmic matter. We have a choice, either mind created matter and the laws that it obeys, or there is no mind behind the universe. If that were the case, we, though we are beings with brains, would have no more ultimate sense of purpose than Phaeton. Eventually, we would destroy ourselves. The history of humanity is a history of the war between good and evil, between avarice and generosity, between love and hate. It was well said that, 'Man is man's ABC. There is none that can read God aright, unless he first spells Man.' We have a great purpose in this universe if we will grasp it, it is to be partners with God in his continuing creative work. This universe, in which we are working partners, needs the inspired mind of humanity. As St Paul put it, 'Now that you have faith you are sons and daughters of God.' What a sense of purpose that should give us."

Shortly after one o'clock, when Victoria arrived at the office in Pall Mall, Eileen said, "Miles wants to discuss a couple of important points to do with finance and agriculture. He said we could talk over a working lunch in his office, or we could meet after lunch depending on the time you got back."

"I know very little about finance, and not much more about agriculture. Do you think he really wants me at this meeting?" asked Vicky.

"He said that you and I were responsible for some fundamental changes which he proposes to make in PI's management structure. Therefore, we must take a continuing part in the dialogue," replied Eileen. At that moment Miles walked into Eileen's office.

"Oh, Vicky, you're back! Eileen, let's have lunch now. Get Alice to bring sandwiches and coffee round. What shall we say my office in ten minutes?" Miles returned to his office.

"Miles," said Victoria, following him, "do you really want me at this meeting?"

"Your presence is essential. We must set in train a thorough reorganisation of PI's administrative set-up and of our global finances. I'll explain it over lunch in a few minutes. I have a phone call to make before we meet."

Vicky withdrew, muttering, "What have I let myself in for?"

★

In Scotland and the north of England the great snow clearance had started. The Rt Hon. Mrs Heather Moor returned by special train to York, where, from a nearby airfield, she intended to fly by

RAF helicopter to many of the places worst hit by the blizzards.

"If this thaw continues, George, we shall have floods, bad ones. I'm asking for more bulldozers to push as much snow as possible into the sea," said Heather.

The Aftermath

"This Compact Disc," said Miles, "is used to record reports from Poundmore International Directors abroad. Our home director is Charles Norton. His office is downstairs. Any time you need figures for the home market, let Charles know and he will screen them."

"All those figures, Miles. I shall never understand them," said Victoria.

"You helped PI to grow in its early days, so don't make excuses. These are the old familiar figures – capital employed, turnover, just a few more companies and noughts these days – millions instead of thousands. And, of course, profit. Those columns are broken down on a monthly basis, by regions and our major businesses. You can see at a glance if there's anything dodgy. And if you ask for figures for a day or a week, you will get those too. It's simple economics, Vicky, and you've got a degree in that."

"Eileen, do you understand all this?" asked Vicky.

"As Miles says, we grew up with it. I'm sure it will soon make sense if you take your time, look up the different regions regularly so that you get to know their patterns. You've met all the key people when they've been over here. I would advise a travel plan so that you see them on their own ground. Find out how each director operates. Attach faces to places, then the personalities will have relevant PI identities. And Vicky, do ask questions."

"That's it. Work with Eileen on a daily basis for a month, and you'll soon be asking the right questions. Over the next six months I intend to devolve some of my responsibilities. The aim is to spread the load without losing our 'hands on' management style. That means two more directors and regular, planned board meetings in addition to the AGM, instead of my spur-of-the-moment affairs. And, if we agree, the sale of some of our shares. We might aim to leave ourselves with fifty-one per cent of the

UK holding company: that means selling seventeen per cent. We would do that gradually, of course."

Victoria was exhausted after her first full day as a PI executive, but, at Miles's suggestion, she agreed to invite Eileen and the Rev Neville Gadsby to lunch the following day, Tuesday. Miles phoned Laurie Colgate who accepted for himself and Angela. The forthcoming meeting in Tunis would launch PI on a venture in uncharted waters. Miles had earmarked potential assistant navigators for that project.

★

Laurie and Sheila worked late into the evening of Monday, 4 October. The Home Secretary had telephoned them from York saying, "Mr Colgate, my helicopter is grounded by blizzards. It is freezing up here, when is that supposed thaw coming?"

"There may be snow storms for a couple more days, but the east wind is giving way to southerlies," Laurie assured her.

★

An eye witness report on the landing of Phaeton's "breakaway" in the Indian Ocean had been passed to London by the Australian Asteroid Tracking Centre. "The report," said the centre, "came by radio from a fishing boat whose crew has not yet been interviewed, and it reads:

At 21.50 local, 16.50 GMT, MV Rover registered Kn77 Kerguelen, steering course 097 approximately 100 nautical miles east of Crozet Islands, sighted a colossal, white-hot glowing object estimated position 48S 65.5E crossing bows left to right distance twenty nautical miles. Object passed between vessel and main Kerguelen Island. Enormous glowing ball estimated diameter 2,000 metres. It flashed low over the sea lighting the whole world; fantastic speed on a heading estimated as south by southeast. There was a sort of boiling bow wave like a great tidal wave in front, a long bubbling wake astern. Sky and sea were on fire for miles behind it. After crossing between Kn77 and Kerguelen, object touched sea, lifted into the air, flew on at high speed trailing white, incandescent clouds, smoke and steam. It

The Aftermath

> spun like a giant catherine wheel showering the sea for miles around with enormous flaming pieces. It hit the water three times, bouncing and skidding. Then there was a violent explosion partly underwater. I turned Kn77 towards the blast expecting a tsunami. The first reached us several minutes later. The sea was boiling. There were muffled under water explosions and eruptions like volcanoes. The enormous size of the object dwarfed Kn77. It travelled like lightning. Position where it exploded estimated as Lat 53S 59E. There were two intense cracking noises followed by a kind of vacuum when it was difficult to breathe. Then there came some loud, prolonged rumblings. Minutes later hot, hurricane-force winds hit us. For an hour we steered various courses, trying to keep our head into the storm, but the wind and the seas came from all directions. We took some damage and a few bruises but, thank God, we remained afloat with no serious casualties. John Beck, Captain.

"It seems to have exploded well away from the sea-bed ridges in that area, and away from Antarctica," said Sheila, "with a possibility that the main force of the tsunamis will head for the southern ice sheets."

"Yes. The Aussies and the French research station on Kerguelen have issued hurricane warnings. We shall get a more detailed report and analysis from them," replied Laurie. "Our main question about 'Breakaway' at the moment is this – what effect will it have on tectonic plates and the world's weather systems?"

★

Eileen, as requested by Miles, arrived at the house in St. James's at 11 a.m. on Tuesday. As they drank coffee Miles said, "In about four weeks I shall have to give a great deal of time to a new PI venture which will entail my being abroad for, say, a month in the first instance. When the prototype schemes bear fruit, the exercise will be repeated. That's why we need to appoint a Chief Executive to take over Group strategy and continue my system of 'hands on' management."

"Have you anyone in mind?" asked Eileen.

"Yes, I have. I want to make a joint appointment. This would mean a clear division of responsibilities, for example one Joint

The Aftermath

Chief Executive would govern personnel, buying, and product ranges, liaising with Directors under those heads. The other would head policy for sales, capital employed, cost effectiveness and profit, and would liaise with Directors. They would work closely together. Obviously the division of responsibilities must be clearly defined and agreed. They would report to the Chairman, and the main board. The Chairman would retain responsibility for the acquisition and sale of businesses."

"You said you had someone in mind?" asked Vicky.

"You two would make a great working team," replied Miles.

"I had a feeling that was coming," said Eileen.

"*Eileen*, I can understand," said Vicky, "but me? You must be mad!"

"I don't think he is. Crafty is the word. If management consultants were asked to advise on the appointment of a Chief Executive for PI, they would first look at our regional directors and divisional managers, most of whom are doing an excellent job. Only one of those could, at present, be considered as a potential Group Chief Executive. A consultant always offers two or three names so that the client has to make the final choice. So they would look outside PI for other candidates. Think of the turmoil and the publicity caused by an exercise like *that*," said Eileen.

"And who is that potential Chief Executive you mention, Eileen?" asked Miles.

"The abrasive, but competent and successful Amos Griffin."

"You're right, but I have other plans for him. Victoria, there is not the slightest tinge of nepotism in the offer of the job of Joint Chief Executive to you. You have the qualifications. You have the interest and the personality. Only you can say if you have the energy and the will," said Miles.

"Eileen, wouldn't I be a drag – a kind of negative equity for you?" asked Vicky.

When the doorbell rang at noon, Miles left Vicky and Eileen talking. He was confident that this key move in his new strategy for PI would work out as he had planned it.

Mrs Brown, Victoria's housekeeper, had opened the door to the Colgates. Miles welcomed them, "I'm so glad you could

The Aftermath

come, Mrs Colgate. I wanted to tell you how much I learned from Laurie on that wonderful trip to Greenland."

"From what Laurie said, Mr Poundmore, I gather that the trip was mutually advantageous," Angela replied.

"Let me introduce you," said Laurie, with a smile, "Miles – Angela."

As they walked into the sitting room, Miles described the impression Greenland's icy beauty had made on him.

Shortly afterwards, Neville Gadsby arrived, and as they talked, Victoria mused about her husband's ability to bring together, in a connected way, people from diverse backgrounds.

During lunch Miles asked, "Does anyone know of a satisfactory definition of the good life?"

"Shakespeare found life good in both town and country, and he had something to say about it," suggested Neville.

"Where does this come from? 'Whoever loves money never has money enough… as goods increase, so do those who consume them. And I'll give you a clue – all is vanity," said Vicky.

"That's Ecclesiastes," responded Neville, "but it's a warning about greed rather than a definition of the good life."

"I can offer something from a country lad who found fame in the city," said Angela, "'And this our life, exempt from public haunt, finds tongues in trees, books in the running brooks, sermons in stones, and good in every thing. I would not change it.'"

"That's Shakespeare. Wasn't he a country lad banished to the city?" asked Laurie.

"I don't think so," answered Eileen, "he chose to follow his destiny and, at the same time, he made provision for his wife and family. When, at the start of *Two Gentlemen of Verona*, Valentine says to Proteus, 'Home-keeping youth have ever homely wits,' he speaks for William, as he does at the end when he says, 'One feast, one house, one mutual happiness.' Doesn't that sound like the good life?"

"Dear old Oscar said, 'Anybody can be good in the country,'" said Neville, "But perhaps Eileen is right, one feast, one house, one mutual happiness – sounds very good. Maybe you've found your definition in Arden, Miles?"

"I admit that my question is unanswerable except in terms of relativity. If you are starving, food might represent the good life," said Miles.

"Miles, I suspect you've got something up your sleeve," said Victoria, "What are you leading up to?"

"I try to be subtle, but Vicky reads me like a book," said Miles. "Actually Phaeton and the ice up north caused me to recall some youthful ideals, and to question a few things that I've been inclined to take for granted."

"What kind of things?" asked Neville.

"A long time ago I read history and economics, and, in numerous discussions in those days, we set the world to rights. In our world, people wouldn't starve. In our world, order would be achieved through diversity. We had seen Communism, Fascism and Nazism and the brutal kind of order they imposed and worshipped. We liked Gasset's definition, 'Order is not a pressure which is imposed on society from without, but an equilibrium which is set up from within.' Equilibrium had to include justice and, of course racial and religious tolerance."

"You said people wouldn't starve in your world. But in countries where there is civil war, power-hungry people slaughter the innocents for political, racial and, or religious ends. Starvation is incidental. You either impose a solution from outside, or let them find their equilibrium from within," said Laurie.

"I believe that mankind is involved in a developing creation, and that the world we have in our mind is the one we actually create for ourselves," said Miles.

"Somebody said that we must find, and live, our own truth, which stems from our personal relationship with God," said Victoria. "Now, if you don't mind, Neville, Laurie, I'm taking Angela and Eileen away. We'll join you later to settle any problems you can't solve."

Mrs Brown brought in a tray of coffee and a decanter of brandy which Miles dispensed, whilst saying, "I wanted to tell you about a 'grass roots' experiment I'm hoping to encourage, by way of five small pilot schemes to begin with. If successful it could help to raise the subsistence level of the poorest members of a society by enabling them to meet their own basic needs. I am

The Aftermath

conscious of a certain truth in Vicky's quote, 'As goods increase, so do those who consume them.' That might imply that the answer is in redistribution rather than increased production. It's a complex problem in which we are morally involved. It cannot be left entirely to a bureaucratic solution."

"We have talked about the good life, food, starvation, production and redistribution," said Laurie, "may we take it that your experiment is in food production?"

"Yes, it is. I started work on it when there was a real possibility of ice once again covering much of the rich agricultural land in the northern hemisphere. Our trip to Greenland was an additional inspiration," replied Miles.

"A television news item said that Poundmore International was extending its interest in agricultural machinery to agriculture itself, so I had an idea that you might be leading up to that," said Neville.

"I'm sure you're right to be concerned about this, Miles, from all the angles you've mentioned, practical, moral, aesthetic – and especially from the angle of mankind's relationship with earth and the universe. Human population is now a potentially disastrous quantity in this equation, demanding more than our planet can supply. For example, at the time of Christ about 200 million people walked on earth. There were 5,000 million in 1987, and now there are 7,000 million. Would increased food production help? Is it possible without the use of chemical fertilisers and genetic engineering which, in the long term, would exacerbate the problem?" asked Laurie.

"This thing began with a businessman's view of a niche in the market," said Miles. "Then I realised that to react only when your own people face the possibility of starvation, is a kind of condemnation. It brings you back to the tribal god, the god of a religion, who loves his own and nobody else. Science, and especially quantum mechanics, has brought us closer to the mind of the God of Creation, the God whom Jesus called, 'Father'. It seemed to me that people starving, or brutalized, anywhere in the modern world is our business if that same God is 'our Father' too. Am I wrong?"

"No, I don't think you're wrong. But how do you propose to go about it when Governments and organisations such as United

Nations, Oxfam and others are trying to deal with such matters?" asked Neville.

"My approach lacks institutional power of any kind, political, religious, military or bureaucratic," answered Miles. "I have arranged talks with four men in Mediterranean countries who could, if they wish, help to get a 'make wastelands bloom' programme started. There are already working models. Jasem Al-Mana, an agronomist in Tunisia, showed me a report he had written on what he called 'The Baringo grass roots' initiative. It was started by a determined woman named Wangari Maathai."

"I read a magazine article about her," said Neville. "She tells a story of an ancient fig tree near her home in Kenya. Not far from the tree was the source of a stream. She used to fetch clean, cool water from the stream for her mother. Downstream grew little forests of green-stemmed, broad leafed arrowroot. The fig tree was a holy tree. Then the area was taken over for tea-growing which would earn foreign currency. The fig tree was chopped down and burnt to make way for tea bushes. The stream dried up and the arrowroot died. Soil erosion followed. The ground became arid and dead."

"The story of how she turned disaster into triumph is one of several from around the world which show what can be done if local people with vision are encouraged to start a grass roots initiative," Miles said. There was a pause, then he continued, "The day after tomorrow, Thursday, 7 October, I am flying to Tunis to meet the four men I mentioned. I wondered if you, Laurie, and you Neville, would come with me, meet these men, listen to what's said, and, if you like what you hear, join in this venture as advisers?" Miles poured more coffee which they sipped in silence.

Neville said, "I'm not sure that I am competent to act as an adviser in such a project. I like the sound of it very much because, apart from any practical, humanitarian gain, a grass roots meeting with the potential for racial, religious, cultural and linguistic interaction is a very attractive proposition."

★

The Aftermath

As she took Angela and Eileen into the drawing room for coffee, Victoria said, "Because Miles is away so much, I have recently spent more of my time in our house in Great Missenden. Although I like the city, I love the country, but Phaeton shook us out of our habits for a while. Do you prefer London or the country, Angela?"

"I like London, but not for too long at a time. We have a cottage in a village near Ipswich where I live. The uncertainty of the Phaeton business led to the creation of lots of new activity patterns, and I must say I've greatly enjoyed these few days. It will be interesting to see if the new patterns develop or fade."

"I'm glad you've noticed that, Angela," said Eileen. "I thought perhaps PI was the only organisation where changes in patterns are occurring due to Phaeton shaking us up. In fact there are likely to be quite staggering changes. Don't you agree, Vicky?"

"Yes, I do agree! Miles wants me to go to Tunis with him on Thursday. He says it's part of my new executive duties, and I can't think of an excuse for saying no. Actually, I could do with a couple of days cruising in Mediterranean sunshine, so I might as well go."

"If I had an opportunity like that, it wouldn't take me ten seconds to make up my mind," said Angela, "I'd go like a shot."

When the three men walked in Vicky said, "Miles, Angela would like to come to Tunis with us on Saturday, if Laurie can spare her for two or three days. What about it?" she asked, looking at Laurie.

Laurie smiled, "Well, yes, as long as it's not more than two or three days."

"Actually," said Angela, "I'm not sure that—"

"Don't say it. It's all fixed. We'll go together," Laurie interrupted. "We shall have to get up at some unearthly hour on Thursday morning."

Miles outlined the purpose of the meeting on *Andromeda* and the Tunis visit. He proposed that, if all went well, and after the other guests had gone ashore, they might sail to Lisbon and fly home from there.

The next morning Laurie and Sheila, at their office in Church House, Westminster, found strange patterns drawn on the meteorologist's charts. Experts were now reluctant to make predictions about weather for more than twenty-four hours ahead.

In the north of England and Scotland, great efforts were underway to dump snow by the lorry load into ditches, ponds, lakes, quarries, and the sea before the snow turned into slush. Every piece of modern blowing equipment, every available bulldozer and tractor was commandeered to help in this prodigious task.

★

Jasem Al-Mana telephoned Ahmed Rahman in Cairo, "Come to Tunis on Wednesday, my friend," he said, "we can have a talk before the meeting. Mary says she hopes Selma will come with you."

"Does The Rain Have A Father?"

"Very business-like," said Eileen when Victoria reported for duty at Poundmore International's headquarters in Pall Mall at 9 a.m. on Wednesday, 6 October. She wore a white-striped, charcoal-grey costume with double-breasted jacket, and single-pleated skirt which dropped about an inch below the knee. A plain white blouse, grey tights, black, low-heeled shoes and grey gloves were complemented by the black, soft leather briefcase which she carried.

"I though I'd better be." She emptied her briefcase onto Eileen's desk. "Here's what I've been reading for the past seventy-two hours. A – the Group Sales Manager's analysis of regional sales for the past year, and targets for the next twelve months, B – the Investment Manager's statement of capital employed and properties included in the PI portfolio, by region, and C – the Cost Accountant's breakdown, by region, of cost effectiveness."

"Impressive," said Eileen, "did it make sense?"

"I'm glad to say it did, and I now have a pressing business matter to start the day with. Is the boss in his office?"

"He's been here since eight o'clock. I thought you'd know," replied Eileen.

"I haven't seen him this morning. I've been busy with Giles and Monica Brown, telling them what our plans are for the next two weeks," said Victoria, as she walked into Miles's office.

"Miles, I asked Charles Norton to get me a desk to match yours. It's coming up now. I think I'll have it placed the other side of the window, opposite yours. I might need your help for a day or two until I get the hang of things. However, the papers I have read during the past few evenings make sense, so I haven't, after all, forgotten everything I learned as an undergraduate."

"I thought you might have a desk in Eileen's office since your work is complementary to hers," he suggested.

"That would not be a good idea. Eileen will shortly have another assistant. And there is too much coming and going in her office. No, this will suit me. You won't be the least bit disturbed by my presence – and I won't be disturbed by you. I am having a telephone, and a computer console next to my desk so I shan't touch any of your equipment. I have drafted my terms of reference as Joint Chief Executive – reporting to the Chairman – with responsibility for Sales, Capital Employed, Cost Effectiveness and Property. I have also drawn up a timetable of visits which I intend to make to our overseas HQs."

Vicky took a sheaf of papers out of her briefcase and laid them on Miles's desk. "Mr Chairman," she said, "I would be grateful if you would read these and sign them if you approve. You will see that I have suggested that my salary should be at the same level as Eileen's."

"I wonder if you'll still find time to go to All Saints once a week? I'll read these papers. You'll have them back by lunch time," he said.

★

Douglas turned from his computer screen, "Laurie, come and look at this, I've been rechecking the temperatures you recorded on your Greenland visit against those given by the Environmental Research Institute. Your readings are within the fluctuations shown on these records. This confirms that the triggers for changes in weather patterns are at present coming from above oceanic surfaces, and not from below."

"That's true as far as the Arctic is concerned," said Laurie. "And, since the Institute holds all the US and Russian research on seasonal ice patterns, it's a reliable check. We also have detailed research and observation for the East Antarctic Ice Sheet. That's the very area where Phaeton's breakaway has upset the balance. Sheila thinks the explosions occurred well away from the sea bed ridges, but there will certainly be repercussions from that region. I've asked our colleagues in the Antipodes to let us know if they detect any tremors. We know that Mt Ruapehu has been unstable in recent years. Something like the Breakaway could, so to speak, turn the heat up."

"If that happens, its effect is likely to be felt longer term through ocean currents, and perhaps from more volcanic activity.

But regarding Phaeton's passage through earth's atmosphere, we shall know in a day or two if that is drawing warm air northwards from the tropics," said Douglas.

*

Severe storms in the Mediterranean caused widespread damage, mostly along the north African shores west of Tunis. Early on Tuesday, 5 October, when the winds and the rough seas had abated, Captain Wenock supervised *Andromeda*'s refloating and exit from dry dock. "We'll pick the crew up, find our sea legs this afternoon, give the ship a good shakedown, and set sail for Tunis at 06.00 hours tomorrow."

"Aye, aye, sir," said Jack. "Any further orders?"

"It's possible we shall sail from Tunis to Lisbon, which is why I gave orders to prepare for at least a week away. PI hasn't yet finalised his plans. Tell the duty officer to check all supplies. I'll inspect at 18.00 hours today. And by the way, I expect you've noticed that the glass is still down. Unusually low pressure. We're in for more gales or more rain, or both."

*

Miles and Victoria rose early on Thursday morning, leaving the house as Giles drove up in the Rolls. "Morning, Giles, you know the way to Mr Colgate's, so away we go. Next we pick up Mr Gadsby at All Saints, along the East India Dock Road."

Ariadne's blue and silver skin glimmered in the glare of the dispersal area lights as the Rolls drew alongside. Eileen, Mike Williams and the stewardess stood on the tarmac by the aircraft's open luggage compartment. Vicky jumped out of the car and called, "Eileen, come with Angela and me, let's go aboard, I'll bet Hazel's got coffee brewing."

The stewardess joined the group of ladies, "You've won your bet, Mrs Poundmore," she said, "I'll bring coffee right away."

"Mike, are we all set?" asked Miles.

"Yes, flight plan filed and cleared. Some dirty weather in the Med, heavy rain storms along the north African coast. The Met man says there's been rain in parts of central Africa for the first time in eight years. Our cruising height is 38,000 feet – ETA Tunis 08.30 hours."

Seven minutes after take-off breakfast was served to the six passengers. The Electronics Officer collected trays for the crew from the galley. At 06.45 hours Miles went forward and asked Mike Williams to see if they could raise *Andromeda* on VHF radio.

"We're out of voice range," said Mike, "but we can signal her."

"OK. Ask Geoffrey for the co-ordinates of his intended mooring at Tunis. I'd like to see how precise this Global Positioning System is after Phaeton. Let me know when you get an answer."

Within five minutes Mike Williams showed Miles the message from *Andromeda*: "Intend to moor off Ile Zembra 37.07 degrees North 10.48.4 East in ten minutes." Miles watched as the pilot set the coordinates on the GPS dial.

At 08.27 hours *Ariadne* flew over the Ile Zembra at 4,000 feet as she descended towards Tunis International Airport. A strong east wind raised white horses over the sea. *Andromeda* had anchored in the lee of the tiny island on the southern side of Tunis Bay. The pilot reported to Miles that the GPS was as accurate as usual.

Miles was surprised when Jasem Al-Mana greeted him at Tunis airport. "Welcome to you and your party," he said. "I asked the Controller to let me know when your flight was due." Jasem's presence facilitated their passage through Customs, after which Miles introduced him to Victoria and the others. At the quayside, he helped his five companions into *Andromeda*'s motor boat. Before joining them he said, "Jasem, I am glad your wife is coming, do you know if Mrs Ramzi and Mrs Osman are coming?"

"Unfortunately they were unable to come, but Mohamed and Hassen are already here. So Mary and I, Ahmed and Selma, Mohamed and Hassen – the six of us – will join you at noon."

"The motor boat will be back here at 11.30 a.m. We look forward to seeing you," he said.

As the boat made its way to *Andromeda*, Miles said, "There will be twelve of us for lunch, Vicky, three may want non-alcoholic

"Does The Rain Have A Father?"

drinks. We'll meet in the saloon at 12.15. Would you and Eileen supervise lunch arrangements please? We'll keep things as informal as possible. I hope we shall talk about 'grass roots' at the table because the interest and support of the ladies is vital."

Miles noted *Andromeda*'s yellow "Q" flag, and the Red Ensign fluttering below the Red flag of Tunisia with its red crescent and star set in a white circle. The weather was unsettled, and heavy rainstorms alternating with brief sunny periods showed the Mediterranean at its best. Rain had settled the dust and washed the landscape so that the sun gave depth, sharpness and vivid colouring to buildings on shore, and a diamond-like sparkle to the choppy sea and a shine to boats in the harbour. He thought of the parched Sahel far to the south, and of God's question to Job: "Who cuts a channel for the torrents of rain... to water a land where no man lives... Does the rain have a father?"

At 11.55 a.m. he went aft to the stern ladder as the motor boat approached. When Jasem introduced Mary, Miles said, "When I first met your husband, Mrs Al-Mana, I was impressed by his command of English and his use of colloquialisms – now I understand."

"Yes," replied Mary, "our three children have grown up trilingual, they are almost as fluent in French as they are in Arabic and English. And please, call me Mary."

"We men became close friends in Edinburgh," Jasem explained, "and we have kept in touch ever since. In fact Ahmed met Selma there at the time I met Mary. Then Mohamed and Hassen drifted into our group. We ended up with an agricultural degree of some sort and I also gained a wife and much improved English, and Mary learned Arabic."

Miles noticed that all his guests had a pre-lunch glass of sherry, except for Mohamed Ramzi who had gin and tonic. Captain Wenock sipped an orange juice, talked to everyone, then excused himself, "The wind is boisterous and changeable," he said to Miles, "we may have to move anchorage. I'll be on the bridge if you want me, sir."

Vicky had produced printed nameplates to facilitate seating. The five ladies and seven men talked "grass roots" as they found their places.

When all were seated Miles stood up, "It is a pleasure for Victoria, Eileen and me to welcome our friends aboard *Andromeda* today. The idea is to enjoy each other's company whilst discussing the need for a grass roots initiative in food production. We have all heard of the dangers of monoculture when biodiversity is thrown to the winds, of the green revolution which destroys genetic diversity on farms, of the white revolution which is destroying genetic diversity in cattle and causing grave under nourishment amongst many rural populations. The needs of the urban market have forced out traditional land management and culture. I have mentioned some of the drastic consequences which are flowing from the ill-considered worship of market forces. We need a grass roots initiative to take grasslands, farms and forests out of the control of banks and governments: they should be controlled by rural communities. Jasem has studied several such projects, at least one of which, The Baringo Food and Fodder Project, has reversed a deadly deterioration and turned it into a continuing success story. Can we, in a small way, encourage and inspire more such projects? That, ladies and gentlemen, is the question."

Miles was surprised when Hassen Osman clapped his hands and everyone round the table applauded too. As the steward and three assistants served, a buzz of conversation followed the lead Miles had given. During lunch he asked Jasem to chair a meeting afterwards to decide if, and how, the embryo group should proceed.

"I will gladly do that," Jasem responded, "and if you agree, I will say a few words about the task as I see it."

Miles rose to his feet and, as conversation died, said, "I have asked Jasem to chair our first meeting, which we will hold in the saloon immediately after coffee."

Jasem then spoke clearly and firmly, "Environmental pollution has reached the scale of a global disaster. This bears directly on our wish to encourage a general grass roots initiative in agriculture. It is widely known that we are poisoning our planet. I will mention a few of the ways in which we do it. Oil pollution on land and in seas, rivers and lakes, industrial pollution from waste products, including nuclear waste, is dumped into the sea, untreated sewage runs into the sea; increasing use of fertilizers and pesticides which leach into water supplies and, in coastal areas, run straight into the sea; pollution of the atmosphere so that the air we breathe, the water we drink, the food we eat may have detrimental effects on human and animal health. It is said that the sea was the source of life on earth, nuclear waste dumped into the sea poisons that source, and its inhabitants, for a thousand years. That poison is already in the food chain. These are some of the reasons why I hope that all of us round this table will feel drawn to the first meeting of GRIP – the Grass Roots Initiative Project."

Mohamed Ramzi, who was sitting next to Eileen, asked her,

"Have you heard of the GIA?"

"That's the Armed Islamic Group, isn't it?" asked Eileen cautiously.

"Yes, they are fundamentalists. Sura two of the Koran says, 'War is prescribed to you.' They use this to justify murder, but neglect to read earlier words in the same Sura which say, 'Fight for the cause of God against those who fight against you, but commit not the injustice of attacking them first, God loveth not such injustice.' These armed fundamentalists ignore the Prophet's teaching. In attacking innocent, defenceless people, they dishonour Islam."

Miles joined in, "Practically all world religions, including Christianity, are struggling to preserve their institutions as if they were the main repositories of truth. Some seek reassurance by emphasising exclusive aspects of their creed. It is a kind of defensive mechanism – a response to the gross materialism of our time – I think it indicates a lack of faith. The trouble is that fundamentalism leads to fanaticism."

Jasem caught Miles's eye and rose to his feet. Glancing at his watch he said, "Miles, let's have a ten minute break before meeting in the saloon."

"Mohamed will have a hard time getting things moving in Algeria," said Jasem to Miles.

"Why are the fundamentalists attacking agricultural communities?" asked Miles.

"Many of these communities support the government – and the government disenfranchised the fundamentalist Moslem party. Targets of GIA wrath are intellectuals, foreigners and government supporters. So Mohamed must move warily," Jasem explained.

"What are my chances of meeting the leaders of the GIA?" asked Miles.

"Remote, and even if you met them, it would be counter-productive. They would regard our project as foreign interference. Such a meeting would be fraught with danger for you and Mohamed," replied Jasem.

There were no absentees from the meeting in the saloon. Jasem said, "At this, our first meeting, I have asked Mary to take shorthand notes. Our aim is to stimulate grass roots agricultural initiatives, with no government involvement and no political colour. We begin in four Mediterranean countries – Egypt, Tunisia, Algeria and Morocco, and in the UK. We will hear a brief statement from each country in that order, i.e. from east to west. Ahmed and Selma?"

"In recent years two major projects have affected the agricultural scene in Egypt," Ahmed began, "one was the Aswan Dam in 1965, the other was a scheme to irrigate almost a million acres, in a multi-million dollar drainage programme financed partly by the International Bank for Reconstruction and Development. Our main agricultural exports are cotton, citrus and rice. We regularly have land reclamation and irrigation schemes, and productivity is generally good. However, there is heavy pollution from oil refineries and tanker traffic, and, particularly in the Nile delta, from heavy use of fertilizers and pesticides. Our peasant farmers work mainly in co-operative organisations which fund, and control, their activities. I have made tentative approaches in areas where marginal land might be reclaimed. As you know, before the Aswan Dam the Nile had an annual rise and fall of about thirteen feet at Cairo. The flood water used to bring rich sediment to the Delta. That no longer happens. Now, the delta is steadily losing land to the sea. Land is also lost through salinisation following careless irrigation in some areas. Population was estimated at 43,000,000 in December 1980, this year it is about 59,000,000 – growing at two point five per cent a year."

"Any questions for Ahmed?" asked Jasem.

"Egypt's tourism declined due to attacks by Islamic fundamentalists, would such people oppose the grass roots plan?" asked Victoria.

"If the grass roots plan develops as Miles suggested, the input would merge with normal agricultural effort, it should not attract attention – political or religious," answered Ahmed.

Jasem said, "Although droughts are a major problem for Tunisia, thirty-five per cent of the workforce are employed in agriculture and fisheries. The chief agricultural exports are textiles, fruit and olive oil. Pollution is a serious problem. Fertilizers and pesticides run into the sea from the intensely cultivated coastal strip. Industrial waste, mostly oil and phosphate residues, is dumped in the Gulf of Gabes and around Tunis. Air pollution is high in and around Tunis. Tunisia's population of about 6,000,000 in 1980 has increased to some 9,000,000 in 2010."

"Algeria," said Mohamed Ramzi, "has suffered from violent political unrest due to a dispute between the government and the FIS, Islamic Salvation Front. Plans for the development of agriculture and industry have not been a great success. About thirty per cent of our workforce is employed on the land, I think a grass roots initiative could be valuable. However, fundamentalists have attacked some of our remote farmers, in some places murdering whole communities. Our main crops are cereals, citrus, olives and grapes. Oil pollution is severe along the coast, and, added to that, industrial waste and untreated sewage are dumped directly into the sea. Our population of about 18,000,000 in 1980 has increased to more than 30,000,000 in 2010. Unemployment is high and many Algerians work abroad."

"Mohamed," Miles asked, "you told me that a majority of your rural people raise livestock and farm small plots along the coastal plains. Is that the kind of area you would look at to reclaim marginal land?"

"Yes, especially in the eastern 'Tell' – the coastal plain. If we can make a success of our grass roots there, where the hills roll into the Medjerda mountains, that would encourage similar experiments west of Oran."

"Morocco employs more than seventy per cent of its working population in agriculture," said Hassen Osman. "Our main products are cereals, citrus fruits, olives, grapes, tomatoes, vegetables, dates and figs. We export some of these, and also cork, wood pulp and esparto grass. There is industrial pollution, and pollution from oil tankers along the Atlantic coast. Population was about 23,000,000 in 1980 and is now about 29,000,000. We already try to extend sustainable agriculture, and the grass roots idea would give further encouragement."

"Thank you, my friends," said Jasem. "Miles's concern for the starving people of our world brings us together. Since 1980 just four of our Mediterranean countries have produced 37 million more mouths to feed. If you look at the worldwide figures, it is truly frightening. When one realises what we are doing to our planet – poisoning the seas, the soil, the atmosphere – the idea of a spreading Grass Roots Initiative Project becomes not only attractive, but urgent and imperative. If glaciers were to spread over North America and Northern Europe, vast areas of fertile land will be lost to agriculture. These, ladies and gentlemen, are the reasons for GRIP. Let us now formally set up our Committee and agree a modus operandi."

The Red Crescent

Jasem Al-Mana agreed with Miles that the initial grass roots committee should include only those directly involved in the project. Thus, within twenty minutes he, unofficially representing Tunisia, with Mary Al-Mana as secretary, met with Ahmed Rahman Egypt, Mohamed Ramzi Algiers, Hassen Osman Morocco, Miles and Eileen PI with Laurie and Neville as independent observers.

The committee agreed its title as the Grass Roots Initiative Project, GRIP. The four Mediterranean members agreed to submit details of the first land to be reclaimed under the scheme: location, area, climate, water supply and condition of soil were to be recorded. They would also name potential farmers, who, in the early days of the project, might need a subsistence allowance. Requirements in terms of organic soil enrichers, water, machinery, shelter, security and support were to be listed. Ahmed Rahman would distribute supplies from his Agricultural Machinery Distribution Centre at Alexandria. At his suggestion it was agreed that implements should, in the first instance, be on loan to individuals through the appropriate GRIP Committee member who would be responsible for them, and for monitoring the progress of the project.

Jasem said, "We must work to tight deadlines, so I suggest the four countries supply the necessary details, by fax, telephone or email within the next seven days. Agreed?"

"We will forward machinery requirements by sea or air once they have been approved," said Ahmed. "Would you also list which supplies, if any, you can meet from your own national resources? It is necessary to monitor individual projects so that we build up records for future guidance. Financial records must be kept for each project, copies to me, please, on a quarterly basis. My office will keep consolidated accounts of expenditure and, eventually, income."

Miles asked, "Do you think a senior official of the Red Crescent could help me to meet the FIS leaders in Algiers?"

After some discussion, Jasem answered "Politically there is little sympathy for the FIS whose position has weakened recently. This has led to excessive violence. On balance, we feel that we might get the worst of both worlds by making official contact with them. To abide by the grass roots nature of our endeavour, we should steer clear of politics and keep our whole operation low key. If Mohamed's efforts in Algeria are threatened, then we must review our policy in that country."

"Would the committee agree that I should visit each country's initial project?" asked Miles. "I think someone should monitor progress, note which methods produce the best results, and circularise details which might be of interest and help to other projects. Incidentally, on our farm in England we have set aside thirty acres of unproductive land for experimental organic farming. Including that, we start with five projects. I propose that we encourage each other with regular reports on progress."

After further discussion of the political situation in Algeria, Jasem, on behalf of the committee, said, "We are agreed that Miles should observe and monitor each project as an unofficial visitor. At the same time he should, if he decides to visit Algeria, look at other farms so as not to draw attention to one particular place. We advise that he should not travel alone to, or in, Algeria. He should consider making his visits high profile rather than clandestine. We suggest that, if possible, Neville and Laurie should accompany him to strengthen the scientific\pastoral nature of the visit."

The next meeting was arranged one month ahead, the venue to be fixed by Jasem.

During their talks Miles noticed that *Andromeda*'s stillness had given way to a gentle rolling motion. By the time Jasem closed the meeting the rolling and pitching had increased, and a discreet hum told him that the ship was under power. He made his way to the bridge. A strong wind from the southwest had whipped up the harbour waters which were grey and choppy. Out to sea rollers and white horses had churned up the relative calm of the morning.

Captain Wenock said, "I've got the Harbour Master's permission to move closer in, otherwise the motor boat would

The Red Crescent

have a long, rough ride to the jetty. There's a string of depressions bringing rain storms across the Atlas Mountains – we're in the path of those storms – we've just had heavy rain, and there's quite a sea running out there now."

"I'll be in the saloon," said Miles, "let me know when you think we can give our guests a reasonable ride back to the quayside."

On returning to the saloon, Miles drew Mohamed Ramzi aside. "Mohamed, how should I dress if I wanted to travel inconspicuously in Algeria, say, for example, to go from Algiers to Oran and Constantine?"

Mohamed beamed at Miles, "I thought you would not give up easily. But you must know that in their present mood, the GIA would shoot you without hesitation. Do you speak French or, better still, Arabic?"

"A few words of Arabic, fluent French," replied Miles. "I realise the danger from GIA gunmen, but I would hope to avoid them. I wonder if I should dress like an ordinary Arab going about his business?"

"There are many ways of betraying oneself," said Mohamed.

"What would you do when the Muezzin calls?"

"Go to the Mosque with my prayer mat – remove my shoes – or pray at my hotel or place of work. Turn towards the Ka'ba in Mecca, kneel and touch the floor with my head three times. If others were present, recite with them the Shahada," said Miles.

"And what are the words?" asked Mohamed, with raised eyebrows.

"I bear witness that there is no God but God, I bear witness that Muhammad is the prophet of God," Miles recited in French.

"I must teach you to say that in Arabic. How do we end our prayers?"

"Assalamu alaikum – Peace be upon you," answered Miles.

"Well well! A western Christian who knows something of Islam," said Mohamed with a smile. "We will talk about dress when we have consulted a map."

"Thank you," said Miles, "it may be a day or two before I can make firm arrangements to come to Algeria. Is it safe to talk on the phone?"

"Here is my office number, phone me there," replied Mohamed, handing Miles a card as they rejoined the others in the saloon.

The intercom handset in the saloon buzzed, Miles picked it up, "We are lowering the motorboat, sir," said Captain Wenock. As Vicky and Mary led the way to the stern step, Miles heard Mary say, "You must come and stay with us when you make your next business trip to the Mediterranean area. We have so much..."

Then Selma spoke to him and he overheard no more... "I hope this 'grass roots' means that we shall have the pleasure of seeing you more often in Cairo," she said.

"Selma," replied Miles, "the trailblazers of Baringo have started something so exciting, we must ensure that our efforts have the same success as theirs. I intend to stay in these parts until our plans take shape. Jasem, Mohamed, Hassen and Ahmed make a very good team, I shall enjoy working with them. When do you and Ahmed return to Cairo?" he asked.

"Ahmed said we shall catch the late morning flight if he has finished his talks with the others," replied Selma.

They reached the stern step and, whilst conversation continued, the six visitors climbed into the motorboat. Miles, standing next to Victoria, said, "Change of plan, Vicky. There's stormy weather brewing up. It would be rough and uncomfortable to sail to Lisbon."

Victoria waved as the motorboat left *Andromeda* and headed for the main Tunis quayside. "What very nice people. I wish there had been more time to talk to Mary. Storms brewing up, Miles?" Vicky looked around, "Nothing serious enough for a change of plan, surely?"

"Geoffrey Wenock says there's a string of depressions coming our way. The centre of the first is southwest of us now. Very strong winds, heavy rain and rough seas. Not the weather for a cruise."

"What's the plan then?" asked Victoria, as they strolled back to the saloon.

"I shall suggest to the others that we find a sheltered, offshore anchorage for tonight, that we dine on board and afterwards watch television or a film. Tomorrow, you take our UK friends to Tunis Airport, *Ariadne*'s still there, and fly home to London."

"And you?"

"I have some business with Ramzi in Algiers," he replied.

"You have some business right here, with me," retorted Victoria. "What about this small farm in England where we have set aside thirty acres for 'grass-rooting'? How is it that I, the holder of PI's property portfolio, know nothing about it?"

"Actually, you do know something about it. You stayed in the farm cottage one night," answered Miles.

"We can't stand here arguing. You'd better explain your change of plan to our guests," said Victoria. Miles obeyed. His guests thought the change of plan a good idea in view of the poor weather conditions. After tea, he took Laurie and Neville up to the bridge. Whilst there, he contacted Mike Williams and arranged *Ariadne*'s flight back to London, to leave Tunis at 11.00 hours local time the next morning.

"Would either of you care to accompany me on a visit to Algeria?" asked Miles.

"Out of the question for me, I'm afraid," responded Laurie, "I'm due back at work in a couple of days."

"I have ten days leave," said Neville, "but the advice I have about Algeria is – stay away – the FIS is anti western tourists."

"Mainly on two counts, I think," said Miles. "Exploitation by the West in the past, and religion. As regards the first, we are not interested in exploitation, we seek co-operation. And as for the second, though they won't yet admit it, Islam is at a watershed, just as most institutional religions are. They have to overcome the psychological barriers that arise when they attempt to freeze a living faith in the religious dogmas of a past age."

"From what I hear, the GIA shoots first and asks questions afterwards, which is hard on the victims," said Neville. "The main weapon of the fundamentalists is fear and their aim is power. Love of God and man has no place in their thinking."

"I believe that's why so many of their countrymen have turned against them. The FIS has lost a lot of ground since 1993. However, it is a dangerous situation to walk into, so I have asked Mohamed Ramzi to advise me. The first step is to meet him in Algiers, discuss ways and means, and only after that should we come to a final decision about travel in Algeria."

"I spent a holiday in Tunisia a couple of years ago," said Neville. "World religions interest me, and I've actually attended worship in a number of Mosques. I made enquiries about Algeria, but was warned off. The precise advice was, go only if you must, and then do not travel inland, especially not to those areas known to sympathise with the GIA. So I stayed put in Tunisia. Really, it was Algeria I wanted to see, and, if possible, its southern borders."

"Now is your chance," said Miles. "You could come with me to Algiers, talk with Ramzi, and then decide whether to get out, or go further." Victoria discussed the change of plan with Eileen and Angela, "Probably sensible in view of the weather," she said, "but annoying all the same. I know you were looking forward to a cruise in the sun, Angela."

"Yes, but not in rough seas," she replied.

"I think there's more to it than weather," said Eileen. "The fact is, in this grass roots business, Miles has experienced the kind of challenge that led him to build up PI. It is timely, because running PI is no longer fulfilling for him. With his drive, and his understanding of the need for grass roots control, sustainable food production could get a great boost. He's right about bureaucratic interference too. While he wrestles with that, our job it seems, Vicky, is to run PI as effectively as he did."

Before dinner Miles telephoned Jasem Al-Mana, telling him of his and Neville's intention to fly to Algiers.

"Have a word with Mohamed," said Jasem, "he is here with me now. You might be able to fly to Algiers with him."

"Miles, you are a fast worker," said Mohamed.

"I wanted to let you know that Neville will come with me to Algiers, but not tomorrow. Probably on Saturday. Victoria is flying back to London with the others at 11.00 tomorrow. I shall be at the airport to see them off. Perhaps we could talk then?"

Shortly after dinner Miles put on a film – Humphrey Bogart in *Casablanca*. Captain Wenock and off-duty crew members joined the party to watch the film. When all were engrossed in the Bogart/Bergman saga, Victoria and Miles took a turn round the aft deck to discuss their business differences.

"The cottage deal was signed up before the farmhouse and land," said Miles. "Furthermore PI owns the cottage, but not the farm. You and I will be joint owners of that."

"You bought a farm without discussing it with me?"

"When I made my first visit to the cottage, the shepherd happened to mention that Newman's Farm would be coming on the market shortly. The farmer had died, neither the widow nor her daughter wanted to run the farm – which is 500 acres – a third arable, a half pasture for sheep. They keep a few horses and cows on the remaining eighty acres, which includes thirty acres of poor land. I went to see Mrs Newman. She and her daughter were keen to sell without the hassle and expense of agents. A neighbouring farmer had offered a low price, which they were considering when I came on the scene. I met their asking price provided the farm came to us as a going concern. They agreed to that. They instructed their solicitor, they have signed the contract, we sign when we get home."

"Horses?" queried Victoria. "What kind of horses?"

"I thought that would interest you. One mare is a prize-winning point-to-pointer, and she has a very promising foal. Four others are hunters – you'll love them," he assured her.

"Who is going to run the farm?"

"The Newmans, now relieved of financial responsibility, are happy to carry on for the time being. Then there's the shepherd, and a general farmhand–cum–tractor driver. If anything, the farm has been over-capitalized with machinery and implements, which are all in good nick. There is a three-year crop rotation on the arable. I'm keeping an eye on that myself. The farmhouse is a grand old stone building. You'll love it."

"I'll never have time to see it! I've been landed with responsibility for a multi-national, if you remember," said Victoria.

"When you and Eileen become accustomed to running PI, you will look forward to spending short breaks on the farm. That's another reason why I got it. And that's when the old shepherd got me thinking about the need for grass roots agriculture."

"Miles, I don't want you sticking your neck out in Algeria. There's a bunch of religious maniacs there who worship the god of hate. If they don't shoot you on sight, they'll stick you in some filthy cellar and hold you to ransom. I'm not taking on PI so that you can run around playing Lawrence of Arabia. No heroics, right?"

"I want this grass roots business to be just that. Low key, no publicity, no politics, no power, and certainly no heroics. Algeria is important because there's a lot of poverty. Produce more food there, and neighbouring countries will, in time, begin to take notice. That's why I must go to Algiers, find out where the GIA operates, and, if possible, avoid those areas when we travel."

"Will you promise me one thing? If Mohamed tells you it's too dangerous, will you leave the Algerian project in his hands?"

"I promise," he replied.

At nine o'clock on Friday, 8 October, *Andromeda*'s motorboat made its first trip to the main Tunis quayside. Neville and Laurie took a taxi to the airport, where they were met by *Ariadne*'s pilot, Mike Williams.

"The senior meteorological officer will be pleased to talk to you," he said. "He has some English and is fluent in French." Mike introduced Laurie and Neville to the Met. Officer, Dr Abdul Mansour, then left to prepare for the flight to London.

Dr Mansour was excited and friendly: "I have watched you, Monsieur le Professor Colgate, on television. Phaeton and the weather. He caused much fires and casualties on the Altai Mountains and Caucasus. Rain in the Sahel and the Sahara, tsunamis in the Mediterranean and the Indian and Pacific ocean. He is not finish with us, I think. Come, look at my charts." Laurie and Neville perused the charts, discussed their implications with Dr Mansour, expressed their thanks and left him to make their way to *Ariadne*.

Miles, Victoria, Eileen and Angela arrived at Tunis Airport soon after 10 a.m. Jasem, Mary and Mohamed met them as they cleared the customs desk. Jasem took the party out to *Ariadne* in his car. As they boarded the plane, Miles steered Jasem and Mohamed to the rear seats. "If Neville and I catch the 08.30 hours plane to Algiers tomorrow, we should clear customs by, say 10 a.m. Would you be able to meet us, Mohamed?"

"I have to be at the airport to meet a visiting VIP at 10 a.m.," said Mohamed. "If I can't meet you myself, my assistant will be there, holding a card with PI printed on it. He will take you to my office to wait for me. I will have the latest information on GIA

The Red Crescent

activities. We shall be able to make a sensible, informed decision."

Before leaving *Ariadne*, Miles, Neville, Mohamed, Jasem and Mary joined with Vicky and the others in a toast to GRIP. A few minutes later they watched as Mike Williams flew the Lear jet away to the southwest, then, in a sweeping, climbing turn to port, the jet flew high over the airfield and Cape Bon, heading towards France and London.

The next member of the party to leave was Mohamed, who boarded the plane for Algiers at 11.50 a.m.

"Miles," said Jasem, "I discussed with Mohamed the possibility of your travelling in Algeria with a senior diplomat from one of the Gulf States, he is known to be an Anglophile. Mary and I are entertaining this man and members of his party this evening. He, I know, speaks English. Basically he is a financier, but he has asked to visit the far south of Algeria, where it runs into the Sahara. As you may know, trees are being planted there. It is another step in an ambitious plan to halt desert expansion by ringing it with green. This would, I'm sure, interest you and Neville. It may involve more extensive travel than you want to undertake?"

"A financier from one of the Gulf States?" Miles repeated. "I have existing business interests with Saudis, Kuwaitis, and, some years ago, I had dealings with Iranians and Iraqis too. I personally would be delighted to travel with such a group. How about you, Neville?"

"It would be a dream come true. If it's on – count me in. I wouldn't miss such an opportunity. It has the hallmark of Arabian Nights."

"I will introduce the matter this evening, diplomatically. No names, just a hypothetical case – suppose a couple of our western friends wanted to observe attempts at land reclamation in Algeria. How could they safely do that in the present political climate?' I have your ship's phone number? Yes – and you have my home number," said Jasem, as he and Mary drove off.

"What an impressive man," remarked Neville. "A Muslim married to a Christian. I wonder how Mary copes in a country which is more than ninety per cent Islamic?"

"Very well. She told Vicky that she and Jasem love the same God. She said that is why Christian and Muslim should love each other."

Compost In Sand

"You know, Eileen, only now have I discovered that, as well as being an entrepreneur, Miles is a clever administrator. Even when there's no-one in this top office, Charles Norton and his staff on the lower floor keep everything working," said Victoria.

"Up to a point," replied Eileen. "The leadership, the acquisitions and the new ideas, the overall strategy, comes from this office. The floor below is the engine room, not the bridge."

"In six months, with your help, I shall have my job under control," Vicky continued. "Guess what my aim will be then?"

"You aim to work yourself out of the job, so that you and Miles can become full-time farmers," replied Eileen. "That's why you're starting your grand PI tour in Australia. You're wondering whether to bring Amos Griffin to London to work with me. A clever move if it comes off. It will look as if Miles had planned it."

"It's not that obvious, is it? When Miles has spent six months working on GRIP, he'll realise that there is a great, interesting, vibrant world outside PI and profits."

"Imagine life without *Ariadne*, *Andromeda* and Giles. Day after day no escape from manure, mangolds and Miles. Are you sure you're ready for such bucolic isolation?" asked Eileen.

*

Aboard *Andromeda*, as Miles watched the Friday late night news and weather in the saloon, his personal phone buzzed. "Poundmore," he said.

"We last met in my country some years ago, and before that you gave me some good advice on investments," said a husky voice with a clipped accent.

"I remember," said Miles. "Didn't you snap up a ten per cent block of PI shares? You must be pleased with them. I recall our meeting in the Gulf." He could picture the man, beardless but moustachioed, about the same stature and build as the late King Hussain of Jordan. He dressed in western-style clothing under a burnous which proclaimed his Arabian roots. There had been an immediate affinity between them. He remembered that he was a senior member of a leading tribe. He took a chance. "Is that Sheikh Al Zebah?" he asked, knowing there were many of that name, and not sure which member, or branch, of the family he was talking to.

"Indeed it is. I thought you might not remember. I hear that you and your wife are as energetic and creative as ever. But I hope we can reminisce tomorrow. My host has told me of your travel plans. I understand that your companion is a Church of England priest?"

"Yes, and a scientist. Mr Al Zebah, am I right in thinking we met in London several times, and once in Kuwait?" asked Miles.

"You are right. I had lunch with you and your wife at your Club in Pall Mall, and again at my country's embassy in Queen's Gate. Mr Poundmore, would you and Mr Gadsby care to travel with me to Algiers tomorrow?" asked Al Zebah.

"That would be an honour," replied Miles, "but there is a problem. I have promised to meet someone at Algiers Airport at ten o'clock."

"That is the time we shall arrive," said Al Zebah, "I suggest you get to the airport at 08.00. Go to the gate for Kuwaiti Airline's flight one. They will be expecting you. I look forward to meeting you again. Goodnight, Mr Poundmore."

"Neville, you mentioned Arabian Nights. That was Sheikh Ali Al Zebah. He is leading a group on a semi-official visit to Algeria. He has invited us to fly with him tomorrow."

"From what I heard, I gathered that you knew him. Is he to be trusted?" asked Neville.

"He was educated at Harrow and Oxford. He had, and may still have, a home in Sussex. He is a big wheel in the Kuwaiti Investment Office, managing a portfolio that runs into billions of dollars. They have an office in London, which is where I first met him. Yes, we can trust him. Jasem obviously thinks so, too. We'll see what he proposes in the morning. Meanwhile, I'm going to the computer room. I have a few things to check, including PI's dealings with Kuwait. Would you like to come?"

Miles read the computer notes of transactions with the KIO. The latest entry on the disk had been made by Victoria. She had arranged a trip to Australia in the third week of October, and, on her way back, she had confirmed a two-day stop in Kuwait for talks with Sheikh Ali Al Zebah. Miles entered details of his latest contact with Sheikh Ali. Vicky was already using the PI computer system to keep herself, and him, informed and up to date. He was impressed. He also read notes of Vicky's talk with Eileen – someone must have inadvertently switched on the intercom and recording machine, so those notes were printed out too. Things were working out better than he had thought they would; he had not realised that Vicky would be so keen on country life.

When Miles and Neville breakfasted at 7 a.m. on Saturday, 9 October, a gusty wind spattered heavy rain on the port side dining room windows. *Andromeda* wallowed uneasily in the choppy waters off the southern shores of Tunis Bay. The engines hummed discreetly as Captain Wenock edged the yacht nearer to the main quay, ready to launch the motorboat at 07.30 hours.

"It's more like a winter morning in Manchester than an autumn one in the Mediterranean," said Captain Wenock. "We shall return to Naples, sir. Usual standby routine until I receive further orders."

"Right, Geoffrey," said Miles, as he stepped into the motorboat.

"We may enlist *Andromeda* on the grass roots operation that I mentioned. If so, you will get orders from Angelo Capelli or me. My thanks to your crew for looking after my guests."

The steward handed Neville's suitcase to the crewman in the boat. Then, with a grin, he said to Miles, "A small suitcase for you, sir. The Captain says you'll be off PI territory for a few days."

"Thanks," said Miles. "I couldn't face the Sahara without a toothbrush."

They checked the flight information board for KAL flight 1, then walked to gate 1. Miles said, "Mr Poundmore and Mr Gadsby."

The official checked their passports, looked carefully at their photographs, then directed them and their suitcases through a metal detector gate. The man smiled, "His Excellency is expecting

Compost In Sand

you, sir. Go along to the second door on the left. There is a guard outside. I have placed a pass in your passport, show this to the guard and he will let you in." He nodded at an elderly Arab in uniform who politely relieved them of their suitcases and led them down the corridor.

There were two armed guards, one of whom inspected their passports and passes whilst the other looked them up and down. The one with sergeant's stripes said, "We must inspect your suitcases before sending them to the aircraft, sir."

"Go ahead," said Miles, "they're not locked." The sergeant's companion knocked on the door, opened it and let Miles and Neville into a smallish room which contained a few chairs, a table, Sheikh Ali Al Zebah and Jasem Al-Mana. Both men wore the headdress and cloak of a white burnous over lightweight, western-style lounge suits.

After introducing Neville to the Sheikh, Miles said, "What a pleasure it is to see you again, your Excellency. And especially to find that we share a mutual desire to co-operate with those who strive to make wastelands bloom."

"Ali, Miles, call me Ali. We are not on duty. I see that you have been in the sun. You are brown." He looked at Neville, "You are pale, but have brown eyes. Jasem, tell them what we propose."

"You will like this idea," said Jasem. "It is based on the fact that most people see what they expect to see." He took two burnouses from a plastic bag and handed them to Miles and Neville. "Remember Gunga Din? 'The uniform 'e wore was nothin' much before, an' rather less than arf o' that be'ind.'"

"That describes a burnous over a western style suit. With sunglasses to hide your blue eyes, you're an Arab. Neville is rather pale, but his brown eyes could be Arabian." Whilst Miles and Neville adjusted their new mantles, Ali Al Zebah told them that his Algerian itinerary included a visit to Oran after he had seen the Saharan tree planting to the southwest of Ouallene.

"You will know," said Jasem, "that tree planting on Saharan borders is being undertaken to stop the desert's advance. There are vast areas where the Sahara is eating up misused grasslands at a rate of thirty miles a year. If we can reverse this disastrous trend by co-operating with our nomadic herders, we might then

Compost In Sand

continue the good work and make more of the wastelands bloom."

"Our route takes us through areas known to sympathise with the GIA," said Sheikh Ali, "but my security chief says there will be no trouble. My party includes two from Saudi, two from Jordan, four Kuwaitis, Jasem, yourselves and, from Algiers, Mohamed Ramzi, with whom you have an appointment, and two assistants, making fourteen in all. We fly south from Algiers to Aoulef Arab. Our security men are already there. Two helicopters stationed there will take us along the south-western border. There are landing pads along the route, so we can stop, observe, and ask questions. You, gentlemen, are *bona fide* members of an international conservation group."

When the private Kuwaiti jet landed at Algiers, it was accorded priority treatment. The passengers were escorted by Mohamed Ramzi to a VIP lounge where they had refreshments before emplaning for the next stage. A smaller aircraft was used for the seven hundred miles trip to Aoulef Arab.

Most of this flight was over a thick blanket of rain cloud which, fortunately, broke up into scattered tufts of altocumulus as they crossed the Tademait Plateau. The tableland, over 3,000 feet high in places, undulated barren and brown to the far horizon. They saw occasional signs of life when they flew low enough to spot herds of goats in isolated places where precious rain had greened the savannah. Soon they saw the desert stretching away to the southwest, but to the east and southeast higher ground led onwards and upwards to the 9,500 feet Ahaggar mountains.

The small aircraft was fast: they reached their destination shortly after 1.15 p.m. Here, a wing in the hotel was reserved for their use. The Sheikh's equerry provided Miles and Neville with maps, an itinerary, and details which showed how well the Arabs had done their homework. There were notes in English about tree planting in Indonesia, the Chipko and Silent Valley campaigns in India, the Green Belt organisation in Kenya, and brief accounts of similar efforts in Colombia and many other countries around the world.

A busy caravan route passed through the oasis at Aoulef, its traffic a mixture of four-legged and four-wheeled drives as old and new modes of transport traversed the same ancient trails. Unlike their companions, the Englishmen wanted to explore the place. Jasem accompanied them, and, with the Sheikh's permission and a member of his bodyguard, they walked in the sweltering heat to observe how old lifestyles persisted alongside those of a modern state.

After sunset prayers, Sheikh Ali said, "Please dine with me tonight. Come to my suite at eight thirty. It would be wise to wear your burnouses when you leave your rooms."

★

"Tonight we are on our own. My equerry is entertaining the other members of our group. This gives us the opportunity to talk freely about cultural, political and religious matters, as well as environmental concerns." The Sheikh pointed to a side table.

"Please help yourselves to drinks. There is wine, spirits, tonic water, ginger ale, soft drinks, ice and lemon. And with our food we may, if we wish, have good Algerian red wine, thanks to Mohamed."

The five men sat round the dining room table upon which a white cloth was spread. There were no plates or anything else on it. Ali remarked, "We are all to some extent involved in the petroleum business. This, together with nuclear arms, agricultural and industrial chemicals, has brought us to the point where we can foresee the end of the human race. When I first heard that kind of comment, I thought it alarmist and exaggerated. But the increase in cancer, the decrease in human and animal fertility, the destruction caused by acid rain, ozone depletion – these are not mere coincidence. Short term they may not seem important. Long term they are about the quality of life our children and grandchildren may, or may not, enjoy."

"Miles's idea of working from the grass roots upwards, is, in my opinion, the best way of changing things in the long term," said Jasem. "Fortunately for us, a great many people around the world share, and are acting on, this view. But governments and organisations in many countries put profits before a healthy environment."

Mohamed agreed, "I had no idea how much this environmental concern had caught people's imaginations until I attended a symposium on the subject. Somebody at that meeting quoted Jonathon Porritt – 'The future will either be green, or not at all.' This truth lies at the heart of humankind's most pressing challenge which is to learn to live in harmony with the earth on a friendly and sustainable basis."

The Sheikh's telephone rang, "Send it right away," he said. Next he answered the doorbell, and shortly afterwards pushed to the table a trolley laden with tureens, plates of bread, and all that was needed for a feast.

There was little talk during the meal, but afterwards, Jasem introduced a subject which intrigued Miles. "Neville," he said, "both Ali and I are married to Christians. We worship God in churches as well as in mosques. Mary and Ali's wife, Christina, also worship in the mosque or the church. The four of us firmly believe that we worship the same God. But Ali and I continue to ask questions to which we have, so far, received either no answer at all, or ambiguous and confusing ones."

"There are questions of faith to which there is, as yet, no answer. There are others which we must answer for ourselves," said Neville, "and then there are matters of basic belief which our respective religions require us to accept."

"I am confused," said Ali, "when I read in the New Testament that flesh and blood will never inherit the kingdom of heaven, and yet in The Apostles' Creed one repeats, 'I believe in the resurrection of the body.' Why resurrect the body if the transitory will never possess the everlasting? Nor can I understand how a new-born baby can be guilty of sin, original or any other kind."

"As a physicist I find the resurrection of the body difficult to comprehend," said Neville. "It doesn't make sense. The modern version of The Nicene creed states, 'We look for the resurrection of the dead' – that presents fewer difficulties. With regard to new-born babies, I agree with you. Jesus said of little children, 'Unless you become as one of these you cannot enter the kingdom.' That surely implies innocence and purity in the little ones."

"I can truthfully say, 'I believe in God,' said Miles, but I don't understand religions that teach people to worship the Supreme

Compost In Sand

Being, to strive for good, to reject evil, to love their fellow humans – and yet attack one another. Not one of the religious institutions man has formed is perfect. The story of the beam and the speck apply to them as much as to individuals. So we ought to work together under God – it is 'by their fruits that you shall know them.' I can see why so many people reject religious institutions, their intentions may be good but their fruit is often sour."

★

When Victoria reached her office in the morning, her first action was to check the computer readings for her spheres of interest. Next she discussed matters with Eileen and, together, they decided on strategy and tactics. "What's Amos Griffin's number two like?" she asked.

"Have you read his file?" queried Eileen.

"Yes, but it doesn't tell me whether he's got the personality to run PI Australasia. He's the right age and he's got the experience, has he got the temperament?" queried Vicky.

"Miles doubted it. But that was, at least in part, because he didn't want to move Amos here. You'll have to talk to Amos about him."

Victoria telephoned later that night. "Amos, would Alexander Boyle make a regional director?" she asked.

"What are you thinking of?" he asked cagily.

"Nothing in particular at the moment. But I can see a promotion opportunity coming up. So I'm looking at our assistant regional directors first," she replied.

"I've put a lot of work into his training. I don't want to lose him. Especially as I'm now taking in PI India Region."

"Who would you put in his place if I move him?" persisted Victoria.

"Young Compton, I suppose. Bit over-confident, but we're knocking him into shape. Give me three months' notice if you decide on Boyle."

"OK. Can you meet me in Karachi a week today? I need a full day with you. If you could time your Bombay visit to fit in with this, we would be able to settle some crucial matters. And congratulations on landing that bridge construction contract."

"The only difference between you and Miles is, he'd have said 'meet me in Karachi' – no 'can you'. As it happens, it would suit me. That's Monday the 16th. Email your arrival time and any other info, Victoria. I'll book your hotel accommodation."

"If I decide it's right, Eileen, I shall transfer Amos to London as Acting Joint Managing Director in three months' time. He'll work with you and me for three months, after which, if, and only if, we both approve, the appointment will be confirmed."

"It will be. Miles will struggle, but he'll learn to accept a PI without day-to-day Poundmore management. And Vicky, what a crafty way of snuffing out the Aussie management tree without telling Amos what's on the cards. Miles could learn a trick or two from you."

★

Miles and Neville were fascinated by Algeria's Saharan borderlands. They learned that Tuaregs and other nomads loved and respected the desert. It was no "wasteland" to them. True, the desert could swallow up villages. It was pitiless to the unprepared and unwary. It would reward those who knew its ways, the people who spent their lives in the desert, who knew where, when, how and what to grow. The recent rains had resulted in rich growth: the sun could kill it as quickly as it had sprung to life. But already, weather patterns since Phaeton's passage suggested that rainfall in the Sahel, far to the south, was set to make up for the years of drought.

The helicopter flew them to the Toulla Chegga oasis. Here Mohamed explained how areas of sand most shaded by trees had, for many months, been fed with compost made from the local community's waste. This was one of dozens of similar grass roots efforts. "Of course," he said, "the winds blow sand about, but because the trees provide a windbreak, this is not enough to interfere with the local growers' crop-rotation plan. In the fallow, which is every third year, we dig in the compost as you see on this strip." He pointed to a strip about ten by one hundred yards,

"Nothing is wasted, kitchen refuse, treated sewage, paper waste – properly activated – it is mulched and left for three years before use. You see, we have built four large compost containers which are rodent- and pest-free, but we introduce normal soil bacteria and worms." Two other strips had root and cereal crops. "We are careful not to overburden the soil. The crop rotation feeds it, the compost enriches it, and so we are learning to sustain roots in the sand."

*

Miles returned to London on 13th October, in time to talk to Victoria before she flew to Karachi. After Miles telephoned her from Algiers, Vicky arranged a welcome home party. He was delighted that the Colgates and Eileen were there to hear about grass roots progress.

Towards the end of the evening Eileen asked, "Are there any reports of damage caused by Phaeton?"

"The dust cleared enough to allow the first satellite pictures of a part of northwest Mongolia over which Phaeton passed at his lowest. For over 700 miles there is a great swathe of devastation, mainly in mountainous and forested regions. It looked as if a giant, superheated blow torch had blasted and burnt buildings, trees and vegetation for about ten miles either side of its path. Dust clouds are still preventing full photographic cover, and, since roads, tracks and communications in the disaster area were destroyed, it will be some time before we get the full story."

"Were any densely populated areas hit?" asked Miles.

"Fortunately the meteorite, when at its lowest, was mainly over mountainous, sparsely populated country," said Laurie. "A few small towns were directly under its path. There are no reliable eye witness reports yet – and there is a communications blackout. UNO has offered all the help that is needed to the governments concerned."

"Thank God it's over," said Miles.

"It's not really. We shall all feel the effects of Phaeton's aftermath to some extent," responded Laurie. "For example, something, perhaps Phaeton's brush with earth, has affected the planet's angle of tilt – granted by only a fraction of one degree – but for us in the northern hemisphere that means less sunlight. Also we suspect that undersea explosions and pressures caused by Phaeton's breakaway have aggravated tectonic plate friction. Early evidence points to Breakaway explosions under the sea as the cause of disturbances along the Southwest Indian Ridge. The shakes and quakes then ran along the mid Indian ridge, through the Owen fracture zone near southern Arabia, and then under Iran to the Mediterranean."

"Sounds as serious as the ice," said Miles.

"Disturbed weather patterns will be with us for some years. They could be years of cool and dry summers for our latitudes. We need grass roots projects now, not because of ice and snow, but because of drought. The water shortage in North America and northern Europe will be severe. Soils that have been subjected to intensive monocropping will become arid and infertile."

*

After Victoria left on her overseas tour, Miles visited the Letcombe farm. He inspected progress on the office block which was taking shape behind the rambling old farmhouse. From the outside the new block might have been an old stone barn, but the inside contained a "Chairman's Suite", with the technological equipment necessary for "hands on" control of a modern multinational company, and a Joint Chief Executive's Suite similarly equipped. On the first floor there was spacious accommodation for Eileen and an adequate suite for visitors. With Amos Griffin and Eileen as Joint Chief Executives, he was sure that he and Vicky could keep a watch on PI, run their farm, and work with the grass roots Initiative Project. Amos could live in the house off St James's. Yes, Miles was pleased that his forward planning was working out so well. If the ice advances in ten years time, as old Hugh predicted, roots in the sand would by then be a going concern.

Printed in the United Kingdom
by Lightning Source UK Ltd.
109225UKS00001B/4-24

9 781844 016495